The *Christmas Wish*

M.A. Nichols

Books by M.A. Nichols

Regency Love Series

Flame and Ember
A True Gentleman
The Shameless Flirt
Honor and Redemption
The Jack of All Trades
A Tender Soul
To Have and to Hold
A Holiday Engagement

Victorian Love Series

A Stolen Kiss
The Honorable Choice
Hearts Entwined
A Passing Fancy
Tempest and Sunshine
The Christmas Wish

The Villainy Consultant Series

Geoffrey P. Ward's Guide to Villainy
Geoffrey P. Ward's Guide to Questing
Magic Slippers: A Novella

The Shadow Army Trilogy

Smoke and Shadow
Blood Magic
A Dark Destiny

Table of Contents

Chapter 1

November 1845
Oakham, Devon

Never kick a hornets' nest. Whether metaphorical or literal, doing so only brings harm—usually to the one doing the kicking. Unfortunately, children tended to learn that pearl of wisdom through experience.

"Aunt Evelyn, why aren't you married?"

Little Gemma's tone held no malice or judgment, and her aunt couldn't fault the four-year-old for voicing the question. However, Evelyn's feelings on the matter were immaterial. Most of the Finch clan were gathered around the large kitchen table, which was quite the feat as there were fifteen in attendance, and they stood there, silent and rigid, staring at the child.

Then the hornets shot from their nest.

"What a question to ask, Gemma!" cried her mama, reaching over to place a hand over the child's mouth as though that might trap the words back inside.

"Don't be rude," chastised her papa, giving his daughter a firm frown.

The others alternated between scolding Gemma for voicing

such a horrendous thing and assuring Evelyn that the question was of no significance and she ought not to countenance it. But the very nature of their boisterous reactions told a vastly different story.

And their agitation only grew when Gemma pulled free from her mother's hold and frowned. "But Aunt Josie was just married, and she's *much* younger—"

Evelyn almost laughed. To her thinking, that was the only proper response when her niece spoke as though there were dozens of years between her two aunts when there were only a mere seven. Gemma's genuine confusion and indignation at her parents' response were natural, and Evelyn couldn't help but find the situation humorous.

However, seeing Bridget drag her daughter towards the kitchen door as tears rolled down Gemma's face chased away any merriment she might've felt.

"Do not send her away," said Evelyn. "She hasn't gotten her wish yet."

Pausing at the doorway, Bridget turned back and studied Evelyn before casting a narrow look at her daughter while Gemma let out a hiccupping breath. With a sigh, Bridget leaned down and gave her daughter a stern look.

"Give Aunt Evelyn an embrace and apology."

"But what did I do wrong?" asked Gemma, wiping her cheeks.

"We will discuss it later," said Bridget, pointing her daughter at Evelyn and giving her a nudge forward.

Receiving affection through maternal dictate wasn't ideal, but Evelyn wouldn't turn aside the opportunity when the sweet girl was of an age where holding still was a herculean feat. She scooped up Gemma, and her niece wrapped both arms around Evelyn's neck and squeezed tight, clinging to her like a monkey. Swaying in place, Evelyn held her close as Gemma gave a watery apology.

Yet rife in the child's tone was confusion, and Evelyn had no explanation to give. What had Gemma done wrong? Express curiosity? Ask a simple question?

The rest of the family turned back to the task at hand, giving the large ceramic bowl their full attention. Cook and the kitchen maids had already prepared the batter, which was for the best as the children were still too young to help prepare the Christmas pudding properly, but neither could they be denied the opportunity to partake in Stir-up Sunday.

Though the event was rife with chaos (and not solely due to Gemma), there was order to the madness as Mama gave instructions for each person to come forward and take their turn. Evelyn basked in the sweetness of having her niece buried in her embrace, her little head resting heavily against her aunt's shoulder. However, all thoughts of hurt and remorse evaporated when Mama called for the child to take her turn; pushing free of Evelyn, Gemma hurried to her grandmother and climbed atop the crate they'd placed there for the children to reach the table.

Holding Archer nestled in her arms, Bridget drew up close and gave Evelyn a smile that might've been appreciated more had there not been a hint of pity shining in her sister's eyes. Evelyn thought she might find an ally in her sister-in-law as Marian had been inching close to spinsterhood before marrying George, but there was a similar hint of concern in Marian's gaze that made Evelyn long to sigh. At least Marian's expression seemed more steeped in sympathy than pity (two emotions Evelyn was coming to know far too intimately), but that was little comfort.

Evelyn was grateful when her mother finally called her to the head of the kitchen table. Gripping the wooden spoon, she stared at the batter in the bowl, and her mind went blank. What ought she to wish for this Christmas season?

As a grown woman with nine and twenty years to her name, Evelyn Finch knew wishes were a childhood fancy, but it felt wrong to eschew the tradition. No doubt, the others thought she was hoping for a strapping gentleman to sweep her off her feet, and Evelyn's heart sank low in her chest as she considered just how accurate that assumption was. How many times had she stood here and wished for a husband?

Working the spoon through the thick batter, Evelyn wondered if the whole tradition of Stir-up Sunday was merely an opportunity to make a game out of such a laborious chore, for it was not a simple task with such a dense mixture. But her spoon had made nearly a full rotation before she had a firm idea of what she wished for in the coming year.

Grasping the first thought that popped into her mind, Evelyn closed her eyes and sent out a silent petition to the cosmos. It was a silly thing to do, but she couldn't help but wish for that mysterious husband to finally arrive. All the other times she'd stood here at this table, sending out her Christmas wish, she'd had grand imaginings for the sort of fellow she wanted, and with each passing year, that image had shifted and altered.

Gone were the details she'd thought important. Handsome looks and a rousing sense of humor were well and good, but Evelyn had seen too many young ladies place such qualities at the top of their lists and end up in miserable marriages.

What sort of man did she desire? In all honesty, Evelyn had no thoughts as to what would make the perfect husband for her, but surely, if he were driven towards self-improvement, then any fault or frailty could be overcome with time. Together. Just as she hoped for a man who would help her become a better Evelyn.

And surely, innate goodness came along with such a quality. Not perfection. Heavens, no. Evelyn knew herself to be too far from that lofty perch to win the heart of someone who had attained it, and she wanted nothing to do with someone who believed himself to be sitting atop it. But a determination to try one's best would make for a happy future.

Beyond that, Evelyn didn't know any longer what sort of man suited her. And even if she wished to come up with a lengthy list of qualities, her turn at the Christmas pudding was now at an end, and she had to relinquish her place at the head of the table with her wish half-formed. Papa stepped forward when bidden to give the pudding its final stir before Cook wrapped it up for steaming.

With the family's attention fixed on the Christmas pudding, Evelyn drifted towards the door, slipping away from the cacophony and into the empty hallway. The door shut behind her, muffling the noise, and she felt like sagging against the wood. Her family were dear people, and she adored them beyond all reason, but they were a raucous crew, and Evelyn's ears rang.

Her slippered feet brushed against the floor, the swipe of leather against stone following her along as she made her way to the servants' stairs; pulling her skirts close, Evelyn crept up the narrow passage, grateful no one was descending, for she was certain they would not be able to pass one another. How did the servants manage it whilst carrying buckets of water or trays of food?

Emerging at the top, she wandered into the house proper. Now that her sisters were all married, Evelyn had a bedchamber to herself, but the library was her special place of solace, so she ducked inside. Thick curtains covered the window seat, and an armchair was angled just so before it, hiding the space from casual glances. That tiny space was a haven that had belonged solely to her when the house had been stuffed full of children running to and fro.

Evelyn tucked herself into it and longed to curl up like she had as a child, but between her longer limbs and voluminous skirts, it was no longer possible. Twisting in place, she contented herself with propping a leg up enough to allow her to stare out the frosty window.

Winter had brought with it a thick layer of snow, covering the trees and bushes in white, though it was nothing compared to the flurries Evelyn had navigated when she was young. The world had seemed buried in snow with thick, thigh-deep banks. But as she considered that, Evelyn supposed her perception was skewed as her thighs were quite higher now than when she was a child.

"There you are."

Chapter 2

Sucking in a deep breath, Evelyn swiped at the window, putting a great streak through the lacy frost, and then turned to face her father with a smile firmly on her face. "As you see."

Papa turned the armchair nearest to her around and plopped himself down to face her. "And how are you faring?"

Evelyn huffed, and her smile turned rueful. "I was afraid you might ask that."

Giving her a shrug, he leaned into the chair. "You left in quite a hurry."

"Our family can be quite overwhelming when they wish to be. I needed a moment to myself."

Papa nodded, allowing her statement to fade into silence, though Evelyn heard the cogs turning in his mind; it took little effort to guess what had him so preoccupied.

"Gemma meant nothing by her question and comment, Evelyn."

"I am well aware of that, but it is clear from the family's reaction that they view my impending spinsterhood with such horror that it ought never to be remarked upon. As though it is something shameful and wretched. Something pitiable."

Leaning forward, Papa gave her a sympathetic smile. "They did not mean to imply that, Evelyn. They were simply afraid Gemma might have bruised your feelings with such a question." Then he paused and grimaced. "And then her statement that followed."

Evelyn pressed a hand to her mouth, stifling a laugh at that memory. "If an adult had said such a thing, I might've been, but she's a child and doesn't see things in such a light. To her, my being unmarried isn't disgusting but merely confusing. Gemma only wished for clarification, so how can I be offended by such a thing?"

"Quite easily," replied Papa. "People often take offense when none is meant."

Shifting in her seat, Evelyn smoothed her skirts as she studied the floral pattern. "True. And it is entirely easy to do so when it is clear from every word and action that others view my state as wretched and pitiable."

Papa straightened, but before he could reply, she raised a staying hand. "Do not try to assuage my wounded pride by assuring me it is not so. Do you know how many people lectured me about 'keeping my chin up' despite Josie marrying before me? I spent the whole of her wedding festivities fending off well-meaning people who could not help but try to lighten my spirits simply because they assumed I was weighed down by crushing disappointment because of my younger sister's good fortune. They assumed I was mere seconds away from bursting into tears."

Evelyn scowled at the memory. "No matter how I tried to assure them, they were convinced I was hiding my pain because they view spinsterhood as so wretchedly awful that it is a miracle I rise from my bed in the mornings. Even when their marriages are filled with arguments and discontent, they still praise the heavens they have husbands as my state is infinitely worse."

Her words sped up, coming faster as her muscles tightened. "It is one thing to have others sympathize with my disappointments, but having people pity me is unbearable. They assume I must be forever disheartened and unable to summon any joy for my dear sister who has found her happiness. Inferring anguish at the prospect without any regard for whether or not I feel that way. Oh, no. They view it as an incontrovertible fact that a spinster must be a miserable creature for there is not an ounce of joy in their life. And to be forced to attend her younger sister's wedding? What torture! Surely, she must be in the pits of despair! Her world is a thing of black despair!"

Sucking in a breath, Evelyn sighed, her body sagging as the air left her lungs. "I wish to be happy, but it is impossible when I am forever being told I must be wretched. Having my family send little Gemma into hysterics for simply broaching the subject has not helped matters."

Papa scooted his chair closer, taking her hands in his. "I am sorry for it, Evelyn. We do not mean to make you feel that way."

"And I do not mean to make it sound as though I am treated terribly," said Evelyn with a shake of her head. "Today was an aberration. The family does not view me as a plague to be reviled, and though Bridget is the worst offender, I know she loves and respects me. She simply doesn't understand."

Papa rambled on about goodness knew what; Evelyn's thoughts were far too preoccupied to discern his words.

Her chest constricted, drawing forth a prickling in her eyes, and she frowned, forcing herself upright again. This was not what she wanted; wallowing in such things was not helpful. This coming year would mark her thirtieth birthday. Evelyn had made her debut more than a decade prior, and in that time, she had spent countless hours primping and preening, waiting and hoping. How many more years would she allow this husband hunt to commandeer her life? If she longed to find her place in the world, perhaps it was time to accept her reality and stop fixating on the aspects she could not alter.

Evelyn frowned at herself as she thought about the wish she'd made—foolish thing that it was. Did she truly expect this year to be any different? For the patterns of the past to suddenly shift and deliver a gentleman to her doorstep, desperate for her company?

Wishes (ones made at Christmastime or otherwise) were silly, and Evelyn gave them no weight. However, she wanted to turn back the clock and alter the one she'd made over the Christmas pudding, for it only continued to feed her foolish hopes. If given another opportunity, she would've wished to find peace with her place in the world whatever that may be.

How did one discern such a thing? The world was a topsy-turvy place, yet some people were content despite any knocks or bruises they received; life did not turn out as planned, yet they soldiered on, content with what they had.

For years, the hope for a husband had consumed Evelyn's thoughts. So much of the world was fixated on marriage and family that it was impossible not to be swept up in it as well. However, Evelyn couldn't blame her burning desire solely on that: she wanted to be loved. That bone-deep longing was woven through her, feeding the hope that one day a gentleman would value her. Cherish her. Desire her.

Yet no man appeared.

"...I know how disheartening it can be to have your life feel like it is not within your control," said Papa, his pale brows twisting as he held fast to her hand.

Evelyn straightened, a smile playing at the corner of her lips. "But it doesn't have to be. I have spent so much of my life fixated on something I cannot control and that will never come to pass. I've surrendered so many years to a fairy tale, telling myself a husband will appear. It is time I let such foolishness go."

Blinking, Papa frowned and drew upright, his hand falling from hers. "What do you mean?"

"Precisely what I said. I am done with hoping for marriage. I am a spinster, and it is high time I accept it." The words tasted sour, but even as her insides squirmed, a sense of rightness settled over her. "Why should I spend my life hoping for something that will never come? It only makes me miserable."

"You speak as though it is impossible for you to marry."

Papa's eyes bore into hers, the furrow of his brow deepening.

"Isn't it? In all the years I've spent slogging through the marriage arena, the only man who has ever looked in my direction was Mr. Townsend, and I needn't remind you how that horrid business ended."

Papa's hands clenched, his lips squeezing together into a tight line. "No, you needn't remind me of that blackguard." Then, forcing out a breath, he relaxed his posture. "But your mother was older than you when we met—"

"But Mama never wanted for suitors. I, on the other hand, cannot find a man willing to stand up with me for a dance. Do you truly think it's possible that a gentleman would finally take notice of me when there are more obvious candidates for their affection? With my complexion and coloring, my chances were never great, and they have only lessened as I've grown older."

The words stuck in Evelyn's throat, and she shook away the shadows in her heart.

"There are plenty of spinsters in the world," she continued, "and there is no shame in embracing my role. Without a husband and children of my own, I can spend my days helping my family and others. I shall be an adoring aunt to my nieces and nephews and support my siblings in their lives. I will find joy and peace in that, Papa. But only if I accept reality as it is and stop dreaming of things that will never be."

Papa moved forward once more, reaching for her hand, and Evelyn allowed it, though she refused to let the sadness in his gaze move her.

"Before I met your mother, I was without hope. My life seemed a dreary mess, and I saw no end in sight. Then your mother swept into my life, upending the whole of it and making it into something new. You do not know what is in store for you, so do not surrender your hopes and dreams."

Evelyn rose to her feet with a shake of her head. "I cannot go on as I have, Papa. Every day, I go out into the world, hoping for someone to notice me, only to have my heart crushed again and again. I cannot bear it any longer."

"But—"

"It is better this way, Papa." Giving him a quick kiss on the cheek, Evelyn smiled, infusing it with the certainty she felt. She strode away, forcing herself to leave behind those silly dreams; there was no good to be had in fixating on what was not to be and hoping that Christmas magic might grant an impossible wish.

Chapter 3

Two Weeks Later

Everyone needed a sanctuary. Comfortable seating and distance from one's troubles were paramount, and if that refuge from the troubles of the world included delectable food and drinks, then all the better. And though Hamilton's was not as fine a coffee shop as those in London or Bath, it met every requirement for a prime sanctuary, and Gideon Payne adored it.

The front room had been outfitted to serve the social needs of Bentmoor's menfolk. Benches and tables were scattered about, ready to be shifted and circled whenever required, and many an hour was filled with raucous laughter and conversations. But the true beauty was found in the backroom, which had more of the air of a gentlemen's club than a public space. Warm colors and overstuffed armchairs greeted the men seeking refuge inside, promising long hours of quiet by a warm fire as they perused their newspapers and books.

But any feelings of solace fled as he stared at Mr. Lewis Finch. Gideon had retired to this quiet space because there was a noticeable lack of chairs, leaving an intruder unable to sit near him. Yet Mr. Finch had stridden in and dragged one over to face Gideon. As if that were not annoyance enough, the fellow had begun spouting nonsense.

"You wish me to pay call on your daughter?" asked Gideon.

Surely, this was a jest. Though Mr. Finch didn't seem the sort to laugh at another's expense, Gideon knew any number of gentlemen who had no scruples about orchestrating such a bizarre situation. One's friends were always ready to mock, after all.

Mr. Finch picked at a speck on his trousers. "It is not—" He paused, shifting in his seat. "I merely wish for you to...pay her special attention—" Mr. Finch leaned forward and then back again with a furrowed brow. "She is a lovely young lady, yet she is too often...overlooked—"

Letting out a low sigh, Mr. Finch lifted a hand to his cravat but stopped short of tugging at it, dropping his hand once more to the arm of the chair.

Straightening, he met Gideon's gaze. "I am not suggesting anything untoward, Mr. Payne. I am merely suggesting that it would be...mutually beneficial—for you and her—if you would...seek out her company. Go on a drive or two. Dance with her. Accompany her to parties and balls and the like. Whatever else the youth enjoy doing these days."

But for all that Mr. Finch assured him otherwise, Gideon thought that sounded very much like courting, and he could not see how it would be beneficial to anyone but the matrimonial-minded.

Before Gideon could say so, Mr. Finch's expression pinched, and he let out another sigh. "I know this sounds ridiculous, Mr. Payne. I am well aware of it. But my daughter is a fine lady who does not receive the attention she deserves, and that has left her feeling—" But Mr. Finch shook his head and changed course once more. "I merely wish for her to be noticed. With a little...assistance, she might—"

Gideon blinked at Mr. Finch as the fellow stammered his way through a rambling explanation. Though they had never formally met before, everyone in Bentmoor, Oakham, and the surrounding areas knew of the family, and anyone involved in Devon's economy was acquainted with Barrows & Finch. So, Gideon was familiar with Mr. Finch's reputation. One did not maintain a successful merchant business like that without a healthy dose of confidence and a commanding presence, but that was not congruent with the awkward gentleman sitting before him. Mr. Finch was not at all what Gideon had expected him to be.

"Simply introduce her around," said Mr. Finch with a wave of his hand, his forehead furrowing.

"As diverting as that sounds," though Gideon's words could not be further from the truth, "I am not one to..." Gracious, how could one describe what Mr. Finch was requesting? Gideon couldn't bring himself to say "court a lady," though that was the proper phrase. "...pay special attention to a young lady simply because her father desires it."

That was something Gideon had never thought to say. "Besides, I am in a poor position to offer Miss Finch any social assistance."

Mr. Finch shook his head. "But that is precisely the reason you ought to do it. This will open doors for you, young man. Your reputation is in such tatters that nothing short of a miracle will mend it. Having a clear connection with my family will be a boon."

"You wish for a scoundrel with a tattered reputation to associate with your daughter?" Gideon hid his self-deprecating smile, though he could not hide it completely from his tone. When he chanced a glance at Mr. Finch, he found the gentleman studying him.

"I do not take my daughter's position or safety lightly, Mr. Payne," he said, his words steadier than before. "If there were any chance you would bespoil her, I would not allow you anywhere near her—just as the rest of the fathers in Bentmoor have done. But though you have not known me until this moment, I have been aware of you for some time, and I do not believe the rumors surrounding you are true."

Gideon's breath stilled, his gaze holding firm to Mr. Finch's. Though he could hardly countenance such an opinion, Gideon saw nothing but truth reflected in the gentleman's eyes. His throat clamped shut, and he tried to swallow past the lump, but his muscles wouldn't work properly.

"I—" What could one say to such a revelation? Turning his gaze to his newspaper, Gideon folded it carefully and tossed it onto the side table as he tried to sort out the puzzle that sat before him and the maelstrom churning in his chest.

"I am not suggesting anything untoward, Mr. Payne," said Mr. Finch, straightening. "But I am well aware of how difficult it can be to manage society when facing it alone. If you desire to thrive in banking or to marry, you will need society's doors opened, and with the proper connections, you would have no trouble securing your place. My daughter has the entrée, but she is often overlooked in favor of those with more obvious charms."

Gideon's brows furrowed as he wondered why Miss Finch required such assistance; the word "antidote" came quickly to his mind, but he was not about to ask the young lady's father if she was homely.

As though he knew precisely what Gideon's pause meant, Mr. Finch clarified, "My daughter is a lovely creature but uncomfortable in crowds. Having someone at her side would greatly ease her fears. And gentlemen are not the brightest of creatures. Sometimes they need assistance to see past their noses. If one of their own paid her marked attention, that would increase her visibility."

"And by association, my standing would improve," Gideon added, his mind churning at this unexpected turn of events. Though there were flaws aplenty in this plan, he couldn't fault Mr. Finch's logic. Gideon had seen many a gentleman's interest piqued simply because another pursued a lady, and his being connected—and accepted—by the Finch clan would elevate his situation significantly.

"If Miss Finch is amenable to this arrangement—"

"My daughter should not know of this conversation."

Gideon stiffened, his brow furrowing as he studied Mr. Finch, whose gaze was fixed on the toes of his shoes. "Miss Finch doesn't know you've approached me?"

The gentleman shifted in his seat, his lips pinching into a sharp line as his gaze bored into the floorboards. Straightening, Mr. Finch met Gideon's eyes, and whatever hesitation had been there a moment ago was absent.

"My daughter would not welcome my interference."

Rising to his feet, Gideon gave Mr. Finch a curt nod. "Then that answers the last of my questions and concerns. I am not the gentleman for this venture."

And with that, Gideon strode towards the exit.

Chapter 4

Mr. Finch raised his hands as he shot to his feet. "I give you my word that I am doing this in the best interest of my daughter."

"I am quite familiar with parental 'good intentions,' Mr. Finch, and I assure you I have no interest in assisting with yours."

Mr. Finch stepped in front of him, his hands still raised in placation. "And I assure you, Mr. Payne, I am asking this because I believe it will further her happiness, not to manipulate her into doing as I please."

Gideon huffed and shook his head, stepping around him. "What you believe will further her happiness may not do so. Being a father doesn't mean you always act in your child's best interest."

Though Gideon had every intention of stepping out of the coffee shop and finding some new sanctuary for the afternoon, Mr. Finch's response made him pause.

"You are correct, young man. Far too many fathers believe they have the right to decide for their children and that those decisions are infallible and indisputable."

Gideon turned to find the gentleman standing there, his

shoulders lowered and his brows furrowed. Mr. Finch's gaze was focused on him, and Gideon felt those eyes burning through him. There was such a hint of melancholy to them, though he wouldn't say Mr. Finch looked downtrodden. There was a sympathy in his eyes that made Gideon feel as though the gentleman understood the meaning beneath Gideon's words.

"The truth of the matter is my daughter has been judged by society just as you have. They have deemed her beneath their notice. And here you are, turning away from something that would benefit you greatly because you feel it dishonorable, despite everyone labeling you a cad and a bounder," he said, stepping closer. "Perhaps together you might alter their perceptions."

Then pushing a square of paper toward Gideon, Mr. Finch bowed. "I have secured you an invitation to the Meechams' ball tonight. You are free to attend regardless of what you choose to do, but I do hope you will reconsider. You both deserve better hands than the one you've been dealt."

With a curt bow, Mr. Finch turned and strode out the door, leaving Gideon blinking and clutching the invitation; the copperplate stood out in stark black against the creamy white paper, and he read the few sentences again and again, as though that might alter the clear words. Gideon Payne was invited to the Meechams' ball. Though by no means the grandest event of the coming festive season, the towns of Bentmoor and Oakham and the surrounding villages and hamlets eagerly anticipated this annual event, which marked the beginning of the holidays.

It had been some years since he'd been allowed to cross the Meechams' threshold, let alone grace their ballroom. The virtues of Bentmoor's young ladies needed protecting from the vile Gideon Payne, and even if a family did not have a young lady in residence themselves (which most did), for the good of their guests, the hosts would not risk the chance that he might taint their goodness even amidst a party—which Gideon might think entirely ridiculous if that was not precisely what had happened. In a manner of speaking.

Frowning, he returned to his armchair and cast the invitation onto the side table, though his gaze never strayed far from it. With the Finches sponsoring his efforts, few doors would remain closed to him. People were quick enough to trust Gideon with their funds—and that ought to be enough—but far too many of the bank's investments were proposed and negotiated at such gatherings. If he didn't wish his father's bank to flounder whilst under his guidance, Gideon needed to make stronger connections in the community.

But courting a lady under such mercenary terms—even if it was only a temporary arrangement—made his stomach sour.

What to do? Such a curt question with far too complex an answer, and despite distracting himself here and there, it followed him as the day passed, lingering in the back of Gideon's thoughts as he stared at ledgers and spoke with clerks. And then there were the interminable hours of quiet when he had nothing to distract him from the fact that the Meechams' ball was drawing nigh.

No doubt, Miss Finch would be there, and her father likely expected him to make some overture to her (assuming Gideon accepted this ridiculous bargain, of course), but the invitation had been given without caveat, and Gideon wasn't about to turn aside an opportunity. Perhaps tonight would be all that was required, and he could avoid this farce.

One moment, he was certain of his decision, and the next, the world shifted, leaving him determined to do the opposite. Even as he readied himself for the ball, Gideon couldn't think what he'd do once he arrived there.

His fingers fumbled with his waistcoat buttons, and he sighed and straightened, forcing himself to calm as he reached for his dress jacket. The black fabric looked somber on its own, but the brightly colored waistcoat beneath breathed new life into it. Stitches stretched across the silk, bursting into a rainbow of flowers and vines that were far too flamboyant on their own, but just as his suit jacket was revived by the waistcoat's vivid appearance, his somber evening clothes lent the colorful waistcoat an air of gravitas and kept him from looking like a peacock. The pattern didn't suit his tastes, but he couldn't imagine sallying forth without it.

With quick movements, Gideon straightened the various layers and turned towards the door. The floorboards creaked beneath his shoes as he tugged at his cuffs while thoughts of Miss Finch followed him through the corridor.

"Are you going out?"

Gideon paused just beyond his father's bedchamber and turned back to stand in the doorway. "Yes, sir."

Lying amongst the blankets and pillows, Father's gaze bored into him. A stern expression pulled at his lips, unmarred by the nightcap tassel hanging jauntily down the side of his face.

"Out carousing while your father is dying." As though to punctuate that morbid statement, Father's lungs seized, and he gave a deep, rattling cough.

Gideon stepped forward, reaching for the teacup on the table beside him and offering it up, but Father batted it away with one hand as he held a handkerchief to his mouth with the other. His dark gaze blazed as though his son were the author of each spasm shuddering through him. Gideon stood beside the bed, holding the cup, and waited until Father's muscles relaxed and his head fell back against the pillows once more.

"I was invited to the Meechams' ball, and I thought it prudent to accept," said Gideon, setting the teacup in its previous place.

Father huffed, though it stirred up another cough. "It is about time you started mixing with the right company, boy. Though I don't know how you managed it."

Gideon's lips pinched, but otherwise, he kept his expression impassive.

"But it is a good sign that they issued you the invitation. Your mother and I attended every year." Father stared up at the canopy above him, his brows furrowing. "At least the family shall be represented this year."

Though the words seemed kind, Father's tone dimmed

their shine, for it was clear he believed the substitution a poor one.

Turning his gaze to Gideon, Father frowned. "This is a golden opportunity, so do not squander it on chasing petticoats, boy. If you ever hope to take my place at Payne & Co., you'd best spend your time speaking with the gentlemen. You manage their money with some skill, but they'll take their funds to other institutions if you ruin their daughters."

And with that, Father closed his eyes. "Now, off with you. Be on your best behavior, and remember whose name you bear."

Ignoring the tightening in his chest that always accompanied that reminder, Gideon swallowed and nodded, as he knew he must. He moved to the door but stopped on the threshold when his father spoke again.

"Is that the waistcoat your mother made you?"

Gideon turned to find Father studying him from the corner of his eye.

Tugging at the bottom, Gideon nodded. "I don't have call to wear it often, and tonight—"

"It makes you look like a peacock," he said, closing his eyes. "Vanity is a sin, boy."

"Yes, sir." With that, Gideon left as there was nothing more to say—or nothing he could say—and there were far more important things to be done tonight.

Chapter 5

There was peace in accepting the inevitable. Hope had its uses, but it often included a string of unbearable consequences, and only when those fantasies proved true was the price worth that cost. Seated in her usual area of the ballroom, Evelyn took a deep breath, letting it out as she reveled in the looseness of her muscles, the steady rhythm of her heart, and the lightness of her spirits.

Having harbored matrimonial dreams for so long, Evelyn hadn't realized just how much strain it placed on her. Romantic eagerness had nipped at her heels, forcing her to seek out every unattached gentleman and consider his viability as a beau, and then the countless minutes praying he would approach, only to have him walk by without seeing her. Evelyn had spent her adult life with bated breath, and now, she could breathe again.

The Meechams' ballroom was by no means grand and certainly was not designed with such a robust gathering in mind. Of course, it hadn't been intended to serve as a ballroom, but the long gallery was large enough to serve that purpose. The room was festooned with greenery and bunting befitting the holiday season, and their hosts had spared no expense regarding candles; the chandeliers and sconces burned bright without even a hint of the cheap tallow so many others preferred. Thank the heavens. The press of bodies was pungent enough; there was no need to add the scent of burning animal fat. And Mrs. Meecham had done her best to offset it all by using aromatic evergreen boughs along the walls and tables, which filled the room with the scent of Christmas.

At the far end sat the musicians, their instruments skipping along with merry tunes as the dancers made do with the oddly shaped room. The long, narrow space had served perfectly for the dances of the older generation when the popular country dances involved long lines of pairs weaving between each other, but the advent of the gallopade, mazurka, waltz, and polka required a little more creativity to maneuver the space. Especially with so many people in attendance.

Evelyn tried not to laugh as Miss Virginia Fernsby shuffled past while her partner attempted to keep the two of them from colliding with the others (despite the young lady's ungainly movements fighting his every lead). Evelyn knew it was utterly uncharitable of her to laugh at the struggle, but she contented herself with the knowledge that her response was kinder than what Miss Fernsby was apt to show when the roles were reversed.

With the room being so long, it left a fair amount of space on the far end, and those who longed to enjoy the music and await the next set gathered there with their friends. There were chairs aplenty, for which Evelyn was quite grateful. Not every ball or party provided such comforts, eschewing the cumbersome furniture in favor of more room for dancing. To Evelyn's thinking, if one was relegated to watching the goings-on without being allowed to participate, then one ought to be comfortable while doing so.

Smoothing her silk skirts, Evelyn hummed along with the music. There was no one near enough to hear, so she indulged herself as her mind wandered to her current book, which sat on her bedside table at home, awaiting her return. Perhaps she ought to have brought it with her, but reading during a ball was an unforgivable sin in society's eyes. Never mind that they had no interest in engaging her in conversation.

Instead, Evelyn played out the story in her mind. She had read *The Ghost of Berrymore Manor* a dozen times, and the plot ran through her thoughts as though she were watching it on the stage. The story was ridiculous and entirely devoid of any literary merit, yet the characters tickled Evelyn's fancy. Winter evenings were the perfect setting for Gothic tales and ghost stories, though the lively dance music detracted from the mystery of the story.

"My dear Miss Finch."

Evelyn had seen Mr. Redding approach with another gentleman at his heels, but even when he spoke, she didn't entirely believe Mr. Redding was addressing her, despite his clear use of her name. The two gentlemen stood there, awaiting her acknowledgment, so Evelyn greeted them with a dip of her head.

"Mr. Redding."

Motioning the other gentleman around, Mr. Redding gave her a smile that made Evelyn's teeth grind together as she struggled to hold onto her own affable expression. The fellow had far too high an opinion of himself, and she was certain she might growl if he used such a ridiculous appellation again.

"My dear..." As if they were friends. Until this moment, they hadn't exchanged more than a few vague pleasantries. Forcing herself not to scowl, Evelyn studied him and his companion, searching for the telltale signs of mockery.

"Allow me to introduce Mr. Gideon Payne," said Mr. Redding with a wave of his hand in the other's direction. "He was practically begging to meet you."

Definitely mockery. There was no mistaking that twist of the lips and tone of voice. Though Mr. Redding did a better job at hiding his teasing than most, Evelyn recognized the signs and sighed. Would he ruin a perfectly pleasant evening?

But it was then that she turned her attention to the man at Mr. Redding's side. Where the first was lanky and tall with fair coloring and features that made ladies swoon, Mr. Payne was quite average. In height and build, he had nothing to recommend himself. Much the same could be said of his coloring and features, but they held hints of something unique that kept him from being altogether bland.

On anyone else, his nose would seem large and ungainly, and Evelyn couldn't say why it did not look so on Mr. Payne, but it seemed to match his cheekbones and ears, both of which were a little too pronounced to be attractive on their own. His hair was dark and unremarkable, but it had just a hint of wave that framed his face in a manner that might look purposeful if Mr. Payne were inclined to fuss before a mirror, though he didn't seem the type.

Evelyn wouldn't say he was handsome, but there was something striking about this Mr. Payne. Yet it wasn't his appearance that held her attention. It was his eyes. Upon closer inspection, she noticed they held a hint of green that kept them from being a bland brown. More than that, they were filled with unspoken irritation for Mr. Redding. Mr. Payne didn't go so far as to sigh or frown, but Evelyn saw a flash of frustration before he hid it away and swept into a bow. Intriguing.

"I am most pleased to make your acquaintance, Miss Finch," said Mr. Payne.

Blinking, Evelyn tried to think what to say in response. True, the words were commonplace, and she'd heard them plenty of times before, but the situation was anything but usual for her. Ought she to express gratitude that he wished to make her acquaintance? That seemed merely self-important. Mimic his words back to him? Evelyn couldn't say if she was pleased or not, though it seemed the most logical thing to say at the moment.

But before she could reply, he spoke again.

"Might I join you?" Mr. Payne motioned towards the chair beside her, and Evelyn nodded. And, thank the heavens, Mr. Redding took that as an invitation to leave. With a parting bow, he disappeared back into the crowd.

Mr. Payne slid into the seat beside her, his hands clasped tightly together as they stared out at the dancers. Evelyn was quite aware of "polite conversation," that meaningless jabber so many employed in company, but whenever placed in a situation where such things were required, her thoughts always fled her, leaving her with nothing (meaningless or otherwise) to say.

Others made it seem so easy to get to know another person, but Evelyn had never found it so. Such things grew naturally, not out of forced conversation. Matters were not helped by Mr. Payne's current reticence. The strains of the music filled the silence, and the tittering groups around them only served to highlight the conversational void between the pair.

"I have often crossed paths with your brother-in-law, Mr. Landry, during my work," said Mr. Payne, though the gentleman went no further.

"Are you a banker, as well?" asked Evelyn, for that was the only thing that came to mind.

Mr. Payne nodded. "My father founded Payne & Co."

Evelyn held back a cringe, refusing to allow herself more than a second of embarrassment. Though not acquainted with the Paynes previously, she knew of that institution and ought to have realized the connection on her own rather than asking the question and making certain Mr. Payne thought her a simpleton.

No matter. There was no reason to fret over what this stranger thought of her. But like so many things in life, that philosophy was easier to espouse than live.

Straightening, Evelyn reminded herself it did not matter. Mr. Payne was just some random gentleman. Not a potential suitor or beau. She was done with that sort of thinking. No more working herself into a dither because she wanted to say the exact right thing to earn his admiration. Evelyn Finch was merely a guest at a ball who had been approached by another guest in conversation.

Granted, there was little of that to be had, for Mr. Payne sat there as mute as she, glancing at her in silence. Why had Mr.

Payne approached her if he had nothing to say? The behavior was quite odd, indeed.

"Your gown is very lovely," he said.

Evelyn's gaze followed his, and she frowned. The dress was by no means frumpy or hideous, but neither was it one of her finer ones. The puffed sleeves and gathers at the bodice allowed for a more comfortable fit, and the cream of the silk flattered her bright red hair or freckled complexion, but that was the most that could be said about the fabric. The embroidery kept the gown from being wholly boring, but the scant flowers along the hem were hardly enough to catch the eye. Which was precisely what Evelyn had wished for. Her natural coloring drew enough attention on its own.

"I am seated, so you can hardly see it," she said with an arched brow.

Mr. Payne cleared his throat. "But what I do see is very lovely."

Evelyn held back a laugh. Why did so many gentlemen ply ladies with false compliments? Even her plain looks and garish coloring had received honeyed words from time to time, but the comments revolved around the beautiful styling of her person rather than the person herself. It meant nothing, but it was as though gentlemen deferred to that mode of communication when others failed or when they felt it was the required opening of a discussion.

Before Evelyn could think of broaching another subject, Mr. Payne spoke again. "Might I see your dance card?"

Her breath caught, her heart stilling as she blinked at Mr. Payne. Her dance card? Those wretched things were a physical manifestation of one's desirability, and whoever invented them certainly gave no thought for those who struggled to fill them. The empty spaces laughed and mocked the plain ladies while more attractive maidens turned gentlemen away with a falsely meek, "My dance card is full." Even when the odd gentleman (usually enlisted by guilt or their friendship with her brothers or brothers-in-law) asked Evelyn to stand up with them, they never requested to see her dance card, for they were well aware of how empty it was.

Surely, Mr. Payne didn't wish to write his name in the space? But there was only one reason a gentleman wished to see a lady's dance card. A maelstrom struck her thoughts, swirling all that was and all that might be into a tangle of possibilities. It filled her, making her heart beat with increasing force, demanding she do whatever he wished. Here sat a potential beau.

Evelyn pulled her heart up short and forced herself to breathe. Be rational. This was precisely the reason she needed to surrender these ridiculous hopes. A gentleman couldn't even ask her an innocuous question without her spinning it into a declaration of love. Mr. Payne was merely asking for a dance. Nothing more. And there were plenty of reasons he might do so that had naught to do with attraction.

Was he merely pitying her lonely state? That was a possibility.

Or was the gentleman mocking her? Wishing to draw attention to her empty dance card? Evelyn's gaze darted around, though Mr. Redding was nowhere in sight. Were the gentlemen making some sport of her? Perhaps Mr. Payne had lost a wager, and this was his forfeit.

Or was she the game itself? Yes, any of those motivations made far more sense—especially with Mr. Redding's mocking introduction.

Just as she opened her mouth (to give what she hoped would be a witty retort), Evelyn stopped. Mr. Payne had said he knew Robin. As neither her brother-in-law nor George was in attendance tonight, perhaps one of them had contrived to find her a companion for the evening. That was certainly within the realm of possibility—more so than Mr. Payne being so over-come with adoration that he insisted Mr. Redding introduce him to Evelyn at once.

Casting a look at her companion, Evelyn considered the fel-low. Though first impressions were not immutable, her in-stincts said Mr. Payne was not the sort to partake in jests that left victims in their wake; his irritation with Mr. Redding had seemed genuine, and her family's interference seemed the most likely reason he was seated at her side rather than with the gentlemen.

Evelyn sighed and frowned.

Chapter 6

"**M**iss Finch?" asked Mr. Payne. Evelyn straightened, realizing that although her thoughts had sped to that conclusion in a matter of seconds, she had been sitting silently for far too long. But perhaps this was precisely what she needed. Mr. Payne was not serious in his attentions but seemed determined to do his duty (whatever that was). Perhaps it was time for her to fully embrace her newfound social apathy.

Lifting her wrist to display the lack of that accoutrement, Evelyn smiled. "I haven't a dance card, Mr. Payne."

The gentleman's brow furrowed.

"The only reason to have one is if you cannot remember your partners," she replied, lowering her hand once more.

Mr. Payne nodded. "You have a good memory, I see."

"I haven't any partners, Mr. Payne." Evelyn laughed, her lips pulling into a wry smile. While the girl she had been might've remained silent, there was freedom to be found in her new state. If Mr. Payne was not a prospective suitor, then why worry about making a poor impression? She was not currying his favor, so it mattered not if he stayed or abandoned her, and thus there was no need to guard her tongue.

When the gentleman shifted in his seat with another frown, she held out a staying hand. "Do not fret, Mr. Payne. I didn't say such a thing to make you uncomfortable. It is merely the truth. I do not employ a dance card."

Not anymore, at any rate. Evelyn did not need that little bit of paper mocking her lonely state, and she would no longer allow it to have power over her.

Mr. Payne watched her with raised brows. "Would you do me the honor of standing up with me?"

Evelyn's thoughts raced through the possibilities. Even without Robin confirming his hand in this situation, she knew something was afoot. In all her years searching for a beau, only one had ever shown any interest in her, and Mr. Townsend had been in love with himself. Evelyn wasn't about to believe the world had suddenly shifted and made her desirable to a stranger. Even at her most fanciful, she couldn't imagine a man looking at her from across a crowded ballroom, suddenly overcome with desire; her future husband would begin as a friend who loved her personality, and eventually, he would see past the freckles and red hair to her beauty within.

No, Mr. Payne was not in earnest. But that didn't mean she couldn't enjoy him while he was so determined to do his duty to her brother-in-law.

"I would love to, Mr. Payne."

Good gracious. No wonder Mr. Finch had resorted to bribing young men to court his daughter; the young lady was determined to keep suitors at arm's length. Gideon was only seeking a conversation and a dance. Nothing more. Yet Miss Finch required him to wheedle and coax her into accepting. The Meechams' invitation had been extended with no expectations, but Gideon owed Mr. Finch at least that.

As the first strains of the song began, they took their places amongst the dancers, and when it began in earnest, Miss Finch proved herself a skilled partner. Not the finest, but despite her wallflower existence, she managed the steps with grace.

Luckily, the lively dance and odd-shaped room required enough attention that conversation was not required, for Gideon knew not what to say to her. How did one go about forcing a connection when such things ought to occur naturally? Making business connections was one thing, but a true conversation about subjects beyond money and politics?

Gideon's eyes drifted towards Miss Finch, though hers took in the swirl of dancers around them as they hop-skipped along the dance floor. Her abrupt manners made it clear why she had no partners, though Gideon couldn't understand why she chased them all away. Mr. Finch would require more than a pretend beau to alter her standing amongst the gentlemen if she insisted on calling them to task for compliments.

"They are not contagious," said Miss Finch with a hint of a smile in her tone.

"Pardon?"

"My freckles. You are staring." Her eyes turned to him, and they were a deep brown. Rich and warm, alight with a silent laugh.

"I was not thinking about your freckles. Now that you are standing, am I allowed to compliment you?" Gideon tried to keep his tone polite, but the words held a hint of sarcasm. Miss Finch may be an odd lady, but she was no lackwit and understood his tone readily enough, earning him an arched brow in return with a humorous twist of her lips as she studied him.

"You may try," she replied with a tone as dry as his own.

"Your gown is very lovely."

Miss Finch sighed, and her eyes dulled with disappointment before turning to watch the dancers around them. Being utterly flummoxed by the situation, he let the conversation lapse. He wasn't here to win her good opinion, after all. This was merely a favor to Mr. Finch. Unfortunately for that gentleman, his daughter seemed determined to remain unattached. Good luck to her and her father.

Only when dance had stretched to impossible lengths, leaving Gideon wondering if they would be stuck here for eternity, did the music finally wind to its close, and he was free to deposit Miss Finch in her previous seat. With a quick bow, he turned away and went in search of more diverting conversations. His obligation was fulfilled, and it was time for him to make the most of the situation. There was no way to heal his reputation in one evening, but there was no reason he couldn't secure the good opinion of a few people here. With the holidays looming, there were events aplenty, and even an invitation or two could put him on the path back into society's good graces.

Turning on his heel, Gideon studied the crowd. There were gentlemen aplenty haunting the ballroom and adjacent card room, but their good opinions were far easier to win over. And only a fool thought it was a husband who controlled the guest list. Gideon spied a group with whom he was familiar. Though he could not count the Tomkins and Doddingtons as close acquaintances, they were not strangers. Taking a steadying breath, he refused to think about his actions before striding to their group.

"Good evening, Mr. and Mrs. Tomkins. Quite a lovely evening, isn't it?"

"Quite." Mr. Tomkins offered a smile in return. Mrs. Tomkins gave the fellow a subtle nudge of her elbow (though not subtle enough for Gideon to miss it). Her husband's brows rose, his gaze filled with confusion.

Before they escaped, Gideon swooped in with another greeting for their companion. "Mr. Doddington, it has been some time. How are your parents?"

"They are well enough," said Mr. Doddington, his tone the picture of polite disinterest, proving he was far quicker than Mr. Tomkins, for Mrs. Doddington had only to tighten her hold on his arm for him to grasp her disapproval.

Clearing his throat, Gideon attempted to speak of the weather, which was met with equally dry responses. Asking about their plans for the holidays fared only slightly better, but only because they were forced to either snub him entirely or offer more than single-word responses.

When Gideon could think of nothing more to say, he bowed and took his leave. Dabbing at his temple, he wandered about the ballroom, searching for any friendly face. At best, he was met with the sort of curiosity reserved for a menagerie of exotic animals. At worst, they turned away from him, refusing to acknowledge his very existence. Or at least, Gideon had thought that the worst. When he caught sight of a young lady standing alone, he approached her for a dance, but her mother swooped in like a hen protecting her chicks from a fox, sniping at him until he scurried away.

Turning, he spied Mrs. Meecham surveying her handiwork. No doubt Mr. Meecham had secured his place amongst the older gentlemen of the party, many of whom had taken up residence in the card room, where they could drink and gamble while avoiding the whirl of the ballroom. It was tempting to disappear there, but gaining their approval was only part of the battle. No, Mrs. Meecham was a far more important ally to win over.

With purposeful strides, Gideon made his way to her side and gave her a low bow. "Madam, I must tell you this evening is a delight. I am honored to have been invited."

Mrs. Meecham's smile was not wholly warm, though it was far from cool. "I am pleased you think so. How is your father? I understand he has been quite ill."

"Unfortunately, he has taken to his bed." The truth of the matter was that Father had hardly left it since Mother's passing three years ago, but that was far more honest than such a polite inquiry demanded.

"That is wretched business," she replied with a frown. "But with your assistance, I am certain he will make a full recovery."

"I hope so." Then, casting a glance about him, Gideon decided it was better to take the risk than retreat, so he hurried to add, "Might I beg your assistance, Mrs. Meecham? I would love to avail myself of the dancing, but I fear the young ladies with whom I can claim an acquaintance are all occupied at present. Would you introduce me around?"

Mrs. Meecham's expression tightened, her gaze darting out to her guests and back to the man Mr. Lewis Finch had foisted upon her. It didn't take any preternatural ability to see the battle waging within her between the duty she owed to one guest compared to the rest. Holding onto his most affable of smiles, Gideon tried to exude as much righteousness as possible, hoping it might convince the lady of his good intentions and character.

"Dear me," she blurted, straightening. "I must speak with my cook. I fear I have forgotten something of utmost importance. Please excuse me for a moment, Mr. Payne. I can assist you when I have a moment to spare."

And with that, she hurried away. Gideon let out a low sigh, certain that Mrs. Meecham would do everything in her power to ensure she was too preoccupied with other tasks to aid Mr. Gideon Payne in corrupting any of her innocent guests.

Turning about, he stared out at the gathering. In all honesty, the others weren't paying him much attention, but it was clear from the whispers here and there that little good had come from attending tonight. His feet pulled him forward, weaving through the crowd until he spied a familiar sight—the Jovials. The label seemed so apropos that Gideon could think of them as nothing else, though perhaps it was a kinder assessment than they deserved: they were more irritating than entertaining.

Every gathering had at least one or two such groups. They were easy enough to identify, for gentlemen of that ilk grew exponentially more boisterous with each addition, caring solely about conquests and wagers. Their joint intelligence dropped by degrees every minute they spent together, pushing them to drink more while discussing the various ladies in manners that, if overheard, would have their mothers fainting and the matrons swooping in to hurry their charges away.

They were an obnoxious lot, far too pleased with themselves and fixated on their status and pleasure to be enjoyable to anyone except other Jovials. They also happened to be just the sort of people who welcomed a man with Gideon's reputation into their ranks, and he was in no position to turn away any allies. Beggars cannot be choosers, as they were wont to say, and Gideon was scraping up any social crumb he could get.

"Mr. Redding," he said with as much of a smile as he could manage, but Gideon could not bring himself to embrace the vapid grins and chortles they preferred. Sidling up to their group, he gave them a firm nod, as though it was a given that his presence was acceptable. Not that he needed to worry about such things; a tattered reputation was guaranteed to earn their respect.

"Mr. Payne." Mr. Redding gave him a hardy pat on the shoulder that had Gideon staggering. Then, placing an arm around his shoulders, Mr. Redding turned him towards the others and gave the introductions. And before Gideon could say anything to divert the conversation into more savory paths, Mr. Redding gave a broad grin, and Gideon knew precisely what sort of introduction he was about to receive.

"This, my boys, is Mr. Gideon Payne—the man who seduced his general's daughter in the middle of a masquerade."

Chapter 7

The others whooped, drawing glances from other guests, though luckily, Mr. Redding hadn't spoken loud enough for his words to carry. Not that it mattered, for though no one else said it in such a bold manner, there wasn't a person in attendance who did not know the story.

"You are a legend!" cried one young man.

"And when can we expect the nuptials to take place?" asked another with a smirk before he downed a glass of wine; there was no reason to respond to the question, for the others all guffawed as though it was the best jest imaginable.

"I do not wish to speak of it," said Gideon through gritted teeth, though he managed to hold onto his smile.

Mr. Redding gave him a playful shake. "Don't be a prude, Mr. Payne. We know the story well enough, and there is nothing wrong with having a bit of fun."

Sucking in a deep breath, Gideon forced himself to relax. Defending Miss Evanston did no good: the fools wouldn't recognize truth if it slapped them in the face (something Gideon's hands were eager to do). Holding his tongue was the only good he could do for that poor young lady. Even until it bled.

"I have nothing to say on the subject," said Gideon.

And so it went, the fellows all taking their turns, attempting to outdo the others' crassness while painting it in the barest hint of wit. Gideon sent out a silent prayer of gratitude that they were in public at a ball, for he knew precisely how wretched the conversation would be without the constraints of propriety. Thankfully, such situations required little input from him; the more he remained silent on the subject, the more the others inferred, feeding into whatever ridiculous imaginings they had conjured.

But it left Gideon feeling as though he needed a bath.

Why could he not have an intelligent conversation? However, one could not expect much when one was passing an hour with Jovials, and at least they included him in their ranks. Any discussion was better than standing alone amongst the outskirts of the ballroom.

"And how did you fare with Miss Finch?" asked Mr. Redding while giving Gideon a gimlet eye.

"Who?" Mr. Durrant gazed about as though the lady would appear at the mention of her name.

"Lewis Finch's spinster daughter," supplied Mr. Hawker with a frown. "The plain, freckled one with the garish hair."

Mr. Durrant snorted, nearly choking on his drink. "What game is this, Payne?"

"Game?" asked Gideon with a frown.

"There is no reason a man like you would pay any attention to such an antidote without a scheme of some sort," replied Mr. Durrant, and though Gideon wished to refute that, several others jumped in with their agreement.

He didn't know which aspersion he detested more—that he was the sort of man who toyed with ladies' affections or that Miss Finch was a repulsive beast. As his reputation certainly supported the former, Gideon couldn't fault the men for thinking it. However, he scowled as he considered the latter.

True, Miss Finch's coloring was odd, which was bound to deter some of the vainer gentlemen, but a perfect complexion was not the epitome of beauty. Her freckles were plentiful, but he couldn't comprehend why fashion deemed them hideous.

And her hair. The brightness of her coiffure was shocking, but Gideon had heard young ladies bemoan the time they spent with their hot irons to form the sort of curls that came naturally to Miss Finch, and hers were certainly lovelier than anything that could be done by a lady's maid.

When one stripped such obvious things away, Miss Finch had much to recommend her. Her features weren't delicate, but they were striking. Rather like the rest of her. Not every lady could be the most handsome in the room, but Miss Finch was not devoid of charms. Far better to be interesting than the uninspiring string of beauties who paraded around the ballroom as though the world owed them every happiness simply because an accident of birth granted them an objectively lovely face.

But no matter how Gideon tried to defend Miss Finch's features, the others merely laughed his statements away. Not that he wished for these louts to pay her any special attention (no young lady deserved such an annoyance), but he ought to defend at least one young lady tonight. Even if it was unlikely to do any good.

Luckily, the conversation shifted quickly enough. Jovials were like bumblebees, flitting about the conversation in a haphazard manner, never resting long on one subject before allowing the winds to carry them on to the next. Gideon had seen enough Jovials from different walks of life, countries, and cultures to know they were found in every corner of the globe, and not one was inspired enough to delve past the superficial. The same conversations. The same irritants.

Gideon nodded and smiled, wondering if he had made a mistake in accepting Mr. Finch's invitation. Of course, that was a foolhardy thought, which he batted away as easily as it came. Something had to be done to raise his fortunes, and clearly, one good invitation wasn't going to undo the damage the rumors about Miss Evanston had done.

Mr. Finch's proposition came to mind once more, and Gideon groaned within. Ought he to accept it? Pretend to be the doting beau? To say nothing of the fact that he would be forced to endure Miss Finch's company. Their previous conversation hadn't recommended her nor been remotely stimulating. Odd was a better description, but not the sort of odd that Gideon wanted to experience again.

From his place amongst the Jovials, Gideon caught glimpses of Miss Finch, seated precisely where he'd left her. Then he found his feet turning of their own accord, taking his leave of the Jovials and carrying him towards her. Still, he didn't know what to do about the lady, but each step drew him closer, forcing him to acknowledge that he was merely lying to himself. If squiring about a young lady for a few weeks would allow him to heal the damage he'd done to his name, it was a small price to pay.

Even if it meant surrendering his dignity.

Breathing deep, Evelyn tried to focus on the scent of the evergreen boughs, but as the evening wore on, it grew fainter as the dancers' aroma increased. When Mr. Dickens had described the Fezziwigs' festive offerings as the height of joy and holiday merriment, Evelyn thought he must've imagined a scene somewhat like this. Thankfully for his readers, scent was something confined to the author's imagination.

That thought brought her to the novel itself, and having already entertained herself quite thoroughly with other literary offerings, Evelyn settled in for a mental retelling of that wonderful story. Redemption wrapped up in holiday trimmings—it was difficult to find fault with the book, and Evelyn lost herself in Ebeneezer Scrooge's winding tale. However, she had to invent some of the details; she well remembered the overarching tale but was not as familiar with the nuances as she was with the other stories that had kept her company tonight.

Evelyn's gaze drifted around the dancers and guests, catching sight of Mr. Payne once more. What an odd fellow. If Robin had thought him a prime companion for the evening, her brother-in-law was sorely mistaken. Perhaps Mr. Payne was a good sort, but he'd said so little that Evelyn couldn't make heads nor tails of him. And despite scampering away at the first opportunity, she caught him spying on her at various intervals.

What was the fellow up to?

Then he started meandering her way. Starting and stopping. Turning away before continuing on a path so circuitous that Evelyn couldn't be certain he was heading towards her until he was a mere twenty feet away.

"Might I join you, Miss Finch?" asked the fellow with a bow.

Evelyn pinched her lips together, but she couldn't hide her smile. Though habit tried to keep the words from emerging, she forced her newfound philosophy to the forefront and spoke her mind. What good had it done to quiver and quake over every word that left her mouth?

"Then you did lose a wager."

Mr. Payne straightened and blinked at her. "Pardon?"

"I am well aware of how gentlemen like the Ninnies pass their time, and they have no qualms about abusing others for their entertainment," replied Evelyn. When Mr. Payne remained there like a ponderous statue, she added, "You seemed quite cozy amongst their ranks."

"Who?"

"The Ninnies." Perhaps she ought not to call them such, but the name was far too apt for that band of gentlemen, and saying audacious things was precisely what was expected of the eccentric spinster aunt; if Evelyn was to perfect that role by the time her nieces and nephews were old enough to appreciate it, she ought to begin posthaste.

When Mr. Payne clearly didn't grasp her meaning, she nodded toward the group, and the fellow's gaze darted in that direction before returning to her.

"You call them the Ninnies?" Mr. Payne's brows rose, but Evelyn refused to let it discompose her; the eccentric spinster aunt thought nothing of such things. "I had always thought of them as the Jovials."

Evelyn huffed. "Perhaps I would think of them more as 'Jovials' if their entertainment was not so often achieved at others' expense, or if they amused anyone but themselves. As they are generally considered irritating to anyone with sense, my moniker is far more apt."

Mr. Payne considered that with raised brows. "You make a valid point. It is difficult to get a sensible conversation from them."

"Do sit down," she said, waving at the seat beside her. However, Mr. Payne looked no more at ease when after accepting the offered chair than he had been while looming above her. For all that he spoke of sensible conversation, he seemed in no rush to supply it himself. Perhaps that was why he was on such amicable terms with the Ninnies.

A wicked impulse pushed Evelyn to tease him, and as she had no reason not to, she embraced it. "And so, you've traveled the ballroom, seeking out sensible conversation, only to find that no one else will supply it but me?"

"Besides those gentlemen, you are the only person here who will acknowledge me."

"Ah, so you are sitting by my side because you have no other options," she replied in a dry tone.

Mr. Payne's gaze widened. "I did not mean to imply—"

Evelyn laughed it away. Whether or not the fellow worded it offensively or not, there was truth to the statement. She didn't know if his presence at her side said more about Mr. Payne's desperation for company or her desirability as a companion (perhaps a bit of both), but regardless, he preferred passing the evening with her to standing alone. That may not be much of a consolation, but plenty of others chose solitude over passing an hour with her.

"Do not fret, Mr. Payne. I am merely teasing you. But I will warn you I shan't be content with awkward snippets this time. If you wish to sit beside me, you must provide me with a stimulating conversation."

Mr. Payne's brows shot upwards, though he looked more

considering than shocked at her statement. For her part, Evelyn was quite surprised at her audacity, but despite the frisson of fear that coiled in her stomach, her heart felt all the lighter for it.

"Might I ask what you were pondering when I approached?" asked Mr. Payne. "It looked as though it was amusing you."

"It was," she said with a nod. "Do you enjoy Mr. Dickens' novels?"

"Who doesn't?" he replied with a furrowed brow.

Evelyn laughed. "A good answer, Mr. Payne. However, I assure you no author is universally beloved. But as to your question, I was thinking about the scene at Fezziwig's, and how much the Meechams' ball looks like what the author described."

With a thoughtful huff, the gentleman turned his attention to the ballroom and studied it. "I don't think there will be any earthly manifestation to match what I pictured when reading that passage. It seemed like a veritable Christmas fairyland."

Here was a subject Evelyn could spend many hours dissecting, and as she rambled on about the book, Mr. Payne's posture relaxed, his attention turning more fully upon her. Their knees turned, pulling them towards each other, their attentions shifting so that they occasionally glanced out at the room rather than sparing the odd glance for the other.

Though focused on his conversation, Evelyn's thoughts could not stray far from his mysterious motivations for being by her side. Even if Robin had petitioned his assistance, Mr. Payne needn't spend the entire evening with her, as was clearly his intention. A dance, some polite conversation, and he was free to do with his evening as he wished. Certainly, any other gentleman who had been enlisted through her brother or brother-in-law's efforts to placate her had done so. Yet Mr. Payne remained as the hours wore on.

Evelyn could not comprehend it any more than she could believe the gentleman was in earnest. There had been too much resignation in his gaze as he'd taken the seat for her to believe he truly wished to be there. But as she thought about his explanation, she realized the truth.

Mr. Payne was lonely. Hadn't he said as much when he approached? No one else desired his company, and Evelyn would never be so cruel as to ignore someone who wished to speak with her. To say nothing of the fact that the fellow was rather interesting.

Though reticent at first, Mr. Payne proved himself versed in literature—something that marked him as decidedly different from the Ninnies, for Evelyn was certain none of them could read. That conversation began as a mere trickle; words here and there that slowly built into a stream, meandering about as all good discussions did. Evelyn couldn't be certain where it would lead, but Mr. Payne seemed as eager to speak as she—as long as a proper subject was settled upon. Politics, literature, travel, and music, their path wound along in a serpentine manner that had the pair laughing more than once.

And left Evelyn thinking about it long after she was deposited at home once more.

Chapter 8

Nothing induced anxiety quite like orchestrating a serendipitous meeting with a lady. What ought to be natural and simple was twisted into a shallow mimicry, but in the world of courtship, such playacting was a necessary evil. Which was rather ridiculous, all things considered. At worst, the object of your affection guessed your feelings, and who did not find such attentions flattering?

Yet it was part of the courting dance.

Which was how Gideon found himself sitting in his father's sleigh outside St. Margaret's church, draped in woolen blankets and furs with a few heated bricks at his feet while forcing his poor horse to circle the building again. Luckily, the village was not so very busy, making the roads easy to navigate even with the thick snow thick.

The maze of streets drew him around the churchyard, and the choir's voices rang out in the evening air, adding to the jingling of Cinnamon's tack and the bells the grooms had attached to the harnesses. Gideon couldn't free his hand well enough to look at his pocket watch, but surely, they had to be finished with their practice soon.

Pulling to the edge of the street, he gave the beast a rest and stared at the stone spire. The few panes of stained glass glowed from the prayer candles burning within, and the low rumble of the organ buzzed through the air even when the notes were not clear enough to hear. Biting the end of his leather-clad finger, Gideon tugged off the glove and pulled out his timepiece just as the church doors swung open.

Shoving the pocket watch back in its place, he struggled to get his glove back on while nudging the horse forward as though they'd always been in motion. As the sleigh drew close to the churchyard gates, Gideon searched the people spilling out but saw no sign of Miss Finch. Pulling back the reins, he slowed Cinnamon until they were hardly moving. He stared at the entrance, willing her to emerge.

Nothing.

The churchyard passed by, and Gideon nudged the horse forward, taking him quickly through the circuitous route they'd employed for the past quarter of an hour while Gideon prayed she'd be there when he finished his round. The church gate came into view, and he forced himself to slow so the flurry of snow and huffing horse didn't give his ruse away. The spire drew closer, and Gideon held firm to the reins as his gaze swept the churchyard.

But the church door was closed once more, and there was no one in sight. Blast!

With a flick of the reins, they moved forward, hurrying down the road. A lady walked just ahead, but Gideon didn't recognize the deep blue cloak. Not that he'd know Miss Finch's wardrobe on sight. Was that a flash of orange peeking out from the back of her bonnet? The sleigh drew up beside her.

"M..." began Gideon, but the lady glanced at him and was most decidedly not Miss Finch. "M...madam."

The lady stared at him. Thankfully, Cinnamon carried him past before either of them could say anything more. Passing a street corner, Gideon glanced down that crossroad and cursed his luck as he caught sight of a green-clad lady meandering away. The road was too tight for him to turn about, so he took another roundabout route, which allowed him to backtrack.

Gideon cursed himself for this ridiculous plan and his luck for making such a muck of it, but now that he was in the midst of it, he was committed and wasn't going to surrender. Urging the horse forward, he fought against the gnawing worry that he was driving too fast; no good would come from hurrying to her side if he crashed before he arrived there.

Then he caught sight of the lady again, and Gideon pulled back on the reins, easing Cinnamon into a slow trot. As he drew up next to her, he spied the telltale hint of her red hair blazing from beneath her bonnet.

"Why, Miss Finch, what a surprise," he said as he pulled to a stop.

"Mr. Payne," she said with a grin. "How good to see you. Do you have business in Oakham?"

Gideon cleared his throat and fiddled with the reins. "I found myself free for the afternoon and have been enjoying a drive."

"Well, you have just found me walking home from choir practice," she replied, nodding down the lane. "We've been preparing for the Christmas celebrations."

"Would you allow me to escort you home?" Gideon held out his hand for her, and though he expected her to take it, Miss Finch merely stared at the proffered limb.

"It isn't far, Mr. Payne."

"Then it won't be out of my way."

Miss Finch stood there, studying his hand, and then turned her gaze to him. Truly, they were quite lovely; those warm, rich brown eyes always seemed to hold some secret laugh within them. If the lady were not so determined to chase off suitors, one would get quite enamored with her gaze.

For a long moment, they stood there, silently studying each other before the lady placed her hand in his. Helping her into the sleigh, Gideon shifted the blankets so she could sit and tucked them around her, placing one of the heated bricks at her feet.

"If this is your attempt to sway me to your way of thinking concerning Mr. Dickens, I shan't be moved," she said, burrowing into their warmth. "He is a brilliant writer, and I adore his stories, but the fellow is long-winded. Forever using twenty words when three would suffice."

Gideon chuckled and flicked the reins. "As he makes his living being paid by the word, it is obvious why he eschews succinctness."

"I have done some investigating and learned that serials are paid by installment—not by the word. So your argument is moot."

Giving her a sideways look, Gideon stared. "You spent time researching my argument to prove me wrong?"

She straightened, raising her head as much as she could without relinquishing her hold on the blankets. "A lady ought to be informed."

"But it doesn't discredit my justification. Whether he is paid by the word or by installment, brevity is not financially sound for Mr. Dickens."

Miss Finch sighed, a heavy, put-upon noise, though her eyes were still alight with humor. "I understand quite clearly your reasoning and why Mr. Dickens does so, but that does not alter the fact that he ruins his gorgeous prose with superfluous words. And once his serials are published in novel form, there is no excuse for it. Books are not paid by the word. If anything, wordiness inflates the cost and drives down the profit."

Gideon opened his mouth to counter that argument, but Miss Finch forged ahead without drawing breath.

"His brevity is why I adore *A Christmas Carol* so much. I hear he wrote and published it in a matter of weeks, so he had not the time to stuff it full of ramblings. It is to the point and still has the hallmark of his heavenly prose, compelling characters, and strong themes."

With a laugh, Gideon shook his head. "I see we will never agree, Miss Finch. It is a hopeless matter."

"I suppose it is. Our friendship is quite doomed."

That earned her another laugh, livelier than the last, and Gideon was left dumbfounded by the odd lady at his side. Despite the passionate nature of her defense, the debate had never grown contentious or disgruntled. There was fire and convictions aplenty on both sides, yet she did not begrudge him his opinions any more than he did hers. He couldn't remember a discussion he'd enjoyed more. If Miss Finch didn't make it so infernally difficult to woo her, Gideon might like the lady.

"What if I were to suggest we postpone your return home and explore the countryside instead?" he asked.

Miss Finch turned in her seat, keeping the blankets carefully snuggled about her, and studied his profile. As Gideon couldn't turn his attention away from the road ahead of them, he couldn't be certain what it was she was searching for, but he felt her attention on him as the silence stretched out for several seconds.

"My family plans to start making our Christmas decorations tonight, so I need to be home in the next hour."

Gideon nodded, slanting a look in her direction. "I will ensure your safe return by then."

"Then I accept."

Chapter 9

Miss Finch smiled and straightened the blanket sliding off Gideon's lap. "I cannot think of a better way to spend my time than driving about in the snow, all bundled up warm and snug, with a friend at my side."

Friend? That was the second time she'd described Gideon as such, and he frowned to himself. He certainly wasn't going to convince anyone of the courtship if Miss Finch viewed it in that light. However, he rather liked the classification. He'd had plenty of chums over the years, but he'd never considered any of the fairer sex amongst their ranks. And despite Miss Finch's oddities, Gideon thought she would be quite a fine friend indeed.

"So, you sing, Miss Finch," he said, turning his thoughts back to the present.

With a wrinkle of her nose, Miss Finch shook her head. "Not in any significant manner."

"You are part of the church choir. That seems significant."

"Only because you have not heard Papa sing. Or Lily, for that matter. Her family are dear friends to mine, and we often spend the holidays together. She loves to sing while Papa plays, and her voice is divine. And her mother is equally talented with the pianoforte." Miss Finch shook her head. "Unfortunately, I was born with my father's love of music and my mother's talent. Middling and unremarkable. Hardly good enough to participate in a small musical soirée."

Straightening, Miss Finch snuggled closer. Gideon nearly jerked away, but she did not seem to notice, merely holding the blankets closer to him so they did not fall as he directed the horse through the town.

"So, I am relegated to the choir. I am a strong alto, and they need as many as they can find, so I am quite happy with my contribution." Miss Finch gazed out across the passing landscape. They did not always have such fine snowfalls, but winter had graced them with an abundance this year, lying thick upon the ground and across the branches; the chill in the air crystalized their surfaces, making the world sparkle despite the cloudy skies.

"I love singing the Christmas carols." Then with a frown at the world, she added, "But I am sad to say there is a shocking lack of songs that feature 'hallelujahs' or 'hosannas.' If we are singing our praises for such a sacred moment, it seems as though every one of them should have an abundance of such words. Don't you think so?"

As Gideon hadn't given it a smidgen of thought, he didn't know what to think about the subject, though Miss Finch's logic was sound. But before he answer, she beamed out at the world and sang a few lines of "Joy to the World." Though Miss Finch was correct in her assertion that she had a voice better suited for choirs, she had been overly harsh in her assessment of her skill. The notes came out clear, ringing through the winter air with a clear pitch, though the beauty of the sound was due more to her exuberance than her tone.

Turning her gaze to him, Miss Finch grinned, and Gideon found himself doing so in return.

"I don't know if I've ever met anyone so outspoken as you," he said, glancing at her. "I am never certain what is going to come from your mouth next."

Miss Finch's cheeks were already pinked from the winter's air, but there was something in the way her gaze darted away and the tightness of her lips that made him think she was blushing.

"I assure you this is a new development for me," she replied with a self-deprecating smile before Gideon was forced to turn his gaze back to where it ought to be. "I have spent my life terrified of everything I said to others, and I've recently decided I'm done currying favor. All it has done is make me miserable."

Gideon considered that. "That is commendable. I wish I were that brave."

With a chuckle, she shook her head. "It is not bravery but exhaustion. I am tired of living as I have, forever hoping things will change when they do not. Even now, my instincts are begging me to ask if you find my company enjoyable, but I will not give in to them. I hope you find me amusing and not irritating, but I refuse to hold my tongue any longer because I am afraid it might drive you away."

"You think I find you irritating?" asked Gideon with a frown.

"I said I hope you do not find me so, though I would hazard a guess that you did during our first conversation."

Straightening, Gideon turned to gaze at Miss Finch again, and she met that with a challenging raise of her brows before tucking the blanket more firmly about their laps. And Gideon had no words to defend himself. Not truthful ones, at any rate. Miss Finch had been vexing at first, but her bald declaration demanded a rebuttal, though her gaze promised he would not win that battle should he choose to engage.

Gideon turned back to the task at hand and said, "Say what you will, I think your honesty is admirable."

"I doubt you would if you knew just how much I shake in my boots," she replied in a tart but teasing tone. "I cannot bear to approach another living soul unless they are a friend or family. And attempting to strike up a conversation with someone is torturous unless it unfolds naturally. As you well know."

Gideon glanced at her to find the lady studying him with narrowed eyes that were alight with humor. "I suppose our conversation at the Meechams' ball was a bit torturous."

"At first."

Cinnamon listed to the right, and Gideon righted the beast, guiding him down the snow-laden lane. "But I have to wonder what brought you to this sudden epiphany. What inspired your sudden bout of unfiltered honesty?"

"I would rather discuss your waistcoat."

Gideon straightened. "My waistcoat?"

Miss Finch leaned over, giving his torso a thorough look, though the article of clothing was covered by several layers. "The one you wore at the Meechams' ball was lovely and so eye-catching. It made me wonder if you have a penchant for unique waistcoats."

"So, you are allowed to compliment my clothing, but heaven save me if I choose to praise your gown?" Gideon turned an arched brow in her direction, but Miss Finch met that with a stern nod of her head.

"My compliment was genuine. Yours was perfunctory. And do not attempt to convince me I am wrong."

"And so, you wish not only to be forthright in your own opinion but for me to be as well?" he asked, certain this was the oddest conversation he'd ever had, even as he wondered what Miss Finch would say next. Society was predictable; she was not.

"Would you prefer to discuss the weather or whatever latest scandal has the area enraptured?" Miss Finch asked in a tone that said she knew what his answer would be. When he gave none, she nodded as though that settled matters. "Then back to the subject at hand. Do you adore colorful waistcoats?"

Gideon huffed. "My wardrobe is more interesting than the weather or the latest scandal?"

"Most definitely."

Brushing away a bit of snow that caught on his eyelashes, he frowned. "There is nothing to say about it. I prefer sedate colors and do not generally wear such colorful or ornate articles, but it was a gift from my mother, so I wear it."

"So, you wear something you do not care for simply because it makes your mother happy." There was a smile in Miss Finch's tone.

Gideon wasn't one to blush, but the heat filling his cheeks and ears at that moment gave him quite the rosy hue. Thank the heavens for small miracles and cold air, for he was certain he would look quite the fool if his cheeks hadn't been already quite reddened from the winter chill.

And though he knew he ought to respond to that statement, he struggled with the words. They caught in his throat, and Gideon frowned, unsure of what to say. Politeness dictated that he ought to make some vague response and gently steer the conversation towards more decorous subjects. But he glanced at Miss Finch and found her studying him, her bright brows twisting together as though she knew the truth of the matter. Some part of him wished to keep it buried, but the lady's determinedly honest nature seemed to call to him.

"My mother never saw me wear it, for she passed away not long after she made it for me," said Gideon.

"I am sorry for that, Mr. Payne," she said with the same sincerity she had employed throughout their conversations—no mere pat on the head, but as though she felt the pain as well. "You needn't mind my nosiness. I may be embracing a liberated tongue, but that does not mean I wish for anyone to suffer because of it."

Turning back to the road, Gideon nodded. "Thank you, Miss Finch, but it has been nearly four years, and the pain is not so acute that I cannot speak of her."

Miss Finch gave a hum of agreement, though it was vague enough that Gideon suspected she didn't believe him. As well she shouldn't, for his words were inching perilously close to a lie.

"What was she like?" asked Miss Finch, repositioning the blankets once more.

With a huff, he frowned at the road ahead. "I doubt you wish to hear about my family."

Miss Finch straightened. "And whyever not? You know I am fully capable of ignoring you altogether if I have no desire for conversation, so I would not ask if I were not curious."

"My mother..." Gideon's lips pinched as he studied the passing landscape. With the sky dulled by a thick layer of clouds, the world looked gray. Only the occasional dots of brown from the tree branches gave it any color, though he knew the view was quite magnificent when the winter sky was clear, the vibrant blue bringing with it all sorts of pastel hues to the white. "My mother loved taking sleigh rides on winter days, always prodding my father to set the horse at a bruising pace."

Gideon smiled to himself, his gaze drifting through the distance as he began speaking of her. That passion and love. The vibrant spirit that had filled his world with light and laughter. Though he knew full well it was human nature to paint the deceased in rosier hues than they were wont to display in life, he didn't think his description was exaggerated. His mother had her faults, like anyone, but she was a good woman to her core.

"My father loved her to distraction, even willing to—" Gideon caught himself, his fingers clamping around the reins until Cinnamon gave a huff of protest. Relaxing his fingers, he forced himself to smile and mumbled something he hoped would not elicit further responses from Miss Finch. His mother's secret—indeed, his as well—had never passed his lips, yet he had nearly divulged all to the lady at his side before he thought better of it.

"I fear my father never recovered from her loss," he said instead. "The physicians say he is wasting away and is unlikely to be with us much longer."

"Oh, Mr. Payne. I am sorry for that," she said with that same earnest tone. "I cannot imagine how difficult it must be to lose both your parents. But how wonderful it is that you've been able to return home and see him through his final days."

Though Gideon wanted to question why he was in such a maudlin mood, it was little wonder when the subject of family arose. There was little other sentiment attached to that subject.

"My mother's passing was sudden. She was gone before I received word of her illness. I only wish—" Gideon's words pulled up short, his brow furrowing as he slid a glance towards Miss Finch, though he was certain she had heard his second slip of the tongue. The blankets were pulled tight around her, and she met his gaze. There was no challenge in it. Miss Finch merely watched him, waiting to see if he would give voice to that thought.

Her gaze was so open, matching her newfound honesty in every way. She had shared so much of herself; perhaps he might share a little in return. The impulse seized him, unwilling to let him go. So, he let the words out.

"I only wish my mother could see the man I've become."

Chapter 10

Turning back to the road, Gideon guided the sleigh towards a copse of trees. "I have not always made good decisions in my life, and I fear my mother did not live to see me settle myself on a better path."

"I am certain she knows it, Mr. Payne." Miss Finch's tone was not the simpering, pitying one that people so often employed in such circumstances, batting away the fears with trite phrases in well-meaning but useless ways. There was sympathy there, as though she felt his pain and clung to that belief with the same fervor as though it were her heart breaking, not his.

"I hope so, Miss Finch."

And as much as he appreciated her understanding, Gideon had no desire to delve further into that somber subject; it was hardly appropriate for an afternoon of courting, and there was little more to say anyway. Yet his companion watched him with knowing eyes, as though seeing far more than he wished.

Gideon needed a diversion. Flicking the reins, he urged the horse faster, and the sleigh jolted as the beast sped up. The chill air sped by, nipping at their cheeks and noses and tugging at their hats and scarves as Gideon pushed Cinnamon faster down the lane. Miss Finch laughed, clutching the blankets as they jostled along.

The path wove through the dense forest, the trees pressing in until they formed a snow-laden tunnel, their branches hanging low. The road was not so narrow as to cause Gideon concern, but he had vastly overestimated the distance between them and those bowing treetops. Twiggy fingers reached down, snatching his hat from his head and dumping a load of snow on him in the process. Miss Finch shrieked, though it was nothing to Gideon's shout as wet, cold clumps snuck in the tender places around his collar.

He yanked on the reins without meaning to, and Cinnamon stopped and whinnied, shaking his head and sending water droplets scattering across their faces.

"Miss Finch!" Gideon twisted in his seat, hurrying to scrape off the layer of snow that now coated her head to foot. Her hands were pressed to her mouth, her eyes scrunched tight, and Gideon let forth a slew of apologies as he began brushing off her bonnet. But when her hands fell away, laughter rang out, her eyes dancing as she reached to clear a clump of snow from his shoulder.

"Well, that was quite the surprise," said Miss Finch with a chuckle.

Gideon grimaced. Though he had never courted a lady before, he was fairly certain dousing her in snow was not among the usual practices. "I didn't mean—"

"Please stop apologizing, Mr. Payne. It was an accident. Nothing more. And a humorous one at that." Miss Finch gave him an arched brow as she glanced back from whence they came. "But I shan't remove myself to fetch your hat. The blanket and brick at my feet are the only things keeping my teeth from chattering."

Gideon nodded and pushed aside his half of the blanket, not realizing that the sudden movement would send another shower of snow atop her. Miss Finch squeaked, but before another apology could leave his lips, she gave him a teasing glare, snatched his abandoned covers, and drew them around her until she was bundled up like a crêpe, burrowing deep until only her face and bonnet peeked out. She grinned at him as Gideon wiped the last of the snow from his jacket and trousers before tromping off in search of his hat.

A better person would be afraid of stealing all the blankets. And in another situation, Evelyn would've been quick to relinquish her cozy cocoon, but it seemed only fitting to tease Mr. Payne by commandeering them all. As it was, she left him his hot brick (mostly because she could not reach it easily). When he returned to the sleigh with his hat firmly back on his head, Evelyn pulled the blankets tighter and gave him a bright smile, which earned her one of his rare grins.

For all that they'd spoken at length here and at the Meechams', Evelyn felt she knew so little about the gentleman at her side. There were secrets aplenty surrounding Mr. Payne, and though she did not begrudge the man his protections (everyone had things they wished to hide away), Evelyn suspected he had far more than most.

No wonder the man needed a friend. Everyone ought to have someone in their life who can make them smile, and Evelyn suspected Mr. Payne had few of those. If any.

And so, she burrowed into her blanket cocoon and didn't give him an inch of the covers when he sat beside her once more. Mr. Payne glanced at his solitary hot brick and then at her blanket cocoon, and without saying a word, he snuck his one source of warmth beneath the folds of her pilfered layers. Then, taking the reins in his hands once more, he set them on the path that would return her to Farleigh Manor.

Such a simple little thing, but the way Mr. Payne had given her his brick without comment or hesitation was anything but. Consideration could never be considered insignificant. Evelyn had seen so little of it in her life from anyone outside her own family that she savored the moment, letting it warm her through as thoroughly as her blankets.

And when Evelyn tried to give his portion back, Mr. Payne waved her gesture away.

"Consider it penance for your snow shower," he replied with a spark of laughter in his eyes. Evelyn liked seeing it. The gentleman who had approached her at the ball had seemed anything but merry, but humor was buried somewhere in him. And Evelyn longed to see it emerge more often.

"Too right," she said with a haughty sniff. Like so many other times, Evelyn found herself wondering if her own humor had overstepped. That little shudder ran down her spine, settling in her stomach like a lead weight as she awaited the verdict. But with each attempt, the fear grew fainter. It was still there—perhaps it would always be—but the joy of seeing him laugh in response was far too strong for her to give in.

Mr. Payne bestowed another smile that was rather like the ones her family gave when their mother spouted off one of her endless jests, which were both amusing and embarrassing when the listener recognized the childishness yet couldn't help but laugh all the same.

A quick tease about Dickens had him grinning, and before long they launched into a discussion about other authors and their literary merits. When Mr. Payne had the gall to disparage Gothic novels and penny serials as "uncouth," Evelyn could not hold her tongue, defending them to her dying breath. Unintelligent they may be, but they never claimed to be anything beyond entertaining.

Every few minutes, a single thought worried its way into her mind, whispering to her that she was speaking too much. Those same fears resurfaced at intervals, warning her that she would chase him away if she weren't careful. She wished they did not have such sway over her heart, for they pricked and twisted it every time, but she batted them away and clung to the Evelyn she longed to be.

And with each smile and verbal jab Mr. Payne gave in return, she was able to relax further.

The road straightened into one of Evelyn's favorite vistas of Farleigh Manor; no matter the season, the trees framed the house in a most pleasing fashion. At present, the snow above and below made it look like a watercolor painting, where the edges bled out into the white expanse of the paper.

The building itself was an interesting sight. A blend of different styles and materials, the facade was a patchwork of its various owners' tastes. In the summer, the grass and flowers helped to blend the gray portions with the ones that had a decidedly tan coloring, but in the snow, the color variations stood out. Others would likely tear it down and rebuild it with a uniform facade, but it was home to the Finches, and they would never part with it. Besides, it suited her odd family.

Mr. Payne guided the horse to the front steps, and Evelyn peeled away the layers trapping her in place. When he hopped from the carriage, she shook her head.

"There is no need to bother yourself, Mr. Payne. I can manage the front steps."

"I have no doubt you are quite capable, but I would hardly be a gentleman if I did not offer my assistance in such slippery conditions."

As he approached her side, a footman emerged from the house to take the reins, leaving Mr. Payne's hands free to help her from the sleigh.

Evelyn's foot touched the ground, and her heart lurched as her boot found nothing but ice beneath it. A jolt shot through her; she knew what was coming but couldn't move fast enough to do a thing about it. With her balance so precarious while climbing out of the sleigh, she had no hope of keeping her feet. Her breath seized, and she steeled herself for the fall that would be all the worse for the gravel mixed amongst the ice; hitting the surface would hurt enough without the ice-encrusted bits of rocks jabbing and poking into her soft bits.

All Evelyn could do was watch as she sped to the ground.

Arms wrapped tight around her, pulling her back. Despite the slippery surface, Mr. Payne held firm, keeping the both of them from disaster.

"Careful there," murmured Mr. Payne as he helped her past it to a clear patch, not releasing his hold until she was on the front steps. Then he guided her across the threshold and assisted her with her jacket. In each moment, Evelyn expected him to bow and hurry back to his sleigh, but even when everything was seen to, he simply stood in the entryway.

Having witnessed so many of her siblings find love and marry, Evelyn had spied many a doorstep farewell. She had even imagined what it would be like to stand with a gentleman, longing for him to remain while knowing it was time for him to go. The bated breaths. The lingering looks. A stolen kiss or two.

She hadn't imagined being flustered. Of course, in her dreams, she was in command of her surroundings and quite confident in herself. And the gentleman was a beau. It was pointless to imagine this moment as anything more than a parting of friends.

"I am glad our paths crossed," said Mr. Payne.

"Yes. Otherwise, I would've had to walk home."

Mr. Payne chuckled. "I am happy to be of assistance, Miss Finch."

And still, he remained in place, his fist knocking against his thigh as he watched her. While this behavior was odd, Evelyn suspected she knew the source of his discomfort. Though he hadn't said much about his father, the little he'd shared did not speak highly of their relationship, and with his mother gone, Evelyn imagined this time of year was quite bleak. Mr. Payne was a lonely man in need of company, but with no friends to fill that chasm in his heart.

"My family and I are preparing some Christmas decorations. You are welcome to join us," she said, motioning further into the house.

But Mr. Payne did not move. "My thanks, Miss Finch, but I do not wish to intrude."

"It is not intruding if you are invited," she replied with a smile. "At the very least, have some hot cider or tea before you venture out into the cold again."

To her astonishment, the gentleman shook his head and began inching towards the door. "That is a generous offer, but I will leave you to your merriment—"

"Nonsense." Bridget's voice cut through his objections as Evelyn's elder sister swooped from behind, startling Evelyn enough that she nearly shrieked. Then, calling out to the footman at the sleigh, Bridget ordered it to be taken to the stables.

"I—" began Mr. Payne, but Bridget deftly removed his hat and jacket, motioning for his gloves, and though the gentleman continued to give weak objections, he did as bidden. Mr. Payne gave Evelyn a wide-eyed look, and she rubbed at her forehead as heat crept up her cheeks. But there was no stopping Bridget as she ushered him further into the house.

The invitation to join them had been earnest and born of a desire to give Mr. Payne a joyful moment during this festive time. However, Evelyn hadn't considered the ramifications before voicing it—a fact that was emphasized when Bridget glanced over her shoulder at her sister with a smile that was a touch too determined for Evelyn's liking. Mr. Payne voiced no more objections while Bridget led them to the drawing room.

Tables had been brought in from every corner of the house, filled with all the makings of Christmas. Gingerbread biscuit dough, dried fruits, and greenery, along with needles, threads, and glue adorned each surface as the Finch clan gathered around in a festive frenzy, the older generations aiding the youngest as they prepared the dressings that would adorn the house and Christmas tree.

"We have a guest," announced Bridget, drawing every eye to the doorway where Mr. Payne and Evelyn stood. The Finches remained fixed in place, staring at the sight with varying degrees of surprise and delight, and Evelyn's cheeks flamed hotter, certain she had never been more embarrassed in her life. Or so she thought.

"Aunt Evelyn, you brought a beau!" shouted little Gemma, clapping her hands as she hopped on her tip-toes.

Chapter 11

ood gracious. Mightn't the ground open and swallow
her whole? That would be a Christmas miracle, indeed.
Gemma's statement was the proverbial stone, and Evelyn and Mr. Payne were the unfortunate birds in its path. This
time, Evelyn supported Bridget's gasp as she hurried to her
daughter for a whispered talking-to about appropriate conversation. It may have been an innocent mistake, but Evelyn
couldn't look at Mr. Payne, and she could well imagine his discomfort.

No doubt he would make his escape posthaste.

"Mr. Payne," said Mama, moving forward and guiding him
further into the room before he could. "Have you any skill with
shaping gingerbread biscuits? I am in dire need of some assistance with the little ones, and I fear I cannot trust my husband
to leave the dough be. We will have only a fraction of the decorations we require if he is allowed anywhere near it."

Taking a deep breath, Evelyn tried to cool her face. With
her coloring, there was no doubt her cheeks were as red as the
holly berries her nieces were stringing together haphazardly.
Mr. Payne glanced over his shoulder at her and gave her another wide-eyed look, though it commiserated over their shared

trauma rather than seeking rescue. And so, Evelyn left him to Mama and joined Bridget in stringing together garlands.

Gemma murmured an apology when Evelyn approached, and she gave the child a quick pinch of her cheeks, making the girl squeal and swat the offending fingers away with a laugh. Finding an empty chair, Evelyn took up another needle and thread and began adding to the growing garland, stopping from time to time to aid Gemma while Bridget's attention was fixed on little Hope, who was doing more to hinder her mama than aid in the work.

"How did Mr. Payne find his way to our doorstep?" asked Bridget, casting an impish look before giving Hope a few more whispered instructions.

With a sigh, Evelyn pushed the needle through the bits of dried berries and fruits. "He was passing as I was returning from choir practice and escorted me home."

Bridget raised her brows and said, in a tone meant to be mildly curious but which had too much glee to be subtle, "It concluded an hour or so ago, and the church is not far from here by sleigh."

"So, is he your beau?" asked Gemma, rocking in her seat.

"He is not," replied Evelyn, more for Bridget's sake than Gemma's, for the former's expression was quite as eager as her daughter's. "I made his acquaintance at the Meechams' ball, and he has become a friend. That is all."

"But do you think it could become something more?" No doubt her sister meant well by asking such a question, but it only reinforced Evelyn's decision to surrender all such silly notions. Could a man not behave in a gentlemanly fashion towards a lady without others making more of it? Heaven knew Evelyn had often been swept up in such ridiculous flights of fancy, but no more.

Unfortunately, telling Bridget anything of the sort would do no good. If anything, it would induce her to lecture about not surrendering all hope as Papa had done. At least he did not meddle in Evelyn's love life; the same could not be said of Bridget. She was just as likely to do something wretched like put out an advertisement in the paper. *Wanted: One husband for a sad and lonely spinster sister.*

She shuddered before giving little Hope a tickle, which made the little one squirm on her mother's lap. Standing, Evelyn gave a vague excuse about being needed elsewhere and escaped. Coming over to where George and Marian stood in quiet conversation while their children were occupied with their uncles, Evelyn stole their youngest from his mother's arms and gave little Christopher a nuzzling kiss.

"That is better," she said with a sigh. "Nothing cures the doldrums quite like cuddling a babe."

George handed a cup of cider to his wife and gave Evelyn a commiserating smile. "I could've warned you how it would go if you brought a young man home."

"Mr. Payne is a friend. That is all," replied Evelyn with a shake of her head. Then bouncing Christopher in her arms, she looked down at the babe and said in a cooing voice, "No one seems to believe me when I say it. What am I to do?"

Returning her gaze to George, Evelyn frowned. "As you are the one behind Mr. Payne approaching me in the first place, I would think you would know full well that seeing us together is unremarkable."

"I did?" asked George with raised brows.

Marian gasped and frowned at him. "George, you didn't! I have told you to leave her be."

Holding up placating hands, he took hold of his wife's free hand, giving it a tender squeeze before threading it through his arm. "I am no fool, Marian. I wouldn't dare go against your sage advice."

"Too right," said Marian, taking a sip and glancing out at the children. "Sadie, do not touch those scissors."

As Uncle Miles's attention was occupied with his nephew on his other side, he was oblivious to the mayhem Sadie was perpetrating on the ribbon garlands. Marian passed her cup back to her husband and hurried to the table, taking the sharp object from the three-year-old's hand before sitting beside her.

George held the cup while his gaze lingered on his wife. In the first months of their marriage, Evelyn had been grateful they'd chosen to let Chumleigh Cottage rather than reside at Farleigh Manor. The newly married couple were never as careful as they thought themselves, displaying more affection than Evelyn was comfortable seeing. Not that she begrudged their marital bliss or wished them less enraptured, but neither did she care to see her brother and sister-in-law locked in the sort of amorous embraces that ought to be reserved for private moments.

It had been some four years since the pair had exchanged vows, and while those overt displays had faded to a more manageable level, Evelyn did not doubt their affection had grown stronger. The manner in which George watched his wife was by no means the smoldering, desire-laden gaze of Gothic characters (as he'd given her in their early days), but there was no mistaking the devotion steeped in his gaze. His attention was fixed wholly on her, and though George spoke not a word, Evelyn could practically hear all the silent, loving thoughts directed at his wife.

Evelyn's own heart warmed, his joy echoing through her as though it were her own while she gave a silent prayer of gratitude that George and Marian had eventually found their way to each other. That dear little family. Chin trembling, she turned her attention to the product of that affection in her arms. Giving her nephew an exaggerated smile, she bounced Christopher until he laughed. It was one of those giddy, unreserved giggles of one just beginning to interact with the world, unaware of anything beyond the love that surrounded him.

"What was that about me tossing Mr. Payne at you?" asked George, pulling Evelyn from her thoughts.

Straightening, she shifted Christopher, transferring his weight to her other arm. "At the Meechams' ball, Mr. Payne sought me out. I had assumed it was Robin's doing, but he denied any knowledge of it. Clearly, you must be the culprit."

With a wry smile, George stared at her. "Or the fellow sought you out on his own."

Evelyn couldn't help the huff that followed that. "George, you have witnessed my abysmal history with men."

"That does not mean all gentlemen are blind to your charms."

That assumed she had charms.

Evelyn sighed at that insidious thought and reminded herself of all the many things she liked about herself, for there were plenty. So she amended the previous thought.

She possessed many charms, but none of them were obvious to a gentleman standing in a ballroom.

But Evelyn didn't need to answer George's assertion. Her expression told him everything she was thinking and feeling, for she did not attempt to hide the disbelief that had her brow arching.

Turning to her nephew, Evelyn gave him another great grin. "At least there are some little gentlemen who adore me."

Christopher punctuated that with a belly laugh, his smile as wide as it could go as he gazed at his aunt with utter adoration.

"Do not be so quick to dismiss Mr. Payne's attentions, Evelyn. Even if he were enticed to dance with you—" When Evelyn shot him a narrowed look, George held up his hands and quickly added, "Not that I am saying he was, and I fully, unequivocally deny having any hand in it."

Evelyn nodded, trusting the instinct that told her George was telling the truth.

Lowering his hands, George continued, "Even if Mr. Payne were induced to seek you out at the Meechams' ball, why would he go out of his way to see you home today? And do not say it was happenstance: Oakham is too far a distance from Bentmoor for him to be simply wandering through. And at the precise time you were in town? That seems highly unlikely. To say nothing of him stealing you away for longer than was necessary."

Christopher squirmed in her arms, but Evelyn hardly noticed; shifting him into a new position without thought, her mind fixated on George's words. Everything within her stilled as she considered that, her breath catching as her thoughts tried to piece the whole truth together from the fragments she possessed.

Coincidences did occur, but could that account for Mr. Payne being on that exact lane at that exact time to meet with her when their paths had never crossed before?

Swallowing past the tightness in her throat, Evelyn shook her head, forcing her lungs to function again. When she tried to speak, her emotions were too close to the surface, pounding against her control until they threatened to spill forth. She would not fall to pieces over the past. She would not.

Only when she gained full control did Evelyn attempt to speak. "I will remind you that not long ago, everyone was convinced a certain man's pointed attentions meant he wished to court me. Everyone was confident he was madly in love, and in the end, he was toying with me."

"Mr. Townsend was a bounder, but—"

Evelyn shook her head. "I am not comparing Mr. Payne to that man. I truly do not think they are alike. However, neither will I allow myself to be swayed by happenstance. I will not infer meaning from a gentleman's actions. I am done throwing my heart after someone who does not want it simply because he pays me a bit of attention."

Drawing closer, George lowered his voice. "I am not saying you ought to plan the wedding, but neither do I think it wise to deny the possibility. You deserve to find a gentleman who values you, Evelyn, and regardless of how this unfolds, I think Mr. Payne's interest is piqued."

Never before had she been grateful for the little messes babies were bound to make. They were amusing at times, certainly, but it was never enjoyable to be on the receiving end or to clean it up after. But at that moment, Evelyn wanted to kiss Christopher, for while he was busy reaching his little hands into her bright curls, he gave a great gushing hiccup.

Evelyn squeaked, lifting him away from her gown, and the majority of his mess landed on his front, though a few dribbles dotted her bodice, making her grateful she was wearing a high-necked day dress instead of one of her evening gowns; there was nothing quite so unpleasant as getting such messes down one's décolletage. In a trice, Marian and George were there with rags to mop up the mess, spouting apologies as Christopher preened from all the attention.

It was not the cleanest of escapes, but it provided enough of a distraction that Evelyn was free to abandon that conversation. No matter what her family thought, Mr. Payne was a friend. Nothing more. And Evelyn refused to believe differently. Only a fool repeated past mistakes, and she was determined to learn from them.

Chapter 12

The afternoon was not turning out as Gideon had anticipated. From the very start, things had gone awry in so many ways, yet as he watched the chaos in the Finches' drawing room, he couldn't say the turn of events was a terrible thing. Even though he found himself now under the watchful eye of Miss Finch's father.

Somehow, Gideon had been sequestered by the Finch matriarch at a table where her son gilded pinecones to be draped from the Christmas tree and evergreen boughs. When Miss Finch had said this was a family gathering, Gideon had anticipated a small affair, but with nine other adults and seven children, the evening was anything but.

Most of the adults were aiding the little ones in their decorations, but some alternated between making ones of their own and chatting. Mr. Robin Landry and his father-in-law were amongst that latter set, standing in one corner as they held a quiet discussion. Though Mr. Landry gave a quick nod in acknowledgment, Mr. Lewis Finch's gaze fixed on Gideon with enough intensity to make him squirm.

Good heavens. If this was how he treated the beau he'd chosen for his daughter, Gideon imagined any gentleman vying for her hand would quake beneath that regard. Perhaps it was not only Miss Finch's behavior that had landed her in a spinsterly bind. Perhaps he ought to have a word with Mr. Finch and explain how that unblinking study of his daughter's suitors was not conducive to finding her a husband.

But such thoughts were quickly lost in the hubbub of the family gathering. Having no siblings, Gideon had never experienced the sort of joyful chaos that was found in such things. Mother had been lively enough for three ladies, but that could not match the Finch clan. Even the smallest children, who had not the words to form proper conversation, were speaking their thoughts with all the fervor of their parents.

The noisier they grew, the quieter Gideon became. Like a boat tossed and turned by a stormy sea, at times he wanted to cry out at the chaos and tell the waves to calm, but in the same instant, he reveled in the feel of many hearts knitted together through shared experience and time. Though at times Miss Finch and even her brother, Mr. Isaac Finch, looked as overwhelmed as he felt, there was still a sense of belonging.

He found himself sitting back and watching it like a play, and Gideon couldn't help but turn to his memories and sift through them. Had there ever been a time when his family had even a morsel of such sentiments? There had been love at times. Happiness. At times. Unity. At times. All mere snippets compared to what the Finches had.

It was clear why Miss Finch did not want to miss such an evening.

"Mr. Payne, is it?" But Mr. George Finch's tone made it clear he knew precisely to whom he was speaking.

Gideon glanced up to find Miss Finch's elder brother moving to take the seat his younger brother had vacated moments ago. "Mr. Finch."

"I am happy you could join us today." Again, the words said one thing, but his tone said another.

With narrowed eyes, Mr. George Finch studied his sister's beau. Gideon's gaze darted to the elder Mr. Finch, whose attention had now been commandeered by his granddaughter and the string of ribbon garland she was making. Clearly, he had not informed his son and heir about this courtship. Or perhaps the fellow did not agree with his father's methods?

"I am happy to be here," replied Gideon, for he couldn't think of what else to say. Despite Mrs. Landry's invasive questioning and their initial surprise, the rest of the family acted as though his attendance was entirely unremarkable.

Mr. George Finch continued studying him, though it was not nearly as unsettling as his father's gaze from across the room. "I understand you've been squiring my sister about."

There was no question there for him to answer, but Gideon felt he must say something. "Yes."

That earned him a low grunt in acknowledgment. Leaning closer, Mr. George Finch's expression hardened. "I give you my word that if you hurt my sister in any fashion, I will destroy you."

"Pardon?" Gideon blinked and straightened, his eyes darting about the room. Perhaps he had been wrong to fear the elder Mr. Finch more. But then, maybe this family regularly handed out threats to guests.

"She has been mistreated enough, and I will not allow her heart to be broken again by some self-serving bounder," he replied in a surprisingly steady tone, despite the heavy subject. Apparently, the entire family struggled with understanding decorum and etiquette. Or perhaps there was a dash of lunacy running through the bloodline.

But as Gideon considered the gentleman's warning, a flame sparked in his heart, skittering through him.

Someone had mistreated her? Mr. Finch's meaning was clear enough, and Gideon didn't believe her brother was exaggerating. Though Miss Finch claimed her open heart was a new development, he suspected it had always been thusly. Hidden perhaps, but just because it was out of sight did not mean it was out of reach, and he could easily imagine how thoroughly gentlemen might toy with her affection; Gideon knew any number who took great pleasure in seeing how they could twist young misses about.

In rapid succession, he dredged up the memory of their first meeting mere days ago, and though he doubted her brother meant to divulge secrets, that bit of context shone a new light on her behavior. The blaze in Gideon's chest settled into a steady burn, and his gaze drifted to where Miss Finch sat beside her niece, helping the child to shape the gingerbread biscuit dough into whimsical shapes. Her expression was filled with that brightness of spirit she shared so readily with the world around her, and pain echoed through him at the thought of someone dimming that light.

Turning to face Mr. Finch, Gideon met his gaze, as certain of his words as any he'd uttered. "I can say with all honesty that I wish nothing but the best for your sister."

That earned him a long, hard look before her brother nodded and rose, leaving him without another word. And it felt more like a stay of execution than a dismissal.

Miss Finch. Gideon didn't know what to make of this revelation. Not for the first time, he thought the Finch patriarch must be lacking sense or he would not have entrusted such an endeavor to Gideon Payne. Nor could he understand why Miss Finch accepted his company at all. Surely, she had heard the rumors and knew his reputation. She didn't seem the sort to suffer fools or scoundrels.

Somewhere in the hall, a clock chimed the hour, drawing his attention to the growing shadows outside. Rising to his feet, Gideon glanced about the familial scene. As much as his conscience warned him the hour was too late for dawdling (as he still had quite a long trip to his father's home), he couldn't help but remain where he was. Just a moment longer.

"Would you care to stay for supper?" asked Mrs. Felicity Finch, looking up from her grandson nestled in her arms. "We have nothing out of the ordinary planned, but you are welcome to share in it."

"My thanks, but my father is expecting me, and I fear I have tarried too long as it is."

"Then I shall send for your sleigh to be readied," she said, rising to her feet. But before the Finch matriarch moved to the bellpull, she added with a laugh shining in her eyes, "But you are welcome to join us any evening you wish."

Only a fool would not recognize the insinuation rife in her words and expression, and Gideon did the only thing he could think to do—he nodded. However, as lovely as that sounded, it wouldn't serve his purpose. If he was going to help Miss Finch find a good beau, he needed to be out in society, not hanging about their home, playing parlor games with her family. Though such an evening appealed to him far more than traipsing about ballrooms.

Rising to her feet, Miss Finch cast a look over her shoulder and motioned for Gideon to follow as they snuck out of the drawing room and into the hall.

"You had best make your escape without Bridget noticing, or you will be subjected to all sorts of tortures and insinuations," she said with a laugh.

When Gideon only stared at her, Miss Finch added, "Bridget has acquired some mistletoe. As she has quite decided you are on the verge of declaring yourself madly in love with me, you had best disappear before she starts trapping you with that pesky little plant."

Leaning in close, she arched her brow. "I warn you that my sister is quite adept at catching people unawares. She takes credit for no less than three engagements because of her strategic placement of mistletoe."

"I have been duly warned," he replied with a chuckle. It surprised him how often he felt like doing so. Gideon hadn't thought himself grim and gloomy, but compared to Miss Finch, he was a wet and muddy day, and he couldn't help but borrow just a bit of the sunshine she exuded.

With a wave of his hand, Gideon motioned her forward, and she led the way to the main stairs.

"I ought to apologize for my family—"

"There is nothing to apologize for," said Gideon. "They are wonderful people. I am quite envious of you."

Miss Finch's eyes brightened. "Then they haven't scared you away? I was half afraid you would flee."

"They are boisterous, but I enjoyed myself." Gideon chuckled. "I fear your niece Sadie was put-out with my abysmal attempts at gingerbread ornaments. Unfortunately, I've not had the practice."

Miss Finch paused at the top of the stairs, turning to face him. "Did your family not spend December evenings preparing your Christmas decorations?"

"My mother's family had never adopted the fashion for Christmas trees, so it was not something she expected, and my father thought so much ornamentation was merely gilding the lily," he said with a shrug. "The servants put up evergreen boughs, but that was the extent of our merrymaking."

That earned him a vague hum of acknowledgment as the lady studied him for a long moment. Gideon shifted on the stairs, turning towards the door, but Miss Finch held up a single finger.

"A moment, please."

And before he could say anything in response, Miss Finch turned and hurried back to the drawing room. With a sigh, he rocked on his heels and stared up at the ceiling, his eyes tracing the swirling lines of plaster that decorated the edge. Quick footsteps echoed in the silence, and Miss Finch was at his side once more with a long string of garland wrapped in her hands.

"The gingerbread ornaments won't be ready until tomorrow, but you can have this now," she said, offering it up.

But Gideon shook his head. "My thanks, Miss Finch, but I cannot take your family's decorations."

"Ridiculous. There are enough of us that we shall have it replaced in a trice, but you and your father ought to have something for the season," she said, forcing it into his hands. "You needn't get a tree, but you ought to have something more meaningful than a few scraggly boughs your servants purchase in town. And it's not gilding the lily, rather it's giving this important holiday its due. Perhaps this might be the beginning of new traditions you and your father can share."

While he knew he ought to push it away, Gideon couldn't make his hands move. He stared at the gift, fully recognizing which bits had been strung together by the children, as many were hanging on by faith alone.

"That is generous of you, Miss Finch, but I fear it would take more than a few ornaments to make my father wish to share anything with me." Gideon froze in place, his hands clutching the garland as he realized just what he had said. The bitterness in his tone was unmistakable, and he was certain Miss Finch recognized it. When he dared to meet her eye, he found those rich brown eyes staring at him with far more concern than he wished to see.

"I cannot imagine that is true." Though there was a lightness to her tone, Miss Finch could not hide the genuine concern etched into the tightness of her brows. "Even if he does not enjoy your company—something I cannot believe as you are quite enjoyable, Mr. Payne—he is your father. He may not show it, but he must care about you on some level."

Father. Gideon's throat constricted, his blood freezing in his veins. When he'd returned home, he hadn't anticipated just how much that word would bother him. At school and in the army, people rarely referred to the relation, but here it was impossible to escape. His father was too much of a fixture in Bentmoor to be ignored.

Though they stood in silence, there was much being spoken in the little movements of her expression. The tightness of her lips. The rising of her brow. Every shift of her heart showed in her gaze, and Gideon wondered if here was someone who might understand. She was not one to gossip. Surely not. Though he'd known her only a short time, Gideon felt to his very core that he could trust Miss Finch.

But this was not his secret to tell.

Letting out a sigh, Gideon blinked, breaking her hold as he wound the garland in his hand, careful not to lose even a single dried berry or nut.

Miss Finch gave him a tentative smile. "From all accounts, he is intending to leave you his business. At the very least, he respects you, or he shouldn't do so."

Gideon couldn't help the sharp bark of laughter or the quick retort. "Rather, he fears public opinion—even beyond the grave. He would leave it to me because it's expected."

Brows pulled low once more, she opened her mouth to speak, but Gideon turned away and affected a casual air as they moved down the stairs to the front door. A footman appeared, helping him with his things before opening the door. The clouds had cleared a touch, allowing a bit of the setting sun to shine through and chasing away the gloom of the afternoon.

Despite his protests, Miss Finch stood on the front steps as the sleigh was brought forward, and Gideon gave her a bow.

"My thanks for this afternoon, Miss Finch. I can say with all honesty that it has been one of the most delightful ones I've had in a long time. Thank you for sharing your family and traditions with me."

Curtsying in return, she smiled even brighter than the sun at his back. "It was my pleasure, Mr. Payne. I am thrilled to have made you laugh no less than thirteen times. I counted."

That drew up one side of his lips as he studied her. "You are a good lady, Miss Finch. Odd, but good."

She laughed in response and folded her arms. "Now that, Mr. Payne, is a compliment I will gladly accept."

Gideon beamed at her and took the reins from the groom before climbing into the sleigh. But as he was about to send the horse forward, she called out to him.

"The choirmaster is determined to work us to death, and I will need a driver on Thursday."

Lifting his hat from his head, Gideon bowed. "It would be my honor, Miss Finch."

With a flick of the reins, his horse took off at a merry pace, though its hooves could not match the racing beat of his heart.

Chapter 13

There was magic in a winter's day. Where a warm summer afternoon invited one to laze about, the December chill pushed one to be out. More than the mere nip, there was something in the air that filled one with an urgent need to do something; the days were shorter, so one had to make the best of the daylight hours. To say nothing of the looming Christmas festivities, which filled every person to the brim with anticipation. There was nothing like it.

The wind rushed by, tugging at her bonnet and stray curls as Mr. Payne guided the sleigh along the snowy lane, and Evelyn breathed deep, hoping to revel in the clean scent of snow but finding a hint of horse instead.

The snow coating the hedgerows on either side made the road feel even narrower and more enclosed, but then they'd crest a hill and see beyond the living barricade to the fields beyond. Each peek was magical. No matter how many times she'd traversed this route, Evelyn was awed by the simple beauty of her home county. Though lacking the obvious color of leaves and flowers, a snowy field was awash with unique hues one couldn't find in June. Yes, white and brown dominated the landscape, but when the sky was clear and the sun sat low along the horizon, it cast the world in shades of purple and blue that belonged solely to winter.

"It is lovely here," said Mr. Payne.

"I certainly believe so," replied Evelyn, but then the road dipped once more, blocking their view until all they could see was the road ahead and the high hedgerows on either side. Slanting a look towards her companion, she began to sing, "'Hark, the herald angels sing, Glory to the newborn king...'"

Mr. Payne said nothing as she continued with the first verse, though with knowledge crafted over the past fortnight, Evelyn knew it was only a matter of time before he would join in. By the second verse, the gentleman added his voice to hers—quietly, for certain, but it was there.

"You would make a fine choir member, Mr. Payne."

"As I have told you many times, Miss Finch, it is impossible. I am not in your parish."

"A detail," she replied with an airy wave of her hand. "I am certain Mr. York would think nothing of having a new member in the congregation, if only temporarily. Our choir is sadly lacking basses and could use someone with your fine tone."

The edges of his lips turned up, and Evelyn couldn't help but grin in response. Mr. Payne was a delight to tease, and the more time they spent together, the more joy she found in needling him into smiles and laughter.

"Are we ever going to arrive at Mrs. Adams' cottage or have you gotten us lost?" he asked, leveling a narrowed look in Evelyn's direction.

She tried to maintain an innocent expression, but it was impossible to keep her smile hidden away. "I may have taken us the long way around."

That earned her an arched brow. "How long?"

"If I were to take the shorter route, then her home is only thirty minutes from Farleigh Manor." She paused only a moment before adding, "By foot."

Mr. Payne laughed and shook his head. "I suppose I ought to have been more circumspect when I offered you that first ride. Apparently, I am your permanent coachman. Ought I to expect a decent wage? Or perhaps a nip of that cider?"

He gave her basket a speculative look, and Evelyn held it further away. "That is for Mrs. Adams. Along with all the other goodies. One must have hot cider and sweets on St. Thomas's Day, and as she can no longer come to Farleigh Manor to fetch it, we are bringing it to her. By a circuitous route."

From the edge of her vision, she spied Mr. Payne's hand inching towards the basket, and her own struck out like a snake, slapping his away before the fellow could pilfer anything. Which only earned her another of his smiles. Evelyn tucked the basket beside her while sliding closer to him.

"I've been given orders to pester you mercilessly until you accept my mother's invitation to Christmas Eve," said Evelyn. "Though I have reminded her many times that you have family and friends who are likely to commandeer your evening."

"Not at all. The invitation surprised me, that is all. Otherwise, I would've accepted immediately."

There was a quality to his tone that Evelyn could not quite identify, despite her best efforts to do so. As much as it felt as though she'd known Mr. Payne for a great length of time, she reminded herself that it hadn't even been three weeks since the Meechams' ball, even if the past fortnight had seen them thrown together every day. Whether it was formal occasions like the Wrigleys' card party or drives out together, not a day had passed without some sign of Mr. Payne.

Evelyn's lips stretched into a broad grin, and she tugged the blankets higher onto her lap.

"And what are you laughing about?" he asked, in a tone that was equal parts humorous and wary.

"I have enjoyed the last few weeks, Mr. Payne. I am glad we are friends."

"Friends?" The gentleman straightened, turning a narrowed gaze at her.

A chill, far icier than the snow around them, ran down her spine, and Evelyn fought to keep hold of her affable expression.

Had she been too bold? Certainly, it was not common for men and women to claim such an acquaintance unless they had known each since childhood, but it was not outside the realm of possibility that such relationships could blossom. Her mind sped with the implications—

The sleigh jerked.

"Whoa, there," said Mr. Payne as he tightened his grip on the reins. "Just a patch of ice, and we shall be right in no—"

But before he finished his assurances, one of the beast's hooves slid out from beneath it. The others struggled for purchase, and Evelyn's muscles tensed, her hand reaching for Mr. Payne's arm as the sleigh drifted to the right, the hedgerow scraping against the side.

Despite being only bushes with no rock or brick to reinforce them, the hedgerows were solid, and when the sleigh bumped against it, they ricocheted. The lane was hardly larger than them, so they slammed into the left side with increased force and were thrust back toward the right again.

Her head snapped back and forth as the two sides batted them about in a bone-rattling game of lawn tennis, and one nasty jolt had her slamming into the side of the sleigh. Mr. Payne followed suit, ramming into her just before they were sent back in the other direction. She clung to the side, keeping herself anchored for a moment before they rebounded back and the hedgerows stabbed at her arms, forcing her to let go.

Inside, she screamed, though she had not the breath to let it out, and Mr. Payne strained against the horse's pull. Evelyn wanted to help, but she could barely keep her seat as the horse leapt forward, trying to shake free of the sleigh bouncing wildly behind him. The seconds stretched into hours, and her heart pounded in her chest, threatening to burst as there was nothing she could do but hope and pray.

A crossroads appeared, and the expanse of hedges opened up, giving them no barrier on Evelyn's side. The sleigh swung wide, and the ice beneath them gave way to snow, making them shake as the runners fought between the force sending them sideways and the rough ground below.

Evelyn clung to the sleigh, though there was little purchase, and when it jerked to a stop, there was nothing to keep her in place as the momentum tossed her from her seat. The blanket tangled around her, giving her some padding as she hit the frozen ground, but pain arched from her hip and knee, thrumming through her with every heartbeat.

A soldier's life was filled with training. Instincts were well and good at times and ought not to be wholly ignored, but often, they did not allow one to see a problem clearly and make the proper choice. Though Gideon's time in the army had been cut short, he'd spent enough years amongst their orderly ranks to have skills and habits so thoroughly ingrained that even when his mind and heart were screaming, his hands knew precisely what to do.

Instinct urged him to hold fast to Miss Finch. She bounced about the sleigh, her weight being thrown about each time they collided with the hedgerows. The only sound she made was a low moan as her body connected with the hard side of the sleigh, but he knew it must be as painful as what he was experiencing on his side. But they had no hope of a safe ending if he gave the horse his head. So, Gideon gripped the reins, pushing against the front of the sleigh with his feet, hoping the pressure would keep him from being thrown into her, though it did little good.

And then Miss Finch was gone, flipping through the side opening, and Gideon shouted, wanting to reach for her—but with the sleigh now lighter, the horse gave another firm tug, and Gideon threw all his weight and strength into holding the reins tight, barely keeping himself from following after Miss Finch. The moment the horse paused long enough, Gideon leapt from the sleigh and rushed to Cinnamon's head, taking hold of the bridle and trying to calm the creature while he searched behind him for any sign of Miss Finch.

Her feet peeked out from around the side of the sleigh, and Gideon's breath stilled. Again, instinct shouted at him to rush to her side, but Cinnamon was still too agitated and liable to hurt himself or them. Gideon's heart froze in his chest as he stared at Miss Finch's feet, willing them to move. The moment they did, he sighed, though his heart refused to beat until he saw with his own eyes that she was intact.

The horse pawed at the ground, trying to prance about, though the sleigh was firmly caught on the corner of the hedge-row.

"Shhh…" Gideon said, giving the beast a few pats on its side. "Whoa, there."

It took several long minutes before Cinnamon calmed enough to be left to his own devices, but the moment it was safe to do so, Gideon scrambled to Miss Finch's side, his shoes slipping on a patch of ice; he caught himself before he tumbled atop her, but his momentum had him down on his knees faster than intended, sending a jolt of pain through his legs. Gideon's gaze scoured the lanes, but there was no one about, despite his calling for aid.

Chapter 14

"Miss Finch!" Gideon reached for her bonnet strings, but she batted his hands away.

"I am fine, Mr. Payne. Just a little jostled," she said. "Can you find Mrs. Adams' basket?"

"Hang the basket!"

"I did not ask you to hang it, Mr. Payne. I asked you to find it," she replied with an arched brow, and only then did Gideon realize his choice of words had been a touch too colorful for a lady's ears. Before he could think better of it, he started feeling her injuries, and Miss Finch jerked away.

"Enough of that, sir. I am whole. I assure you."

Gideon scrubbed a hand through his hair (his hat had gone missing somewhere, though he couldn't spare a moment to care about it) and felt like growling or hitting something. Anything. Guilt pressed down like a lead pillow, smothering him; he couldn't breathe, and his thoughts were a jumbled mess as he tried to think what ought to be done, but his training had not covered what to do when your lady was tossed from a sleigh on an icy road. The pressure of those feelings only increased when the lady lying in the road began to chuckle.

"I could've killed you, Miss Finch!" Gideon sat there like the hand-wringing fool he was, trying to sort out what he could do for her, yet uncertain what she required. And with that, a litany of apologies spewed forth.

In the time he'd known her, the lady had proven herself to be intelligent enough to recognize mortal peril, but at present, she was proving herself quite incapable, for she met that statement with a wave of her hand.

"It was an accident, Mr. Payne," she said, brushing a lock of hair out of her face. "It is an unfortunate possibility when one drives at any time of the year, but most especially when the roads are icy."

Sitting back on his heels, Gideon stared at her. The blood drained from his face, leaving him feeling ready to fall over, and the only reason he remained upright was the knowledge that he could not compound his sin by abandoning Miss Finch to fix the situation.

"An accident?"

But before Gideon could list all the many reasons he deserved her censure, Miss Finch gave him a narrowed look.

"Did you purposefully drive the sleigh into the hedgerow, Mr. Payne?"

Gideon shook his head.

"Or cause the horse's hooves to slip?"

Another shake.

"Did you, in fact, act to the best of your ability to calm the creature and get the sleigh under control?" Miss Finch spoke with such certainty that Gideon found himself blinking, though the answer to this question was the same as the others. And Miss Finch did not wait for the answer at any rate. Reaching forward, she gave Gideon's hand a firm squeeze. "I admit it was terrifying, and I am sore and bruised, but it was not your fault, and you did your best. What blame can you possibly deserve?"

Gideon struggled to swallow. He'd been able to do so minutes ago, yet now, his throat clamped shut, refusing to cooperate. Miss Finch merely gazed at him in that open, unapologetic manner of hers, her eyes echoing the confidence she'd expressed in her words and tone. Gideon could not trust himself to speak at present.

"Now, would you go and see if Mrs. Adams' basket is intact?" she asked, twisting in place as she tried to spy it.

Rising to his feet, he held out a hand to her, but Miss Finch shook her head.

"Give me a moment to collect myself, Mr. Payne."

"We need to get you off the snow and ice, lest you catch a chill as well."

But she waved him away, and Gideon turned on his heel, hurrying to the sleigh. Crouching, he studied the runners. Thankfully, they were straight, and except for a few scrapes, the body was intact. Moving to the other side of the sleigh, he leaned down and found the runners stuck amongst the naked branches. With a quick tug, he was able to free it, though Cinnamon gave a start and began prancing in place. Hurrying to the beast's head, Gideon gave him a few more rubs and pats, his voice low and soothing as Cinnamon calmed enough that he could trust the horse not to bolt.

"Miss Finch, what do you think you are doing?!"

The question burst out the moment Gideon stepped back around to find the lady on all fours—or attempting it if the grimace of pain was any indication. With a wave of her mittened hand, she drew his attention to the ground behind her where the basket lay scattered across the road.

"Silly woman," he said, scooping her up before she could protest. Miss Finch proved herself not wholly without sense at the moment, for she drew her arms around his neck and held fast to him.

"What do you mean by hauling me about like a sack of potatoes, Mr. Payne?"

"I mean to keep you from causing yourself another injury because you are too impatient to allow me to fetch the basket after I have seen to you and the sleigh."

"I can walk. I couldn't get to my feet because the road was too icy for me to get any purchase from that angle. If you had offered me a hand up, I would've managed it in a trice."

Gideon huffed. "I did! And if you had taken the hand I offered, you wouldn't have had any issue—"

Then he turned his gaze to Miss Finch and found that arched brow of hers staring back at him.

"You are all too easy to tease, Mr. Payne."

But Gideon couldn't focus on her words. Holding her thusly, he was quite aware of how close she was, but upon turning his face towards her, he was taken aback by the proximity. Close enough that he felt her warmth seeping into him. He tried to identify the color of her eyes, but he could not give it a name; dark brown, to be certain, but that was far too pedestrian a description.

The shade reminded him of the Pendletons' home; as the building had been in the family for generations, they took pride in maintaining the original Tudor styling with its dark wood interiors. Gideon recalled the holiday he'd spent there and an evening when he'd stood at the parlor window, looking out at a winter day not so different than this. In the summertime, the dark brown made the rooms feel heavy at times, but with the grand fireplace blazing and frost coating the windows, the rich color made the space feel inviting. All warm and cozy like a blanket wrapped around one's shoulders. Fashion now favored light colors on the walls with white trims, but for all their light and airiness, the rooms always felt chilly.

The memory surprised him, both the suddenness of its appearance and the comparison to Miss Finch; Gideon rarely gave his school days much thought anymore. But the parallel was apt, for her eyes matched the color of the wood and radiated that same warmth and comfort.

They call eyes "the windows to the soul," and if that was the case, Gideon felt certain no soul shone as brightly as Miss Finch's, for her gaze was always aglow—even in the darkest moments. A smile tickled the corners of her lips, speaking as much with that little quirk as she did with words. She always found a reason to tease and jest, and though it was often directed at him, it was not at the expense of his pride.

Those lips. Gideon's gaze drifted to them, and his footsteps faltered as time slowed, holding him captive as he studied that little bit of perfection.

Having read quite a few novels with sweeping, melodramatic twists that thrust hero and heroine together until they were irrevocably enamored, Evelyn had imagined being carried by a gentleman. As much as she enjoyed silly stories, she was not a silly woman unable to see that reality wouldn't play out as it did in those tales. However, there was a world of difference between believing and knowing. The former allowed her to ignore reality and embrace the realm of "perhaps" and "what ifs."

Now, Evelyn could say with absolute certainty that such moments were not romantic. But then, bruises never were, and her backside would be purpled within the hour. To say nothing of her heart, which felt like a handkerchief on wash day, scrubbed, mangled, and wrung out, and no matter how she tried to calm herself, her body did not seem to understand that the danger had passed.

And of course, there was the carrying itself, which was far more terrifying than those fictional heroines portrayed it. Evelyn tensed, her breath stilling as Mr. Payne held her up, and she forced herself not to cringe with each step; the ground was icy, and despite all this gallantry, there was no guarantee she wouldn't end up in another heap on the ground. So, she held rigidly still, hardly blinking so as not to throw off his balance. Especially when he was staring at her rather than paying attention to the path ahead.

"You can set me down, Mr. Payne. I have the use of my limbs."

Blinking, he seemed to pull himself from whatever daze he was in and continued over to the sleigh. Evelyn hid her frown as she studied him and searched her thoughts for something to say that might alleviate the guilt he unnecessarily bore. His eyes darted between her and the sleigh, and Evelyn gave him a bright smile, but before she could say something cheeky to set him at ease, he spoke.

"I could set you down, but how else am I to demonstrate my masculine prowess without hauling about my lady fair?"

There was something odd in his tone, a shakiness that Evelyn had not heard before and seemed unconnected to the situation at hand. There was none of the fear or guilt that she suspected still lurked in his heart (and would likely do so for some time), and if she had to give it a name, Evelyn would say Mr. Payne was nervous, though she could not imagine why.

Chapter 15

Before Evelyn could think of what to say, Mr. Payne deposited her in the sleigh, though her joints and rump protested. He retrieved the blanket and tucked it around her, his brows pulled low as he fluttered about, and though the gentleman said little more, Evelyn heard his thoughts grinding like a bit of grit had gotten lodged in his gears.

"The basket, Mr. Payne," she said, forcing his attention away from his fretting.

With a jerky nod, he scurried back to where it had fallen and reappeared with the contents shoved inside, though he held a dripping jar at a distance.

"I fear the cider did not make it," he said with a frown.

Evelyn sighed and frowned. "Poor Mrs. Adams. She adores our cider and always looks forward to getting a taste of it. I suppose we will deliver what we can and send replacements for everything else."

Mr. Payne straightened, lowering the jar. "You do not wish to return home?"

"We have not finished our errand," she said with a furrowed brow, though it took no great leap in logic to suspect what was concerning him. Leaning forward, Evelyn held his gaze, speaking with as much authority and certainty as she felt. "I am not afraid to drive with you, Mr. Payne. This was not a pleasant experience, but it was nothing worth noting. I've had other similar scares with my brothers, my father, and even on my own. This was not in your control, and you did your best to keep the situation from growing worse."

Having spent so much of her time on the outskirts of society, Evelyn had often wished for a silver tongue. Her mother and several of her siblings (Miles, in particular) seemed possessed of an ability she could not mimic; with a few words, they altered opinions and won favor, but Evelyn had not a shred of their talent. Never had she desired that ability more than at this moment.

But the gentleman gave no sign that he believed her, though he nodded and climbed in beside her. The sleigh lurched forward, and the sedate pace at which they moved attested to Mr. Payne's nerves. He said nothing, except to murmur something about his missing hat before lapsing into a heavy silence.

Evelyn frowned, but as much as she longed to reinforce her assurances, she knew the value of holding her tongue. She couldn't claim to know what Mr. Payne was pondering, but if the furrow of his brow were any indication, it was a weighty subject and encompassed more than the last few minutes. And so, she waited. If he wished to speak to her, then he would speak, but Evelyn wouldn't rush things along. No matter how much she longed to.

Of course, that sort of patience was easier in the abstract than in the execution, and as much as she knew it was necessary, Evelyn occupied herself with all the reasons why she needn't wait. Perhaps Mr. Payne needed a conversational nudge. Or was too shy to share and needed reassurance. Lips pinched together and brows pulled low, she fought herself to give the fellow time. There was nothing else she could do, but the pressure of those unspoken words built within her, and when Mr. Payne finally shifted in his seat, Evelyn felt liable to burst.

"Why do you trust me so, Miss Finch?"

All the tightness released, leaving her deflated as she stared at him. "Pardon?"

"You speak with such certainty..." His voice was so low she nearly missed it beneath the sounds of hooves and crunching snow, his words faltering as he finally met her gaze. "What have I done to earn such faith?"

The words were sour on his tongue, and Gideon grimaced at the silence that followed his question. He ought to have kept his own counsel. No good would come from such a conversation, but the last few minutes had left his thoughts a scattered mess, eradicating what little good sense he had.

Miss Finch canted her head to one side as her brows drew close together. "What have you done to earn my distrust?"

Gideon scoffed and scowled. "I haven't done anything to earn anyone's distrust, but there's not another person in town who shows such faith in me. Or any."

There was no softening the sharpness in his tone; Gideon couldn't control it any more than he could silence the words that kept slipping free of his grasp. Matters were not helped when Miss Finch watched him with those eyes that called to him, shining with a kindness and sympathy he did not deserve.

"I am well aware of how quickly people judge someone without knowing them, Mr. Payne. But I know you are a good man."

"You do not know me, Miss Finch. A fortnight ago we were strangers."

"It is almost three weeks, not two."

Gideon huffed, his spirits darkening despite Miss Finch's teasing tone. In his mind, he imagined that spark in her gaze and the curve of her lips when she thought she was particularly amusing, but he couldn't bear to look over and see it.

"When you can measure our acquaintance in weeks and not

months, you cannot claim to know me well enough to trust me so implicitly." Gideon's voice threatened to give out when the truth settled on him like a lead cloak, weighing him down as he realized that she did not know the rumors. If she did, Miss Finch would not speak so lightly.

"But neither can you say we are strangers, Mr. Payne, when you consider that we have spent so much time together cumulatively. You've had ample time to turn into a ravening beast, but I've received nothing but kindness from you."

Miss Finch meant to comfort, but those assurances wrapped around him, squeezing and twisting his heart. She didn't know. Couldn't know. And the time of his reckoning had arrived.

"Did you know I was in the army?" he asked.

With an overly dramatic gasp, Miss Finch leaned away. "You were! I cannot believe it! To have kept this from me is inexcusable!"

Gideon sighed and shook his head. "I am in earnest, Miss Finch. Please do not mock me."

Shifting in place, the lady turned towards him, her hand resting upon his forearm. "I apologize, Mr. Payne, but you made that sound like such a terrible confession. I didn't mean to make light of your turmoil, but do not forget that it was you who made light of my feelings first. Do not presume I must either be ignorant or foolish to think well of you."

Gideon's gaze rested on her hand, unable to turn towards the lady herself, for he could not bear to see the tenderness he knew was there.

Straightening, she pulled away and shifted the blankets around them. "And I am well aware you were in the army. As it happens, that does not make you a terrible person. My father served for many years as well."

"That was not the point—"

"And I know why you left their ranks."

Ice slid through his veins, freezing him as thoroughly as the hedgerows around them, but it was not her words that startled

Gideon so as much as the blasé manner in which Miss Finch spoke. Though she must have thought it would comfort him, it did nothing of the sort; clearly, she did not know the whole truth.

"What have you heard?" he asked.

Silence followed, and Gideon felt Miss Finch's attention fixed upon him, but without seeing her, he couldn't tell a single thing about her mood—and he was not about to his attention from the road. Keeping his hands firmly on the reins, he guided the horse along, his gaze searching the road for problematic patches, all while his thoughts played out what was to come.

He was not ready to say farewell to her.

"I know you were in the calvary, like my father, which is how I know you handle horses with skill, even in treacherous conditions," she said pointedly, though the accident was now far from Gideon's thoughts. "And rose to the rank of lieutenant, serving as your regiment's agent before you were forced to sell your commission and return home, taking a position at your father's bank."

"But that is not all people say," he murmured.

"No, it is not," replied Miss Finch with a scoff. "The fools claim you were a charlatan of the highest order, drinking and carousing for years until you dared to seduce a general's daughter during a ball. When you were caught, you refused to do your duty and left the ruined girl to her fate, flitting back to Devon to escape the consequences."

Gideon's throat tightened, and he forced himself to relax as he asked with a fair approximation of calm, "And is this where you tell me people can change, and that whatever I may have been in those days, it is clear that I mean to mend my wicked ways?"

Miss Finch frowned. "Absolutely not."

Straightening, Gideon hazarded a glance at her, and she hurried to add, "Not that people cannot change—I firmly believe that is true when they desire it. I only meant you do not need to 'mend your wicked ways' because you did not do what they claim."

Gideon pulled back on the reins, forcing the sleigh to stop as he turned in his seat to stare at her.

"You needn't look so shocked, Mr. Payne," she replied with a smile. "I will not say I wasn't disturbed by how many people have cornered me over the past few weeks to tell me all of your misdeeds and their colorful descriptions. But as I said, I know you. Not everything about you, by any means, but enough to know you are not the sort who would do such a thing. I am well-acquainted with gentlemen who make sport of others, and unless *you* tell me the stories are true, I cannot believe you capable of such cruelty."

The words acted like billows, stoking a fire in his chest that swept through him. Gideon's throat clamped shut, leaving him unable to speak, but even if it were functional, he didn't trust his voice enough to attempt it. Though his thoughts tried to make sense of this revelation, they could not align it with the world he knew. The number of people who showed such faith in him could be counted on one hand, and none of them had done so with such little knowledge of him.

"Tell me I am wrong," said Miss Finch, her tone matching the challenging raise of her brows.

Turning back to the road, Gideon urged the sleigh forward, blinking sightlessly at the road ahead. With effort, he was able to relax his throat, though it was another moment or two before he knew he could form the proper words.

"You are not wrong, Miss Finch."

She didn't bother to hide her glee at being proven correct, giving a sharp hum of satisfaction, and she drew closer to him, though careful not to impede his arms.

"Now, you should say, 'And you are entirely correct about Dickens. I was a fool to disagree.'"

Chapter 16

Gideon laughed, the sound creeping up and surprising
him despite all the wretched things that had proceeded
Miss Finch's statement. It was quickly followed by another blaze of heat as he thought of her, imagining in vivid detail that triumphant smile of hers and the spark of humor in her
gaze, and though he longed to see it, he didn't trust himself to
face her for he was certain his awe for Miss Finch was stamped
across his face.

"I was a lieutenant in the army, serving under Captain
Gregory Reynolds and General Douglas Evanston, two of the
greatest men I have ever had the pleasure to know." Gideon
paused and sighed, glancing at Miss Finch; her attention was
fixed on him, which did little to settle his thoughts.

Turning back to the road, he tried to think how to tell a
story he'd never shared before.

"I suppose I ought to start with my last months at school."
Gideon paused, stepping past the incident that had precipitated
those disastrous months; there was no need for Miss Finch to
ever hear about that wretched moment. "I fell in with some lads
who were not the best of influences. They weren't wicked, but
they certainly strayed far from the rules and dictates of our

headmaster. I'm afraid I was swept up in their antics and found myself shouldering the blame for a particularly nasty prank."

"What was it?" The question was quiet, tentative, as though she needed to say it but would not demand an answer.

Gideon sighed and shook his head. "A rival group of boys was plaguing us, so we snuck into their dormitory and stole all their uniforms."

"That is certainly poor behavior but not worthy of expulsion," she replied.

Shaking his head, he murmured, "True, but several of the lads decided thievery was not enough and burned the pilfered clothes—not only destroying the other boys' property but nearly setting the dormitory ablaze in the process."

"Oh." Miss Finch's solitary word carried a weighty tone, conveying far more understanding and shock than was possible in an entire sentence. "Yes, that would do the trick."

Despite the solemnity of the subject, the prim manner in which she spoke made Gideon laugh.

"I know it isn't humorous, Mr. Payne," she added in a rush, "but with several brothers of my own, I am familiar with the ridiculous things young men do to entertain themselves and the utter lack of self-preservation they possess. It is a miracle any of you survive to adulthood."

Gideon nodded. "Too true. And unfortunately for me, the only good sense my friends had was to distance themselves from the mayhem, leaving me to bear the brunt of the punishment. No matter what I said, the headmaster refused to believe in my innocence. My father followed suit and shipped me off to the army to teach me responsibility."

"That must've been difficult to bear. To be judged so poorly and then cast aside from everything you knew."

Another nod and Gideon guided the sleigh towards another crossroads, but Miss Finch tapped his forearm and motioned ahead instead of toward the turn he was supposed to make.

When he sent her a questioning look, she replied, "I am not ready to surrender this conversation yet. This direction will give us a few more minutes."

Despite his cowardice demanding he end this discussion posthaste, Gideon did as bidden. His head ached from the conflict waging inside him; he hadn't thought it possible to dread and desire something at the same time, yet he was stuck firmly in the middle of that dichotomy. It had been some time since he'd had such a ready confidant, and though his heart revolted at the thought of giving Miss Finch any reason to despise him, Gideon's lonely soul begged to let his secrets free to someone who had proven herself a loyal companion.

Shaking free of his turmoil, Gideon forged ahead. "I struggled for many years and for more reasons than I care to share at present, but that all changed when Captain Reynolds took command. I do not know what he saw in me—"

"Your intelligence, your innate kindness, your honesty..." Miss Finch rattled off the traits, ticking them off on her fingers, and Gideon felt like smiling anew.

"I will not make the mistake of arguing on that score again, but you did not know me then. Though I never did anything terribly wicked, I fell in with the same sort as I had at school. Believe me when I say I was not an easy soldier to have under his command."

"When the world sees you in a poor light, it is easy to sink to their estimation of you."

Gideon straightened and cast her a look, his brows pulling low. Her expression was as open as ever, displaying the same honesty with which she had spoken those succinct words. "I hadn't seen it in such a light."

With a slanted smile, Miss Finch's expression softened. "I am certain Captain Reynolds did."

Frowning at the reins in his hands, Gideon longed to drop them and take her hand in his. But with that thought came others, and he lost himself in a moment as he wondered what it might be like to kiss Miss Finch, though he was growing more certain that no matter how thoroughly he pictured it, the reality would be far better.

Gideon cleared his throat and turned to the task and conversation at hand. "With time and his aid, I rose in the ranks, and eventually, he helped me to secure the post as the regiment's agent."

"With a banker for a father, it is little wonder."

Gideon's breath stilled at that. Stepping past that statement, he continued, "Unfortunately, I was still foolish enough to run with a crowd that had a poor reputation amongst the regiments."

Miss Finch huffed. "Which is saying something, as soldiers are not known for their polite behavior."

"That is putting it mildly," said Gideon with a grim pull of his lips. "But I couldn't bring myself to abandon my friends and comrades who had welcomed me amongst their ranks for so long. They had accepted me when others wouldn't, and I did not participate in their antics, so I saw no harm in keeping them company. Until my mother's passing."

Miss Finch shifted in her seat, turning towards him, and raised her hand as though to take hold of his, though they were occupied with the reins.

"My mother never lost faith in me, but I know rumors about me had made their way home, and she was not well pleased with my choices." Gideon paused for a moment, uncertain if he should tell her the whole of it, before diving in. "When it was clear she wouldn't heal from her illness, she wrote me a final letter filled with praises I did not deserve and hopes for my future that I knew would never come to pass if I continued on as I had."

Gideon took a moment for his throat to clear and waited until he was certain he could speak. "I did not cut them from my life, but I refused any more questionable invites. In truth, I had never been as rowdy as the rest, so it was not difficult to distance myself, but it was noticed. They thought I was becoming priggish and wanted to 'shake me up.'"

Lieutenant Claridge's words echoed in his head. The fellow

had said them often enough that Gideon recalled the very in-flection he'd used. Though the words themselves had the ring of friendship and were spoken as though they bestowed some great favor on Gideon, the sneer buried beneath it testified that Claridge's actions had been anything but well-meaning.

Though Gideon knew it was unnecessary, he turned to Miss Finch, holding her gaze. "Do you give me your word that you will not repeat a word of what I am about to say?"

"Certainly," she said with a nod. "I wouldn't dream of it."

Worry for Miss Evanston had kept his mouth shut, but he needed one person unconnected with the affair to know the truth. And not just anyone, but the lady who had shown such faith in him; Miss Finch deserved to know it was not misplaced.

Guiding the horse along the curve of the road, Gideon sifted through his thoughts. Cottages came into view, peeking up above the hedgerow, and though he longed to speed past them, he guided the sleigh as directed toward Mrs. Adams' front door.

"Those former friends of mine sent General Evanston's daughter notes and presents from me, and during a masquer-ade ball, one of them approached her, claiming to be me. I dare not disclose what happened between him and the young lady, but needless to say, she was compromised. When they were dis-covered, he maintained the lie long enough for the gossips to think it was I who had done the deed, and he escaped when he could."

Miss Finch sucked in a sharp breath. "That wretch!"

The sleigh came to a stop, and Gideon held fast to the reins, studying them in his hands. "My only consolation is that her family knows the truth. Though everyone else demanded satis-faction, they refused to allow me to shoulder that burden."

Straightening, Miss Finch shifted in her seat, placing a hand on his forearm now that it was safe to do so. "You offered to marry her."

There was no question in her tone, but Gideon nodded all the same. Miss Evanston's face surfaced in his memory, her eyes devoid of all feeling, though their redness and the deep purple crescents beneath bespoke of her broken heart.

"The poor woman deserved better than a forced marriage, and luckily, her father was not the sort to think any marriage was better than ruination."

"But now, you are tainted by her scandal and unable to clear your name without causing the young lady more pain," she whispered.

Gideon knew he ought not to be surprised, for though she struggled to navigate society, Miss Finch understood people well enough to surmise the truth.

"Rumors damage, but facts destroy, Miss Finch. There are whispers aplenty, but little can be substantiated. They know something happened, but they cannot say what precisely. Beyond simply saying it isn't true, I can offer no believable defense for myself without confirming Miss Evanston's scandal. The only aid I can offer her is my silence."

Miss Finch's eyelids fluttered, blinking away what looked to be tears, though they were there and gone so quickly that Gideon could not tell for certain. But the smile she gave him was unmistakable. As tender and warm as a thick blanket, it wrapped around him, stoking his heart.

"You are a good man, Mr. Gideon Payne," she whispered. With a squeeze of his arm, she turned and alighted from the sleigh, leaving Gideon to stare after her.

At that moment, he knew he wanted Miss Finch. Undeserving he may be, but he wouldn't turn aside the stroke of good fortune that had dumped her in his lap. Marriage had not been foremost in his mind, but Gideon was certain that even if he scoured the whole of Bentmoor, Oakham, and all the rest, he'd not find a wife as fine as her.

And for some reason, she enjoyed his company.

Could a man love a woman after only three weeks? Gideon hardly knew what the word meant, let alone how to identify its presence, but he had to imagine it felt like this. His heart seemed too big for his chest, the erratic pulse sending his blood zipping through his veins; it filled him to bursting, making him feel as powerful as a god yet infinitely unworthy of such a gift.

"Are you going to sit there gaping at me or are you going to bring the basket?" the lady in question asked, giving him a saucy raise of her brow as she glanced at him from over her shoulder.

Gideon hopped free of the sleigh, tying off the horse on the fence that surrounded the cottage's garden, and then he was at her side, offering up his free arm.

Chapter 17

"You're not fooling me, Miss Evelyn Finch. Stop cleaning, and sit down," said Mrs. Adams.

The old widow sat in a patched and worn leather armchair, which was far nicer than anything found in the nearby cottages despite its age. Every time Evelyn saw it, she couldn't help but recall all the many times she and her father had shared it when the seat had been situated in his study, and she was happy to see it so loved and well-used.

"I am not cleaning," replied Evelyn, even as she wiped the table with a washcloth. "I am performing an ancient ritual to protect your home from fairies."

Mrs. Adams huffed, and though bowed with age, she gave Evelyn a gimlet eye that reminded her of the old cook who had scolded the children for stealing sweets from the larder.

"My home is quite fairy-free, young lady, as I always sprinkle salt across my doorstep and keep rowan and ash branches hung by my windows." Mrs. Adams lifted the St. Thomas Day basket and peeled back the linen covering it. The food had been cold even before the tumble, yet still, she took a whiff of the fruit cake and frowned. "That new cook of yours is too stingy with the ginger. I shudder to think what her gingerbread cake recipe is like, and that is your father's favorite. The more spice the better."

Evelyn grinned and reached over to stoke the fire. "Mama has already spoken with Cook twice about the matter. Her previous employer had either a mild palate or a stingy budget, but she is learning."

Setting aside the basket, Mrs. Adams gave another harumph, and Evelyn knew what was coming, which was well and good, for she had reached the extent of her cleaning expertise.

"Come and sit, Miss Finch. Your poor young man is stuck lurking in the corner until you do," said Mrs. Adams.

Freezing in place, she held back a wince over the label Mrs. Adams had given Mr. Payne, and though she did as bidden, Evelyn couldn't bear to look at him and see the shock or horror that was likely there. She thought of many retorts (for Mr. Payne was in no way "hers"), but none of them felt like the right thing to say. Best ignore it, and perhaps Mrs. Adams would leave it be. For now.

"I shall sit, but only if you promise to tell us ghost stories," said Evelyn with a smile as she stepped over to where Mrs. Adams sat, straightening the woman's lap blanket before taking the seat opposite.

The bruises and aches on her backside made themselves known, and only by sheer strength of will was she able to keep the wince from her expression and the groan from her lips; Mr. Payne needn't bear another ounce of guilt for something that was an accident, and she felt his attention on her, noticing every stiff movement. Surprisingly enough, other than the first few steps, moving about had been far less painful than expected.

"Are we to be entertained with ghost stories?" asked Mr. Payne as he dragged a kitchen chair over to the hearth and joined the pair.

"Mrs. Adams tells the best ones," replied Evelyn.

"I thought you were bringing me my a-gooding treats," said Mrs. Adams with a playful frown. "I didn't realize I would be forced to work for it."

But the protests were feeble, for Evelyn knew the old cook enjoyed telling the tales as much as her audience loved hearing them. With another feigned objection, Mrs. Adams launched into the tale of the Gray Man, who roamed the fields of Oakham in search of his lost dog. It was a story Evelyn knew quite well, for the children had often acted out the old tale at harvest time, making little dogs from twists of ripened wheat stalks, with which they played a spookier version of hide-and-seek.

Mr. Payne listened with rapt attention as Mrs. Adams wove the tale with the skill of a bard, and with such an eager audience, Mrs. Adams continued with her string of stories. Evelyn knew each well enough to give all the proper responses. The gasps. The wide-eyed wonderment. The laughs. But it was Mr. Payne's voice she heard in her mind.

Evelyn's heart burned like a lit coal, and her throat tightened, threatening to strangle her even as tears rose to the surface. She refused to let them take hold, but neither could she erase them as she pictured it all in vivid detail. But more than anything else, it was his tone that held her captive.

"Why do you trust me so, Miss Finch?"

Though she doubted he'd intended to reveal so much, Mr. Payne's tone held the echo of a thousand wounds; given over the years through the hard judgments and cold treatment, each cut might be small, but cumulatively, they were bleeding him dry. Her heart ached at the thought of such a good man being so misused.

Evelyn had never been a gossip, but as one who enjoyed a titillating tale, she'd been known to indulge in the "have you heards" and "did you knows." However, she hadn't considered just how much pain even her little indulgences might cause another, even if the rumors weren't malicious.

With each hour spent in his company, she grew more confident in her assessment of Mr. Payne's character, and though he seemed determined to devalue himself, Evelyn was glad to call him a friend. Sending out a quick prayer, she hoped she might help him heal from the damage of so many undeserved criticisms.

Despite the hapless fashion of their first meeting, Evelyn had sensed goodness inside Mr. Payne. They say one should never trust first impressions, but she suspected that was because most people did not notice all the little details that gave a person away—what they chose to speak about, the tone they used, their attitudes toward their family and friends. Even amongst the sterile chatter of ballrooms, one could surmise much about another's motivations and philosophies simply from how they described the weather. If nothing else, there was a feel to a person, as though their heart and soul radiated outwards, giving off a hint of who they truly were.

And despite being a tad awkward and uncomfortable at first, Mr. Payne seemed a good man. No matter how many times well-meaning acquaintances insisted on telling her the "truth" about her new friend, Evelyn hadn't been able to reconcile the blackguard they described with the man who longed for friendship and connection, who bore his father's apathy without complaint, who disagreed with her at times but never criticized, who found joy in a drive through the country, and who was more concerned with her comfort than his own.

Hearing his story didn't serve to change her mind. It only proved her instincts correct.

"I fear the time is getting away from us," said Mr. Payne, glancing at his pocket watch before getting to his feet.

"I do apologize, Mrs. Adams," said Evelyn with a frown. "Unfortunately, it took us longer to arrive than we'd anticipated—"

The old cook waved the apology away and said with a wicked grin, "No doubt you were finding more pleasant things to do with your time together."

Evelyn's cheeks heated. "I assure you it was nothing of the sort."

For goodness' sake, why must everyone insinuate more than what was? Could Mr. Payne not simply enjoy her company without wild speculation?

The gentleman in question offered her his hand, and Evelyn was grateful for the gesture, though it made it more difficult to hide the stiffness in her joints, as she had to rely quite heavily on his assistance to rise from her chair. She managed to keep her expression as placid as ever, but when her gaze met Mr. Payne's, there was a pull of his brow and tightness to his lips that made her think he knew the truth.

Evelyn kept herself from hobbling, but as she stepped to Mrs. Adams' side, her movements were as unsteady as the old woman's. She tried to crouch down and rearrange the blankets on the cook's lap, but her body protested the movement, and Evelyn stopped herself before there was any serious trouble.

"I am sorry we weren't able to get you your cider, but I promise that once the last of our visitors have left, I'll send over every drop we have."

"You are a good girl," said Mrs. Adams. "Now, go off with your young man and make the most of the day."

With Mr. Payne at her back, she was able to wince without him seeing it, and she rubbed between her eyes where a pain was making itself known, though it had naught to do with the fall she'd taken. Evelyn had almost convinced herself to say nothing when the woman spoke again.

"And you, young fellow, had best take good care of our Miss Finch," said Mrs. Adams. "Treat her well, or you shall have me to contend with."

Evelyn sighed. "Mrs. Adams—"

"I fully intend to," said Mr. Payne. "Heaven knows I lucked into finding such a fine lady."

Straightening, Evelyn's gaze darted to him. "Pardon?"

But Mr. Payne met that with a furrowed brow, while Mrs. Adams seemed not to notice.

"It's about time someone snatched up our dear Miss Finch," she said with a solemn shake of her head. "I do not know what's wrong with the young men that they cannot see what a treasure she is."

And still, Evelyn remained fixed in place, unable to do anything more than blink as Mr. Payne grinned and said, "Their loss is my gain."

Mrs. Adams reached for him, and he stepped forward so she could take his hands in hers. Giving his cheek a motherly pat, she murmured, "Good boy. Now, you've already spent far too much time indulging an old woman. Go take your young lady out."

Evelyn's mouth dried up as though she'd eaten several handfuls of sand, and she wished the fairies Mrs. Adams so often spoke of were real and would spirit herself away. When Mr. Payne returned to her side, Evelyn couldn't meet his gaze, her mind flowing through all the possible things she might say to ease his discomfort. Perhaps Mrs. Adams' faculties had deteriorated more than they had realized, or perhaps the old cook was as mule-headed as her family was, but either way, she had inferred too much.

Helping Evelyn with her things, Mr. Payne offered her a strong arm to hold as they returned to the sleigh, giving her far more assistance than she would normally need, and demonstrating that despite her efforts to pretend otherwise, he knew she was in pain. With the care of a nursemaid, he bundled the blanket over her lap and then disappeared back into Mrs. Adams' cottage to fetch their bricks, which had been warming by the fire.

Evelyn wanted to call out to him and give him some excuse—anything, really—why he oughtn't to go back in. Who knew what else the woman would say? But Mr. Payne disappeared before she could and reappeared in a trice, settling the bricks at her feet and leaving none for himself.

"Mr. Payne—" But her protests died when he gave her a firm look that said she would not win this argument, and so Evelyn relented, settling into the warmth and comfort of the blankets and bricks.

If only she could erase the unease left by Mrs. Adams' well-meaning but unwelcome interference. As much as Evelyn longed to forget it or pretend it hadn't been as bad as all that, her insides twisted, studying every twitch of Mr. Payne's eyebrows and turn of his lips for any sign that he was upset about that inference. Men spooked easily when anyone implied a romance when there was none, and even the laziest of men sprinted away with the speed of a racehorse when faced with such implications.

Evelyn's mind produced a string of images, showing all the possible outcomes of this afternoon. Mr. Payne depositing her on the doorstep with a curt bow, never to be seen again. Or abandoning her on the side of the road to walk home alone. Or worse, running off to laugh with the Ninnies about Miss Finch throwing herself at him. A dozen different scenarios played out, and though she knew Mr. Payne wouldn't be cruel about it, no man would tolerate his name being tied to a young lady for whom he harbored no romantic feelings.

And she couldn't keep the words inside any longer.

"It is kind of you to play along with Mrs. Adams, but I hope you know I did not encourage her in any way—"

"Play along?" Mr. Payne glanced from the road ahead, giving her a raised brow. "What do you mean?"

Evelyn sighed. "I adore Mrs. Adams, but like my family, she is too apt to assume."

Mr. Payne frowned, his gaze narrowing as though he was trying to decipher her meaning. "I beg your pardon, Miss Finch, but you are speaking nonsense. If you wish me to accept whatever apology you're trying to make, I will freely do so with a bit of context."

Good heavens. He was going to make her spell it out in detail? Evelyn wanted to pinch her nose but couldn't bring herself to disturb her blanket cocoon. Instead, she sank further into it. As euphemisms and hints weren't doing the trick, she was forced to take a more direct approach.

"She is under the impression that our relationship is more than friendship."

Mr. Payne gave her a half-smile. "That is bound to happen

when we are courting."

Evelyn straightened, the blankets falling free from her neck, but she couldn't give a moment's thought to the chill. "Pardon?"

His brows pulled tight together, his gaze darting between the road and her. "As you have pointed out, we've spent every day together in some fashion. We've danced. We've been seen together at parties, and when there isn't a ball or gathering to attend, I'm at your home in the evenings. We drive out often. By even the most conservative definition, that is courting."

The world froze in place, and Evelyn stared at Mr. Payne. His succinct description of their time together was accurate, but those were also the actions of friends. Weren't they? But Evelyn didn't know why she was questioning it. The gentleman had stated baldly that they were courting. Had done so without any hesitation or fear. No caveat or clause. Simply stated the truth as he saw it.

Only the sound of the horse's hooves and the jangle of its tack broke the silence as she sat there, trying to grasp the reality laid before her. But how could one accept that the world had gone topsy-turvy?

Good gracious, Mr. Payne was courting her!

Chapter 18

The world snapped back into place as time zipped forward, making up for those lost moments when Evelyn had been trapped in her shock. She smothered a laugh, her wide eyes turning to stare at the gentleman's profile. Luckily, his gaze was on the road ahead, though she felt his attention fixed on her. Shooting her eyes forward, her mind raced through the past weeks, sifting through everything and seeing it anew. Her heartbeat picked up, threatening to beat right out of her chest.

Not just as a chum or acquaintance. A beau! And not just any beau. Mr. Gideon Payne! He was courting her because he felt her capable of being his one true love. The possibilities unfolded before her, bringing with them a myriad of fantasies. All those long-ago dreams of family and children, which she'd thought were erased, sprung forward with even more power, for now, they were more than hypotheticals.

Energy thrummed through her, threatening to shoot her right off the sleigh's bench, and Evelyn felt like shouting it to the heavens. She didn't know how she could contain it all inside her, for it pulsed within her, begging to be let out.

And all the while, Mr. Payne sat quietly at her side.

Ice ran down her spine, dousing all those happy thoughts and feelings until she was as frozen as the ground beneath them. Gaining a beau was one thing. Keeping him was another altogether.

Burrowing into the blankets, Evelyn tried to stamp out the fingers of frost that folded around her heart. But the image of a turtle popped into her head, and she straightened again, trying to keep the blankets draped in an attractive manner. Was there such a thing? She tried to imagine what Mr. Payne saw, but the only image that came to mind was a turtle with her own goofy grin, its head pulled back deep into its shell. That was certainly not the sort of comparison a woman wanted when a man looked at her.

"Do you often visit Mrs. Adams?" asked Mr. Payne, slanting her a look from the corner of his eye, his brows pulled low. Even though she could not see the hint of concern from this angle, his tone conveyed enough of it.

She was ruining it already! Breathe, Evelyn!

With effort, she forced herself to ignore the current situation and focus on the Evelyn of the past few weeks—the one who was not concerned with whether or not Mr. Payne liked her. Only when she thought herself capable of answering, did she give him a broad smile.

"She was our cook."

Mr. Payne paused. "Yes, I gathered that from the conversation."

Evelyn tried to swallow, but her thoughts were so filled with all the things she might say wrong that she found herself nodding like a fool. "She was with our family for many years. I knew her when I was a child. She was very nice to me."

"Is something the matter?"

Her pulse jolted, picking up its pace at his tone. Even a generous appraisal would say he was confused, but a more apt description would be unsettled. Forcing in a breath, Evelyn let it out in a big huff, puffing out her cheeks.

"Everything is wonderful, Mr. Payne. And I do try to visit

Mrs. Adams from time to time. She was always so kind to me."
There. That wasn't so terrible. Not brilliant by any means, but
it was coherent, relevant, and held not a hint of the panic that
had her muscles tensing beneath her blanket.

"Isn't it beautiful?" Evelyn forced herself not to wince. Despite her valiant (though not so clever) attempt to shift the conversation, her tone was too brittle and strained. As much as her
rational side screamed at her to calm herself, she couldn't seem
to stop another attempt at conversation.

"The weather is so very fine."

That ushered in more awkward, stilted conversation, and
Evelyn couldn't be certain what she was saying, except that her
mouth was moving, and she couldn't make it stop. It was as
though her body had seized control, leaving her mind at its
mercy as it laughed too hard, spoke too quickly, and kept doing
silly things like slapping Mr. Payne on the arm with more force
than could be considered "playful."

It was like watching the sleigh crash again. The disaster
raced towards them, bringing with it a world of pain and anguish, but she was unable to do anything but bounce about in
her seat and hold on as best she could. Perhaps they could crash
again; a strong jostle might be enough to set her thoughts to
rights once more.

But no matter how she tried to regain control of herself, beneath every word, every movement, every expression, pulsed
the thought that Mr. Payne cared for her. Not as a friend, but as
a woman. Unfortunately, that revelation brought with it the
truth of her own feelings—Evelyn cared deeply for Mr. Gideon
Payne.

And she was going to ruin it.

Having never spent much time amongst eccentric people,
Gideon hadn't realized there were varying degrees of oddness.
From the beginning, Miss Finch had proven herself worthy of
such a description, but now, her behavior was even stranger

than before. Glancing at her from the corner of his eye, Gideon studied her as the lady rambled on. Heaven knew Miss Finch was a talker, but this was bordering on frenetic.

"There is nothing finer than a sunny winter day, don't you think?" she asked, her words clipped and speeding along like a child being forced to say her prayers, though there was a brightness to her voice that reeked of falsehood. To say nothing of the chuckle that followed that inane comment, which sounded like someone had upended a jar of glass beads across a stone floor. Then Miss Finch began expounding at length about the various weather patterns and their merits, ranking each according to her preferences.

And then nothing. Miss Finch clamped her lips tight, her gaze shooting towards the frozen hedgerow as though it was the most fascinating of sights. As she seemed disinclined to tell him what was amiss, Gideon thought it best to keep his own counsel, though that did not keep his thoughts from speculating wildly about the sudden shift. And it took no great leap of logic to sniff out the source.

Had Miss Finch only wished to be friends? She'd thrown about the term often enough that he wasn't surprised that his declaration had shocked her. Clearly, the lady hadn't believed his overtures were romantic. And Gideon couldn't entirely blame her: they hadn't been at first. As he, himself, had only just arrived at the revelation that he wished for something more, he couldn't fault Miss Finch for not doing so.

The silence stretched on, and Gideon's heart sank with every passing minute, his pulse slowing until he wasn't certain it was beating at all. Could there be any clearer message than her instant discomfort? He had never seen anyone so at ease with their surroundings as Miss Finch, and now, she sat like a statue, shoved to the far side of the sleigh, her gaze never wavering from the wall of hedges at her side. And though the nip in the air made it difficult to decipher, he couldn't help but think her cheeks were redder than before.

Gideon had opened his silly mouth, and now she was embarrassed.

Though the journey to Mrs. Adams' cottage had taken a fair amount of time, the return to Farleigh Manor was far quicker, the gates to the house appearing before he knew what to say or do to salvage this wretched situation.

"I apologize if I offended you," he said, steering the sleigh onto her front drive.

Miss Finch turned to him once more, but that fretful energy returned in full force as she gave him a wide and all-too-forced smile. "You didn't, Mr. Payne."

Gideon pulled the sleigh to a stop at her front steps, and though he moved to help her down, Miss Finch alighted before he could do more than shift in his seat. With a wave over her shoulder and a quick word of farewell, she scurried up the steps, the front door slamming behind her.

Staring at the dark wood as though it might provide some understanding of what had just occurred, Gideon stood there like the fool he was. Miss Finch didn't return his feelings.

Chapter 19

Fire blossomed in Gideon's chest, sparking to life without warning as it burned through him. He forced himself not to take his mood out on the horse as he urged Cinnamon away from Farleigh Manor, but his fingers clenched around the reins. What had he been thinking? He'd spoken to Mrs. Adams of his courtship with such confidence.

Gideon let out a groan, the long, heavy sound releasing the pressure like a valve, and his shoulders slumped, his gaze drifting off into nothing as the road stretched before him. He couldn't say whether it was lucky or not Cinnamon knew the route home for the horse required little guidance, but it left Gideon's mind free to wander through the disaster that was today.

Firstly, he'd nearly done her real harm by crashing the sleigh, and then he'd blurted out that they were courting. Gideon winced, his head dropping.

And beneath all the worry and frustration, the anger and regret, he couldn't get the image of her in his arms out of his mind. The feel of her pressed close to him. That look in her eyes as she'd smiled, her face so close to his. Thank heavens he hadn't followed his instinct and kissed her! If this was her reaction to simply being told he was courting her (or attempting to, at any rate), Gideon couldn't imagine what she would've done had he taken such a liberty.

Or rather, he could. While daydreaming about the softness of her lips sent a spike of heat racing through his veins and served as quite an entertaining diversion, the resulting horror and anger that she would've turned in his direction dumped a bucket of ice water on his ardor.

Gideon straightened, forcing himself to focus on the road ahead while his thoughts ticked off all the reasons he was a fool and how much better the afternoon could've been. It was fitting that clouds rolled in, covering the sky in a pall of gray as he arrived home. He left the sleigh and horse to the groom as his thoughts wandered through the past, present, and future, picking apart the known and the unknown, the reality before him and the hypothetical of how this would play out.

His feet carried him up the stairs, following the familiar path, and he poked his head into his father's bedchamber. The nurse was fast asleep in the corner, as was her usual state, but at least she didn't reek of gin this time. Sitting amongst a mountain of blankets and pillows with a tea tray resting on the bed beside him, Father had the newspaper open, his gaze perusing all the tiny script packed into those pages.

"You look better today," said Gideon.

The paper dipped, and Father spared him a glance over the top of his reading glasses before returning to his reading. "You've been gone a long while. I was starting to think you'd packed up and abandoned me to Nurse Johnson's tender care."

"Not at all, sir. I was out with Miss Evelyn Finch."

Father dropped his newspaper, casting aside his glasses to give Gideon a proper stare. "And how did you manage that?"

Gideon shifted in place, sorting through what he could say to that, but Father merely huffed and returned to his newspaper.

"I suppose it doesn't matter. Seize the opportunity while you can, and do your best not to ruin it."

The words struck their target, though Father couldn't possibly know just how well. They were spoken with a tone that was certain that ruin was the only possible future, and Gideon hoped his father's dire prediction had not proven true already.

"They are good people," added Father, and Gideon recognized the unspoken message accompanying it, for he'd heard that lecture many times before. The Finches were good people, and he mustn't taint them by association.

A sigh built in his chest, though Gideon knew better than to let it out; such actions only led to more lectures, and he could bear no more today. As there was nothing more to say, he turned but stopped when Father spoke again.

"And I do not like your friends showing up on my doorstep," said Father, the paper rustling as he turned the page. "You may choose to associate with anyone you wish, but I do not want them lurking about my home."

Again, there was no point in questioning why Father felt the need to say such a thing or in defending himself from accusations; either would earn him a torrent of sermons, starting with the weakness of the flesh and ending with the inherent evil of men. Best to nod and sneak away.

Gideon's feet felt like they were made of stone as he tried to climb the stairs to his bedchamber. Holding fast to the handrail, he relied heavily on it to help him, for his strength was quite spent. At the top of the landing, he found his door ajar while the reason for some of his father's disquiet lay on the bed.

"Charles!"

"Dash it all, Gideon. Your father is a grim fellow," replied Charles with a shudder before hopping up from the bed. "Nearly gave me apoplexy, staring me down as he did. If I hadn't cried for mercy, I fear he would've tossed me back out into the snow. When he allowed me to stay, I was certain he was going to flay me alive."

Shaking Charles's hand, Gideon motioned for him to sit again, and his guest took full advantage, kicking up his feet and crossing them at the ankle as he reclined against the pillows.

"I thought you were in London," said Gideon while he took a seat in a nearby armchair. "I was starting to think you'd never return to Devon."

Charles sighed and waved an airy hand. "Pater insisted I come for the holidays and make up sweet to Mater. The bounder even threatened to withhold my allowance, so I had no choice but to stir myself. I don't know why it matters so much. I see them often enough when they come to Town."

"I imagine they wish for their family to be together at this time of year," said Gideon, which earned him a frown.

"And that is precisely the reason I avoid it at all costs. With my sisters and brothers multiplying like rabbits, the house is filled to bursting. It's pure chaos and not the good sort. Mater always scowls when I reach for another drink or sneak away to find some proper sport."

"It sounds wretched," replied Gideon in a dry tone. The image Charles presented was just the sort of scene he'd found at the Finches, and a smile tickled the corner of his lips. Except that it reminded him of Miss Finch, which resurrected the memories of this afternoon. Even Charles was not distraction enough.

"But that is why I told them I was staying with you," replied Charles.

"Pardon?"

Charles gave another dismissive wave of his hand. "Your house is so empty at this time of year. It's a tragedy, and as both a good friend and a Christian man, I ought to be here to bring a bit of merriment to your life. Mater almost looked teary because of my selflessness."

And with that, the sigh Gideon had been holding released, but he clung to his smile and didn't bother to point out that Charles had neither asked nor been asked to invade Linden Place. Sighing doubly, Gideon considered how to broach the subject with Father. That was a battle for another time.

"Oh, and Mater insists that you and your father join them for Christmas dinner," said Charles.

"I'm afraid I have other plans," replied Gideon, his gaze drifting away from his friend as he picked a bit of lint off his trousers.

"Ah." Charles spoke that one word with such a wealth of understanding that Gideon struggled to keep his countenance calm. When he did meet his friend's gaze, Charles studied him for no more than a moment before clapping his hands and hooting. "It's a lady, isn't it?"

Gideon remained impassive, not allowing even the slightest hint of emotion to play out as the fellow scrutinized him. But there was more than one reason Gideon had never developed a love of gaming, and it took less than a heartbeat for Charles to start hooting again.

"Quiet up there!" called Father, making the pair wince.

With a nod, Gideon said in a low voice, "I have met a lady."

How he spoke those five words evenly was a mystery, though judging by the gleam in Charles's gaze, his tone was not as calm as he'd wished it to be.

"But it is complicated," he added.

With a huff, Charles dropped back against the pillows. "That is to be expected when women are involved. I met quite a comely barmaid on the journey here, and she led me on a merry chase. They enjoy twisting us around their fingers until we are thoroughly caught in their spell."

"I am thoroughly caught, Charles."

That was met by a long beat of silence. "Truly?"

Gideon considered that and gave him a nod. "Unfortunately, I have frightened her away."

Charles huffed and rose to his feet. "If we are going to talk about your courting woes, we shall need a change of venue. A drink is required. Several, in fact. Speaking of which, I told The White Hart to send my bill here. You were gone for such a long time, and I couldn't bear to spend it all lurking about when your father was so determined to scowl me into an early grave. I would've spoken to you first, but I knew you wouldn't mind."

Holding back another sigh, Gideon followed his friend out

of the room. "I will cover it."

"You're a good sport," replied Charles, moving lightly down the stairs with a hint of a hop. "Pater will read The Riot Act if I send another to him, and he already gives me so little. He doesn't understand that gentlemen of means must have means. The fellow demands I spend my money getting here for Christmas, and then won't give me a little extra to cover the added expense. This time of year is costly, and he cannot comprehend the financial burden I am under."

Creeping past his father's bedchamber, they slipped by unnoticed, though Gideon didn't release his breath until they were bundled up and out the door.

"Now, we have much to discuss concerning your mystery lady," said Charles with a waggle of his brows, "but first, I must tell you about that luscious little barmaid I met on the journey here. The White Hart has a decent bevy, but this woman was quite the prize..."

Clinging to his smile, Gideon nodded, though he turned his thoughts far from the conversation at hand. Charles was quite skilled at monologuing, and from his tone, this was a discussion in which Gideon's participation was not required. Thank the heavens for that small miracle.

Unfortunately, that left Gideon firmly stuck in his thoughts with nothing to distract himself.

Chapter 20

C hristmas Eve was the best of the holidays. Certainly, others received more fanfare, but this beautiful day ushered in the Twelve Days with so many things Evelyn adored. Father sat at the piano, his fingers nimbly running across the keys in a never-ending medley of carols, while Mama alternated between duetting with him and directing the troops as they festooned the parlor with all the trimmings of the season.

Being amongst the older of the children, Evelyn recalled the time when their tree had been a tabletop affair. With each additional child and grandchild, the thing had grown to provide enough space for everyone to have a hand in decorating it. Their handcrafted ornaments were joined by little treats and presents, which would find their way into the children's hands during the holidays. Whistles, mittens, drums, tops, dolls, and books were tucked along the branches, including a few treats for the elder generation, and Evelyn made note of a particularly lovely necklace of coral beads.

To one side, Bridget and Robin worked together with their four children to drape an evergreen bough over the mantle. Marian held Christopher in her arms as she crouched next to her little Sadie, motioning to where the child ought to hang a biscuit, which may have been meant to be a dog or a horse but had transformed into a fanciful creature that defied biology, while George kept a tight hold on Adam's hands as he toddled around the tree, attempting to strip it bare and undo all their work.

With care, the candles were lit, though the bottom third were left alone tonight as they were well within the little ones' reach. It left the tree looking a bit lopsided and undone, but even with that imperfection, it was a marvelous sight. All other lights were extinguished, and the tree stood out even more amongst the shadows.

The flames flickered off the bits of metal like sparkling mirrors, making the tree sparkle as though coated with pixie dust. Though smaller, the candles on the tree weren't any different than those that hung in the sconces and chandeliers, yet they had a light unique to themselves. Perhaps it was the Christmas music playing in the background or the festive scent in the air that lent it something more. Something magical.

The scent of gingerbread biscuits mingled with the evergreen and the spicy and sweet taste of hot cider on her tongue, completing the tableau. Christmas was truly here.

When Evelyn's gaze finally broke from the sight, she glanced at her family gathered around and was struck anew. Mama and Papa sat, side by side, on the piano bench as she turned the pages for him. Bridget and George stood with their families gathered close. Miles and Isaac had their heads together, deep in conversation. And Evelyn remained alone.

Her heart clenched, and she shook away that thought. She wasn't alone. Her family adored her and cared deeply about her happiness and well-being. Yet she stood apart. Together yet separate. Solitary.

Miles and Isaac weren't the closest of friends, but they gravitated toward each other much as Evelyn and Josie had done before her younger sister had married. Her relationships with

George and Bridget had altered with their marriages and ensuing children, for their lives now revolved around the families they'd created. Though they and their children adored Aunt Evelyn, she was not the focus of their world.

Evelyn huffed at that. It was selfish to look at the bounty around her and feel deprived simply because she was not the central figure in another's heart and mind. That was the nature of relationships. Friends and siblings married. That shift was natural, and she did not fault them for it, but it left her feeling alone even amidst her family. Surrounded by love yet not its central focus.

If Mr. Payne were here...She shook away that thought. It was dangerous ground.

Evelyn stared at the tree, refusing to allow self-pity to ruin a beautiful evening. She had love aplenty. It may not be the sort she desired, but that did not negate its beauty.

Drifting towards the piano, she hummed along with the runs and trills that took the simple and familiar carol tune into something magnificent. Rather like their ornaments had done to the Christmas tree.

Mama looked up from Papa's music and stood to take Evelyn in her arms. "Happy Christmas, dearest."

"Happy Christmas."

Turning, they faced the tree, and Mama sighed. "It's a shame the rest of the family cannot be here. They have lives of their own, and that is well and good, but I cannot help but wish it wouldn't alter things so completely."

Evelyn had nothing to say to that, for she understood the sentiment entirely. Work had stolen Benjamin and Mason away from Devon, and with it being her first Christmas as a married lady, Josie was occupied with establishing her home. Would her family ever be together for the holidays again? But Evelyn banished that thought, for she wouldn't wish her siblings' good fortune undone, even if it left her behind.

"I think it may be time for us to end this Christmas Eve tradition. George and Bridget deserve an opportunity to build new ones with their own families," murmured Mama. She studied the adults as they showed their children the tree from various angles. "As much as I love to hold onto things the way they are, it's not good to cling to such things. Life changes and we must adapt."

Though her heart sank at the thought, Evelyn considered it. "Perhaps we might come up with new traditions next year."

Mama nodded and smiled at her daughter. "And perhaps you will have new ones of your own."

Evelyn stiffened at the implication rife in her tone, and she thanked her good fortune that the candles from the Christmas tree were not strong enough to show just how much she was blushing at the insinuation.

"Is something the matter?" Mama's brows pulled low as she studied Evelyn for a long moment.

Shifting from foot to foot, Evelyn glanced at the room. "Of course not."

With a huff, Mama shook her head. "You are a wretched liar and ought not to attempt it."

Evelyn frowned. "Then I will amend my statement. I do not wish to speak of it at present."

Or ever. Though she often found solace in speaking through a problem, this was not one of those times. Heat filled her cheeks, making her feel like a roasting chestnut ready to burst. How would she even describe this disaster? Her feelings and thoughts were in an indecipherable tangle.

Besides, Mama would only dole out a heap of assurances with that little smile that was meant to soothe but implied that Evelyn was making a mountain out of a molehill. No amount of conviction would convince Mama or the rest of the family that her last meeting with Mr. Payne had been a disaster. Evelyn knew better.

Thankfully, Mama accepted that and nodded, and they basked in the glow of the Christmas tree. Yet Evelyn struggled to recapture the magic when she knew time was speeding by. She couldn't see the clock face in this light, but it had to be close to when *he* would arrive.

Forcing air into her lungs, Evelyn clung to the last shreds of her calm. She could do this. She could. She had managed intelligent conversations with Mr. Payne before his courtship declaration. She could do so again. She need only ignore the fact that he had stated his intentions. And the way her heart leapt at the possibility. And wipe her mind of one of the most embarrassing moments in her life. And behave as though nothing had altered between them.

Simple.

She puffed out her cheeks and let out a heavy sigh, which drew her mother's attention. Evelyn shook her head, attempting a smile, though it was no more convincing than her bald-faced lie. Clearing her throat, she forced her thoughts to clear. Mr. Payne was a friend. She could treat him as such.

The parlor door opened, and the footman spoke the words that Evelyn had been anticipating and dreading all at once. "Mr. Payne is here to see you."

Chapter 21

Though her siblings had the good sense to say nothing while the servant was there, the moment he disappeared, the room erupted like that metaphorical hornets' nest. They all spoke at once, so there was no way for Evelyn to decipher one word from the next, but the tones and expressions of delight on their collective faces were enough to convey their meaning, and she groaned.

"Enough!" said Mama, giving them all a gimlet eye. "Stop teasing your sister, or I will happily dredge up every embarrassing story I know of you, and my memory is vast."

Miles and Isaac hardly looked repentant when they agreed, but with Marian glowering at him, George managed a far more earnest apology. Bridget was undaunted; however, her outburst had focused on matchmaking rather than teasing, and no threat would deter her.

The clock chimed, and Evelyn straightened. "We are going to be late if you do not hurry."

That set the group in a dither for a new reason as everyone scurried off in search of their winter clothes. The room fell silent once more as Evelyn stood alone in the light of the Christmas tree, reveling in the moment of quiet as she girded her loins. She was capable and intelligent; there was no reason she could not seize control of her tongue. She was its mistress, and it was time that it learned its place.

Leaving the candles and mess to the servants, Evelyn took a fortifying breath and hurried to the entryway. The chaos in the parlor had transferred there. Despite having done so many times before, the adults struggled to fit little hands and feet into their mittens and boots as the children wriggled and squealed, fighting against the constraints. With the mayhem to contend with, her family gave only a passing nod to Mr. Payne as he stood to one side, watching the stairs.

His gaze was fixed on the top, spying Evelyn the moment she appeared. Mr. Payne's eyes looked darker than usual. Though they had candles lit for the caroling, the shadows stripped the green from the hazel, leaving them far more brown than usual. Evelyn tried to swallow, but for all her plans to behave naturally, she hadn't anticipated his unblinking gaze watching upon her as she descended.

"Good evening, Mr. Payne. How good of you to join us this evening for the evening activities this evening." How many times had she said "evening?" Forcing herself not to wince, Evelyn tried again. "I am glad you came this evening."

Mr. Payne nodded. "I said I would."

Her heart ceased beating, her thoughts quickly speeding through all the implications in those four little words. Examining every twist of his lips, glint in his eyes, and shift in his tone, she tried to piece together the sentiments beneath his statement. Was he here because of that obligation? Was he pleased?

"I hope your father isn't upset that we stole you away this evening." She hid another wince as that word wormed its way into her vocabulary again. "I think it will be a fine evening. I only wish he were well enough to join us this evening."

Stop saying that word! Of all the ones to latch onto, "evening" may be the silliest. At the very least, she ought to use a synonym, but none came to mind.

"He isn't well enough to go traipsing about in the night air," he replied, and something in his tone made her wonder if he was quoting the gentleman in question.

A footman handed over her things, and Mr. Payne took her jacket, helping her into it with far more ease than George was managing with Adam, who had flopped onto the ground at her feet while his papa attempted to force little feet into little boots, all while grumbling about that they shouldn't have given the nursemaid the evening off.

Mr. Payne studied the child for a moment before sending a bright look at Evelyn, his brow arched in silent laughter. It eased the tightness in her chest, allowing her to breathe once more.

"I have missed our time together the past few days." Evelyn knew he deserved an apology, but she couldn't admit the reason behind the separation. Mr. Payne may think her enjoyably eccentric, but her thoughts were in such a convoluted mess of late that she would likely shift from delightfully strange to deranged in his eyes; a lady ought to ease a gentleman into such a thing and not spring all her oddities on him all at once. And until today, she hadn't been certain she could maintain her poise.

Keep her answers simple. Succinct. Rein in her tongue. She could do that.

"I have missed it as well. I could've used a distraction from my houseguest. It is cruel of you to abandon me to him without any respite." Though the words were delivered in a dry tone, there was a spark of mischief in Mr. Payne's gaze that had Evelyn smiling.

"And you abandoned him tonight?" There! She had managed something moderately close to her usual tone.

"Charles's family lives nearby, and he is spending the evening with them."

Evelyn's thoughts fled. Just as she had managed a few coherent sentences, her mind emptied, leaving her blinking at Mr. Payne like the fool she was. Luckily, conversation halted as Mama and Papa herded the rowdy group toward their sleighs.

Clinging to the last shred of her hope, Evelyn reminded

herself she was an intelligent, capable woman. Mr. Payne was a friend and already prized her company. All that was required was to breathe and behave as she had the many times they'd spent together. And as tonight's focus was mostly singing, she needed only to keep hold of her tongue between songs.

Surely, that shouldn't be difficult.

...

Caroling and Christmas went hand-in-hand, though Gideon had never participated in that tradition himself. Like many houses on this all-important Eve, Linden Place had been visited by those spreading their holiday cheer through song, but since his mother's passing, his father never lit the lamps in the window that invited the carolers to stop, and Gideon rather missed it.

The Finches gathered with others in their parish, holding their candles and lamps aloft as they filled the air with song. The children struggled with the words, singing with more gusto than accuracy but ushering in a new spirit that the adults could not manage alone. And few withheld their purses when the little ones shuffled forward with the alms box.

Miss Finch stood at his side, the candlelight playing off the planes of her face. Her dark eyes sparked with golden hues, and though the fiery brilliance of her hair was muted in the shadows, the flickering flame caught hints of reds and oranges from beneath her bonnet. More than that, a brightness shone from within her as she sang. Gideon had witnessed it during the choir practices and when she'd given him private concerts on their drives. Now, in the dim Christmas light, she glowed as her voice rang out with the notes of the carols.

The alms box rattled as coins dropped inside, and the child holding it beamed, wishing the giver a "Happy Christmas" as the song drifted to a close and their group meandered on to the next house.

"The donations are for a Twelfth Night party," said Miss Finch in a crisp tone. The edge of her smile tightened as he helped her along the slippery street. "It is the parish tradition to gather funds for it, and then everyone is invited so that everyone is afforded some celebration during Christmas. It's a wonderful evening full of music and dancing and food..."

And Miss Finch was babbling again, extolling the virtues of their cause, how the parish didn't neglect important charities as well, and listing off the highlights of the past parties and caroling. After attempting and failing to stem the flow of words many times before, Gideon knew better than to try again.

Were he inclined towards megrims, he was certain he would have one at present. Gideon couldn't even think of her as a puzzle—unless it was one whose pieces were missing or turned the wrong way so he couldn't see the image he was attempting to create. One moment Miss Finch was at ease, losing herself in the moment and behaving precisely as she had in the past weeks. The next, she was chattering at a speed that would make a locomotive proud, barreling along at fearful rates.

Even if her verbal cues didn't make it clear she was ill at ease, Gideon saw the moment she shifted from the first to the second state of mind. Miss Finch tensed, and that glint in her eye took on a panicked edge while her smile tightened to such a degree that she looked more determined than gleeful.

Despite the unease, she remained at his side the entire evening. Though they were separated at times, Miss Finch made her way back to him every time. Surely, that meant something good. Didn't it?

Gideon replayed his scant conversation with her brother, and he was left to wonder once more just what Mr. George Finch had meant by saying his sister had been "mistreated." His words had implied another gentleman had toyed with her affections but without saying anything truly helpful.

Patience was touted to be a virtue, yet Gideon couldn't help but think that if things continued in this fashion, there would be nothing to salvage soon.

Slowing his steps so they were a few paces behind the rest, he lowered his voice. "What is the matter?"

Miss Finch halted amidst an inane recitation of the history of their parish choir, and her wide eyes met his. Before she could voice any halfhearted objection or assurance, Gideon hurried on.

"I am no fool, Miss Finch. You've been ill at ease in my company ever since you realized I wish to court you." Gideon's throat tightened at the thought of saying the next bit, but he forced the words out. "If you do not desire my company or wish for nothing more than friendship, you need only tell me. I hope you can return my sentiments, but if not, you need only say the word, and I will leave you be."

While her expression had been feigned calmness mere seconds ago, that strain eased into a semblance of the real thing—mixed with more than a hint of surprise. Gideon didn't care for the wideness of her gaze or how her brows rose, but he loved seeing her soul shining through her eyes as the dim candlelight darkened the brown until he couldn't tell the difference between her iris and pupil.

Gideon stepped closer, and the toes of his boots tucked beneath the edge of her skirts. Lowering his voice, he held her gaze, hoping she saw the tenderness thrumming through him and sensed what he wished her answer to be.

"What would you have me do, Miss Finch?"

Chapter 22

Surely, this was a dream. A fantasy. Perhaps her consciousness wandered off somewhere between sleep and waking, trapping her in this perfect moment. For Evelyn was certain there was no better feeling than having a man standing before her, pleading to court her. Those were not the precise words Mr. Payne used, but the meaning was clear enough.

Evelyn stilled, certain that any movement might wake her and relegate this moment to the realm of dreams and impossibilities. After years of wishing into the Christmas pudding, her deepest desire had sprung to life.

Mr. Payne stood there with only the slightest furrow of his brow betraying his anxiety. She raised the candle, and the light caught the flecks of green in his hazel eyes. No one had ever gazed upon her in such a manner before, watching her with such intensity as though her answer was as important as the very air in his lungs.

"I—" Evelyn's mouth dried, and her tongue turned to jelly. An answer was not difficult to speak when one knew the response to give, and everything within her screamed for her to tell him.

But then her gaze fell to his lips.

Speak, you fool! Tears gathered in her eyes, but Evelyn forced them back. Then Mr. Townsend's words came back to her, echoing across the years to play through her thoughts as though he were standing beside her. Throwing herself at another man, was she? It would end just as poorly again. Evelyn shook that aside. Mr. Payne had sought her out of his own volition, desiring her company again and again. Now, he stood before her, asking that she take him as a beau.

"Miss Finch," he said, drawing close enough that they were nearly touching, and his gaze held hers with a silent plea that echoed his words. "Please, speak to me."

"I am not—" Evelyn let out a sharp huff, her brow furrowing. Her heart wrenched in several directions, begging her to speak up while warning of the consequences. Though she'd mentioned her lack of male admirers in the past, Mr. Payne hadn't believed she wanted for dance partners, how could he understand that she knew not how to behave around a beau?

Many claimed courtship was an easy thing. Entertaining, even. But then, most practiced such interactions in their younger years, testing themselves in the art of flirtation and coquetry and honing such skills as they sifted through their list of candidates. Evelyn's attempts were laughably limited and had taught her avoidance was better than embarrassment.

Evelyn's cheeks burned at the thought of explaining it to Mr. Payne. Even if she could explain the battle raging inside, how could she admit that he terrified her? That her fears were so bone-deep she could not form comprehensible words? That while she didn't doubt his honorable intentions, Mr. Townsend's specter haunted her, taunting her with how unappealing she was?

One day she would say or do something to sour Mr. Payne's feelings, leaving him running for the hills like all the rest. She would spoil everything.

"I have never—" she attempted again. "I—"

Evelyn dropped her head, covering her eyes with her free

hand as she wished the ground would swallow her whole. Was there any point in explaining it? Was there any excuse that wouldn't make her seem like a Bedlamite? Or some pathetic creature, uncertain of what to do with the only man who wished to court her? The desperate spinster.

Mr. Townsend filled her thoughts, and Evelyn cringed. Her family knew much of the story, but no one knew the whole of it. That cad had suspected the truth, but even he did not know how thoroughly and entirely she'd thrown herself into loving him, determined to have him simply because he was the only applicant. And it wasn't as though Mr. Townsend was the first— merely the cruelest.

Mr. Payne's gloved hand brushed a touch along her arm, drawing her gaze as his fingers wrapped tentatively around hers.

Her head jerked up, and she met his eyes, which were far closer than they had been a moment ago. With the moon waning, there was little light other than the stars above and the candle in her hand, though the snow coating the ground and houses brightened up the darkness. The rest of the carolers had continued down the lane, their lights fading into the black, and she and Mr. Payne stood together on the side of the road. The cold nipped at her, but with Mr. Payne's gaze holding hers, Evelyn felt no chill.

"I understand if you are uncertain or afraid, and I can give you whatever time you require to sort your feelings, but know that as long as there is a chance I can win you, I will not surrender." The corner of his lips tipped upwards while his fingers entwined with hers. "I am quite fond of the woman I've come to know over the past weeks. Even if she is running mad at present."

Evelyn couldn't move from her spot. She didn't dare blink, for she was certain Mr. Payne had snatched these words straight from her fantasies, giving her precisely what she'd always longed to hear. They stood there in the snow, the lights twinkling in the heavens as his warm breath puffed out into little clouds. For her part, Evelyn couldn't breathe and was certain she never would again.

Encircled by the light of her candle, Evelyn's gaze drifted to his lips. She couldn't form the words, but her heart cried out for him to close the distance. What would it feel like to have him pressed up against her? To feel his touch? Tingles ran down the length of her as the image played through her mind.

Evelyn leaned closer, her body drawn to him like a magnet. If she could not speak the words, perhaps she could show him where her heart lay. Her breaths mingled with his, and she felt his warmth against her skin, her hand clutching firmly to his.

Her first kiss.

What if she did it wrong?

Between one heartbeat and the next, her mind flooded with that grim possibility. Evelyn had imagined this all-important moment many times in her life and had made a thorough study through books and observations (her siblings truly weren't circumspect enough in their displays of affection). Theory was well and good, but practical application was another thing altogether. Ought she to touch his arms? Holding hands seemed strange at this angle. Which direction ought she to lean? And at what time? To close one's eyes or not? Each question brought with it a myriad of uncertainties—none of which would result in a proper first kiss or strengthening Mr. Payne's feelings.

Their lips nearly grazed, and Evelyn's muscles tensed as she fought to clear her mind. It was only a kiss. Many people did it. Surely, it was not so difficult.

But a man of his age likely had some experience. And expectations she couldn't meet.

Mr. Payne's brow furrowed, but he did not move away. His hand drifted from hers to brush against the edge of her jaw. "Miss Finch—"

Something collided with her legs, and little arms wrapped around her thighs with a bright, "Aunt Evelyn! Mama was wondering where you had gotten yourself to."

Mr. Payne's hand jerked free, and Evelyn nearly knocked Sadie down as she sprang away from him. The child snatched her aunt's hand, tugging her toward the rest of the carolers. Evelyn remained in place, her gaze holding Mr. Payne's. His eyes echoed the beautiful things he'd said, seeking answers she still hadn't given him.

Her tongue still felt like it was tied in knots, but she had to say something.

"You are still coming for dinner tomorrow?"

Cocking his head to the side, Mr. Payne considered that. "If you wish me to."

"Yes." The word came quickly to her lips, and Evelyn put all the certainty she felt into it. She may not know her own heart or what else to say, but she could say that.

With a dip of his head, Mr. Payne smiled. "Then I shall be there."

Taking the candle from her hand, he lifted his arm in supplication, and Evelyn slid her hand through it while Sadie clung to her other as the trio followed after the distant strains of "The First Noel."

Chapter 23

"**S**top fidgeting," murmured Father, and Gideon stilled, though he couldn't help but shift in his seat one more time. The high-backed pew offered little in the way of comfort, though it wouldn't have mattered if it had been the plushest of armchairs. Glancing at his father, he didn't know how the older man managed to sit still when Mr. Moss was determined to stretch his Christmas sermon into a daylong affair.

But Father was determined. And scowling at his son.

"Apologies," murmured Gideon. Affecting a properly attentive expression, he watched as the choir rose to their feet once more. St. Benedict's boasted a larger congregation than the Finches' parish, yet he thought St. Margaret's music far finer.

With twice as many singers, he'd had high expectations, but their choirmaster had chosen complex arrangements that, even to Gideon's uneducated ear, were beyond the choir's ability. Well-done simplicity always outmatched moderately executed extravagance, and he forced himself not to wince as the choir struggled to achieve the harmonies and runs the composer demanded of the singers.

Glancing to the far end of the nave, Gideon spied his friend seated amongst the Moffit family. Charles's head bobbed, jerking back upright as his eyelids fought against gravity, and the only thing keeping him upright was his two large brothers squashed on either side of him (and the occasional well-aimed elbow in Charles's ribs).

As much as Gideon tried to distract himself, Miss Finch invaded his thoughts. It was impossible not to think of her when the choir began a far inferior rendition of "While Shepherds Watched Their Flocks at Night." Having heard St. Margaret's choir sing it several times during his time as Miss Finch's coachman, he couldn't help comparing the two any more than he could stop himself from reliving last night.

Miss Finch had reinforced her invitation for tonight, which seemed a good sign. If only he could do something to set her more at ease. And she hadn't turned him away. Gideon's lips stretched into a grin as he held fast to that, and the image of her standing so close. If only that blasted niece hadn't interrupted, he would've seized the opportunity—and Miss Finch.

Thankfully, the last prayers and blessings were given, freeing the congregation to their personal Christmas celebrations. It was some hours until he would leave for Farleigh Manor, but the time was drawing ever closer.

Standing, Gideon moved to the aisle, his jacket catching on a particularly large evergreen branch. The person in charge of decorating the church for the special service had adorned the end of each pew with a bundle of boughs held together with a massive bow. Unfortunately for the parishioners, the overzealous decorator had not considered how far the branches stretched or how easily they snagged the parishioners climbing in and out of the pew. Gideon plucked at the needles, freeing them from the edge of his jacket, and wiped at a spot of sap staining the fabric.

Father scowled at the decorations. "There was a time when the vicar didn't see the need to tart up the church. The joyful spirits of the congregants were all the decorations required. It seems indecent. Like a painted lady."

Gideon ignored that comment just as he had all the other times his father had made similar complaints since they'd arrived, and he offered his arm to the gentleman. But Father smacked it away.

"Don't rush me, boy. This is the first time I've been well enough to leave the house in weeks. I wish to speak with Mr. Little for a moment." With a shooing motion, he added, "Go off and amuse yourself for a few minutes. I'll call you when I'm ready to leave."

With a nod, Gideon turned on his heel and disappeared into the crowd. With no fireplace in the nave, jackets and cloaks were required at all times, but it was still warmer than what the churchyard offered, so the congregation remained wedged between the pews or drifted into the aisles as the nave filled with the sounds of chatter. Children fairly hopped by their parents' sides, demanding they return home posthaste for all the Christmas morning extravaganza, but the parents were unmoved by the pleas, preferring to reconnect with people they saw weekly.

Straightening his jacket, Gideon surveyed the room, and though he wished to believe there were far less disdainful looks sent in his direction, he found no welcoming expressions that invited him to join in their discussion. Weaving through the horde, he made his way to Charles's side.

"I was just telling Mater that you were counting on me for Christmas breakfast." Charles put an arm around Gideon's shoulder and gave his mother a bright smile. "You wouldn't want me to abandon him and his father to themselves? And we do not have the space for them to join us."

Mrs. Moffit sighed and shooed them away, though Gideon didn't feel like moving. The lady's posture stooped, her gaze full of resignation as she turned away from her son, and Gideon felt like pushing Charles in her direction. But the fellow's arm gripped him tight, guiding him away.

"Thank you for rescuing me," whispered Charles. "I had only just laid my head down when they dragged me from bed.

You'd think they could be a bit more compassionate on Christmas Day."

But Gideon couldn't think of anything to say to that as they stood off to the side of the Payne family pew. Sparing his father a glance, Gideon merely nodded as expected.

"You're always welcome to join us, but I will warn you we have nothing special planned—"

"You will never believe it! I received a letter from Ford yesterday, and our old school chum had some very interesting news to share," interrupted Charles with a wide gaze. He leaned closer, his eyes gleaming with that eagerness every gossiper had when relaying the juiciest of tidbits. "It seems there is a scandal afoot."

With a sigh, Gideon gave his friend a wry smile. "I hardly think church on Christmas Day is the appropriate venue or time for such things."

"But as I'm standing in a holy place on a holy day, surely that negates any wickedness," replied Charles with a laugh, clapping a hand on Gideon's back. "You recall Peterson?"

Gideon frowned, his brows pulling tight together.

Before he could say a word, Charles clarified. "The chap from school who lived out in some tiny village in Cumberland." When Gideon gave no other sign of recognition, he added, "The lad who was so enamored with mathematics that we called him 'Nought.'"

Gideon's smile tightened at the liberal use of "we," but he nodded. "I recall the fellow."

"Well, it seems he did fairly well for himself," said Charles in a tone that warned poor Peterson's life would take a poor turn. "Married a lady with a decent dowry and settled in London. Ended up teaching mathematics or some such nonsense."

Charles waved a dismissive hand and then stepped closer, his voice lowering until there was no way anyone beyond the pair of them that might overhear.

"His wife got an itch, if you know what I mean." Charles waggled his brows, though his tone held enough insinuation that even the greatest of fools would grasp his meaning. "Turns out she got herself in the family way and tried to pass it off as Peterson's."

Gideon's breath caught, his muscles tensing as he clung to his calm expression, not allowing even the slightest bit of surprise to register. Charles's brows furrowed.

"Do you not find that shocking?"

With a jerky nod of his head, Gideon arranged his features into polite interest, hiding how his stomach roiled and his lungs refused to work. Nothing was amiss. This was simply a bit of gossip. His parents had kept their scandal secret for his whole life, and there was no reason for Charles to infer any connection between the Petersons' story and Gideon's birth.

"What—" Gideon cleared his throat. "What happened to Mrs. Peterson and the child?"

Charles huffed. "What do you think? He's tossed her out and is suing for divorce. No man of sense wants to keep an unfaithful wife or raise someone else's leavings—"

"Are you going to stand about, gossiping?" Father's voice had Gideon snapping to attention and turning to face their pew, where his father sat with his brows raised. "I turned away for one minute, and you fled to chatter with your friend."

Gideon didn't bother pointing out that Father had been the one to suggest he do just such a thing, for disagreeing with the old man never did any good. Reaching down, he helped Father to his feet, and they shuffled towards the exit, where their groom had the carriage waiting for them.

Taking the reins in hand as Charles settled in behind them, Gideon tried to focus on the road, but his thoughts were fixed on the Petersons. Charles had recited their fates as though it were a clear and undeniable truth. What man would accept his wife's baseborn child into their household? From the corner of his eye, Gideon studied a man who had done just that.

With so many people leaving the church at the same time, Gideon was forced to keep a close watch on the road ahead, but his emotions swirled about like the drifts of snow behind the carriage. As a child, he'd never understood why his father disliked him. Though Mr. Winslow Payne could be stern and unyielding, Gideon had witnessed the little tendernesses he'd heaped on his wife, showering her with affection Gideon had always longed to see directed at himself.

But he was grown now and understood the truth behind the coldness. What did he expect of the man who had given him a home and his name? Who had protected him from a wretched life? Ought he to demand tenderness? For weeks, he'd watched the Finches, envious of their affection, but how could he be so selfish as to expect so much from a man who owed him nothing? Who had already given him more than most men would?

"Remember whose name you bear." Gideon had heard that admonishment so many times that the words had become a mere background noise in his life, yet they ought to be his lodestone. Gideon Payne. Who knew what his true surname should be, but Mr. Winslow Payne had given his freely.

Chapter 24

Thoughts of his father followed Gideon as he guided the horses along. Charles was wise enough to remain silent while Father expounded on the vicar's sermon. Though clouds covered the sky, they were alight with the sunshine; not allowing it through directly, but turning them to a brilliant shade of white. They passed houses, many of which were alive with the thrum of Christmas cheer as families played games and sang, and the scents of a hundred breakfast feasts filled the air.

When they pulled to a stop, the groom alighted, taking the reins from Gideon while Charles hopped from the back, shoving his hands in his pockets as he stared out at the nearly empty streets. Stepping down, Gideon offered his hand to his father, helping him down with as much care as possible with the snow and ice around them. Father groaned, his lips pulling into a wince, and Gideon guided him toward the front door.

"What are we having for breakfast?" asked Charles as they stepped through the front door and divested themselves of their winter gear.

"The usual," replied Gideon, turning to give his father his arm once more. Casting a glance over his shoulder, he added, "I told you we have nothing special planned this morning."

"No Christmas breakfast?" Charles's tone rang with such horror that one might think Gideon's pronouncement was the greatest evil ever to be released upon the world.

"You wouldn't listen," replied Gideon.

"Ridiculous popinjay," murmured Father with a scowl for good measure.

Charles huffed. Gideon couldn't turn his attention away from assisting his father up the stairs, but he heard a shuffle before his friend said, "I guess I'll just have to go beg Mater's forgiveness."

And with that, Charles Moffit strode through the front door, shutting it behind him.

"I don't know why you keep company with such fools," said Father, though the last few words were little more than a wheeze.

Gideon paused, allowing him to catch his breath. "We do not entertain anymore. Perhaps we should put your bed in the parlor—"

"No." Father practically barked the word, forcing his feet up the stairs, clinging to the handrail and Gideon. "I am not as infirm as all that."

But the weakness in his father's limbs proved he was.

Gideon said nothing, merely waiting as needed, providing him an arm and any strength he required as they made their way up the stairs. Father didn't look at him, leaving Gideon free to study the fellow, but the tightness in his chest forced his gaze away. How many times had he bristled at his father's disdain?

Even knowing the extent of Father's benevolence, Gideon longed for something better. This man had given him every-thing, and it wasn't enough. What an ungrateful creature he was.

They arrived at Father's bedchamber, and Nurse Johnson took over, assisting him with his jacket and waistcoat as Gideon wandered away. There was little reason to go downstairs as nothing awaited him there, so he wandered to his bedchamber and reclined on his bed. Miss Finch's garland hung from the mantle, and a few of her gingerbread ornaments had found their way to his collection, dangling from the arms of the window latch and any other makeshift hangers, filling his room with the faint scent of ginger, nutmeg, and cloves.

Gideon's traitorous thoughts kept dredging up images of the Finches' Christmas breakfast. He saw them all gathered around the table, heaped high with a veritable feast of baked apples with sweet cream, buttered toast, griddle cakes with maple syrup, broiled smelt with tartare, ham omelets, and sweet rolls galore. The Christmas tree alight as the children searched the branches for their treats. Charades and parlor games while the little ones played with their new toys. The air thick with voices, music, and laughter.

Linden Place was silent. No doubt, Cook had something squirreled away for breakfast, but Gideon was not hungry. Had this house ever felt like home to him? During his younger years, there had been moments, but a void stretched between those times and now.

Yet did he have any right to feel the loss?

Straightening, Gideon considered the tiny bits of Christmas decorating his room, and it struck him how little he'd done to make this place his own. The whole of that burden had been placed on his father, and Gideon, in all his pride and bitterness, had refused to lift even an ounce of it while ignoring just how much the man had done for him already. If he wished for a home, perhaps it was time he did something to make it so.

Gideon rose to his feet, holding fast to his resolve as he left his bedchamber and strode to his father's. His palms grew clammy, and he rubbed them on his trousers. Standing just beyond the doorway, he tried to sort his thoughts and feelings into words, but they failed him. How did one go about such a task?

Shoving aside his trepidation, Gideon stepped into the opening and stared at the figure lying on the bed. Why was Father's door always ajar? Even in the dark of night, he left it open, and Gideon hadn't given it much thought. It had simply been a quirk of his father's personality. But at that moment, it struck him as excessively odd. Did his father not want that barrier between them? Gideon didn't know if that was inferring more than he ought, but it gave him courage.

Father looked up from his breakfast tray, one hand occupied with his dry toast as Nurse Johnson prepared his cup of tea.

"What is it?" he asked.

"Might I speak with you, sir?" asked Gideon.

That was met by a furrowed brow as Father gave him a long, hard look. Then with a wave, he sent the nurse away and motioned Gideon closer. As the nurse shut the door behind her, he slid a chair to his father's bedside and sat.

Gideon's thoughts fled, leaving him staring at the man in the bed. How did one broach such a tender subject? As he considered it, Gideon realized he had no experience with doing so. His friends were not the sort to delve into sensitive subjects. Father certainly had never sought him out for a tête-à-tête; lectures were not the same, for they simply began with a loud accusation, followed by verbal castigation. There had been Mother, of course, but between being shipped off to school and then the army, Gideon hadn't indulged in such conversations in many years.

Only Miss Finch ever seemed eager to see past his surface.

"Are you going to sit there, gaping like a lackwit, or are you going to speak, boy?" said Father, sending him a narrowed look before biting into his toast.

"I have been thinking about the past—" Gideon paused. "I heard a story this morning—"

Father sighed. "I am hungry and have no interest in listening to you faff about. Get to the point."

Gideon nodded. "I know the truth."

"And what truth is that?"

"That I am not your son."

The air fled the room, and only the ticking of the clock broke the silence as they sat there, frozen. Father's toast hovered just beyond his lips for several moments before he cast it down onto his tray, shoving the whole thing to one side; Gideon shot from his seat to help, only just keeping it from spilling across the bedclothes.

"Ridiculous," said Father with a scowl. "What put that fool thought in your head?"

"It's not foolish," murmured Gideon as he took his seat once more. "You've never been happy with me no matter how I've tried to please you."

Father huffed. "And now you wish to whine and moan that I was not sweet and tender enough? I've worked hard to make you into something better than you are. To mold you into a man who rises above the baseness of this world. Perhaps I ought to have simply patted you on the head any time you made a mistake and passed it off as childish folly? Even with all my efforts, you've made a muck of your life. How much worse would it have been if I'd been complacent?"

"I know I have fallen short of your expectations," said Gideon, forcing the words out, though his throat tightened against it. "But there is more to this story. I know it."

"What do you know?" asked Father, his tone tinged with mockery.

Continuing on his previous thread, Gideon continued, "I often wondered why you..." He paused, searching for the proper word. "Despise" came quickly to his mind, but Gideon cast it aside. Such a hard descriptor would hardly put his father in a proper frame of mind. "...you never seemed to care for me. And then I heard the rumor that altered everything."

Father shot upright in bed, the tea tray clinking beside him. He tried to speak, but a racking cough took hold of him, and he fought for breath. Gideon rose and rescued the teacup from the breakfast tray and handed it to his father, though he waved it away with a scowl.

"What...?" Father wheezed, his scowl deepening, though that burning gaze was turned inwards. When the coughs finally subsided, he took a drink and spoke, his words weak and shaky, "What did you hear?"

Gideon swallowed, his stomach turning as he tried to speak the words; they'd been a silent presence in his life for years. His heart revolted against giving them voice, for it felt as though they were a betrayal to his mother. But they were merely the truth, and there was no hiding from it.

Swallowing, Gideon dropped his gaze to the floor. "Mother was unfaithful, and for some reason I cannot fathom, you accepted her child as your own. We've never spoken of it, so I haven't been free to say what I ought, but in this time of giving, it seems only right that I acknowledge the gift you've given me—your name, your protection, and your home."

Silence fell again, and when Gideon hazarded a glance at his father, he found those dark eyes fixed on him as Father's pallor grew more ashen.

"How...?" Father swallowed. His throat bobbed as he struggled to form the words, but Gideon guessed his meaning.

His own throat struggled with the words as the memory flooded his mind. He'd been only sixteen years old when his world had been turned on its head. Peter Smith had offered up that bit of local gossip as a demonstration of just how ridiculous rumors could be, never dreaming it was the truth.

"A young man told me it was common knowledge that Mother had left several months before her confinement and returned home with me." Gideon cleared his throat. "I was told it in jest, for though there was some vague speculation about the odd behavior, no one truly believed Mother capable of such a thing or that you would hush it up. But I saw the truth in it. Finally, I understood why my father showed no paternal affection for me, for there are few reasons why a wife would leave during such a time, and I cannot imagine you allowing her to travel in such a condition alone unless she'd been sent away."

Father opened his mouth, but Gideon continued quickly, "I do not know why you forgave her or accepted her child into your home, but I am grateful for it. I hope you can forgive me for the damage I've done to your name. I assure you I've tried my best, though I've fallen short at times."

During his speech, Gideon's gaze drifted away, unable to stare into Father's face as he laid his feelings bare. Despite having no hand in the business with Miss Evanston, Gideon had allowed it to darken the Payne name. Hardly a suitable recompense for his father's kindness and generosity.

But buried beneath that twist of guilt, Gideon felt a flutter in his belly—a bright, hopeful thing that imagined what their future might be, now that the past had been cleared of its secrets. Their time may be short, but perhaps they might finally build something of a friendship. Mutual respect or even kinship. It was too much to hope that Father might view him as a true son, but the possibility of something more friendly developing had Gideon's muscles strung taut as he waited for Father to speak.

They would never be the Finches, but perhaps they could be better than the Paynes.

"I..." Father's words cut short, and Gideon's gaze jerked up to find him gaping. "How could you..."

Blinking rapidly, Father took a slow breath, his eyes darting back and forth as though sifting through the thoughts and emotions surging through him. Then his hand darted out, snatching Gideon's sleeve with far more strength than he'd thought his father capable of.

Yanking him close, Father's eyes blazed as he whispered, "Give me your word you will never tell a living soul."

"But—"

"Do not let a single word of it leave your lips again." Giving Gideon's arm a shake, Father scowled, his words a low growl. "Promise me!"

"I give you my word."

Father released his hold and fell back against the pillows. His lungs heaved and his gaze fixed on the canopy above him. Gideon opened his mouth to speak, but his father waved a hand at him, shooing him away without another glance.

"Leave."

Gideon rose to his feet but couldn't quite turn away from

the unmoving figure on the bed. Shifting in place, he drummed his fingers against his thigh. "I am thankful for what you've done—"

"Leave, boy," Father repeated, his tone as cold as the wind outside.

Swallowing past the lump in his throat, Gideon nodded and hurried from the room.

Chapter 25

Despite the snow and frigid temperatures, the festive days during the darkest part of the year shone brightest; from Stir Up Sunday to the final Twelfth Night, each day was filled with anticipation. Music and laughter wafted on the breezes, mixing with the scent of clean snow and Christmas puddings. Goodwill warmed even the coldest of hearts as all found reason to give a little more and spread their joy abroad. It filled the soul, renewing it for the coming year.

During any normal Christmas dinner, Evelyn found herself surrounded by family, recounting the happy moments that had passed, planning what was to come, and discussing any random subject that popped into their heads. It was the conversational equivalent of billiards, one topic speeding forward and then connecting with another, causing both balls to ping across the table, colliding with the felted sides before zipping off in other directions. At times, they included the table as a whole before splintering off into smaller discussions, eventually regrouping to include them all.

Today's meal was no different, except Evelyn's thoughts were unable to keep pace with the chatter around her. Of course, she'd never had a beau dine with them before. Mama had Mr. Payne situated between herself and Bridget (no doubt to give them free rein to interrogate him), and Evelyn couldn't decide if she was grateful or irritated about it.

But then, she couldn't decide what to do about the man himself—though that wasn't entirely true. Evelyn's vivid imagination conjured up a multitude of things she'd like to do with him. However, there was a disconnect between her rational thought, her words, and her actions, eroding her ability to function.

Thick candles stood as sentinels down the center of the table, with ivy and evergreen sprigs circling their wide bases. White flowers scattered between them like snowdrifts, filling the few empty spaces between dishes. A goose, roasted to a luscious golden brown, sat in the place of honor, surrounded by pigeon and squab pies, fricassee of rabbits, boiled chicken, asparagus rolls, rhubarb soup with sippets, custard pudding, and several other dishes Evelyn could not name.

Yet she found herself staring at her plate more often than the feast before her, for if she raised her gaze even the slightest, it inevitably drifted to Mr. Payne.

Cursing her wretched heart, Evelyn tried to calm its rapid beat. She clung to his assurances of the night before, but as much as she longed to believe his feelings could not be so easily swayed, she had a lifetime of experience that told her the opposite. And every time she attempted to behave sensibly, her words grew ever more jumbled.

How she wished she could return to her previous state of innocence. While knowledge was power, in this situation, it was more like a poison eating away Evelyn's strength by degrees. If Mr. Payne had not said a thing, she would've remained blissfully unaware, able to be the woman she'd embraced of late. Now, his declaration hung over her, making her evaluate every action and word.

Evelyn poked her goose and stuffing with her fork and scowled at herself. Even when she had thought Mr. Townsend had feelings for her, she hadn't acted such a fool. But then, she hadn't truly cared for him. She had reveled in the possibility he presented, but it was her pride more than her heart that had been broken by his mistreatment.

"I have been quite interested in making your acquaintance, Miss Finch," said Mr. Moffit. Though there was a smile in his tone, Evelyn's stomach sank at the admission. Her dining companion had been so occupied with inserting himself into the other conversations that she'd hoped he wouldn't notice her.

Evelyn forced a smile and took a bite from her plate. Despite her conflicted feelings at present, the flavor burst on her tongue, the meat fairly melting in her mouth, and she savored Cook's talents.

"I requested this seat so I might have the opportunity to speak with you."

With raised brows, she patted her napkin to her lips. "I hope I do not disappoint."

"Any lady who can tie my friend in such knots could never disappoint." Mr. Moffit gave her a speculative look as he sipped from his glass.

As Mr. Payne was not privy to the conversation, it was far easier for her to allow that knowledge to wash over her and settle into her heart in pleasant fashions as there was little fear of making a fool of herself.

"When he admitted he had an invitation to dine with your family, I knew I must come and meet this mysterious Miss Finch."

Evelyn's brows rose. "It's a shame his father was unable to join us."

Mr. Moffit waved a hand with a huff. "The fellow would only sit about blustering about how we are making ourselves too merry."

Giving his wine glass a hard look, Evelyn tried to recall just how many times Mr. Moffit had refilled it. He was making himself quite merry, indeed, but at least it kept his mouth occupied.

"When you two are hitched, you ought to convince him to come to London."

Evelyn stiffened, her eyes widening. "Pardon?"

Mr. Moffit waved a hand. "Surely, you're not so enamored with the country, like our dear Mr. Payne, that you cannot see London's beauty. We would have such fun, and I would introduce you two all around."

The gentleman continued to extol the virtues of London while Evelyn blinked at him. Clearly, Mr. Moffit was too far gone to realize it was not the second half of his sentence that had her gaping. But Evelyn chose to ignore it.

Forcing herself to refocus, she sought out a new subject with which to occupy the lush. "I understand you and Mr. Payne attended school together."

Mr. Moffit chuckled. "Ah, yes. Those were wonderful days. We got into quite a few scrapes. Has he told you about his little incident with the fire?"

"He mentioned something about it," said Evelyn in a tone she hoped would not invite any further questions, but before she could think of another subject, he launched into a retelling. His laughter and animation drew the attention of the others, and soon the table was held in rapt attention as Mr. Moffit told the tale in far more detail.

There were polite smiles around the table, but Mr. Moffit did not sense the falseness of those expressions, and Evelyn glanced at Mr. Payne, whose gaze held more than a hint of resignation.

"They were running around like fools, trying to find their clothes, but we had secreted them away in the shed behind the school," he said. "I cannot recall whose idea it was—Parker? Billings? I suppose it doesn't matter—but as the headmaster got more worked up about the matter, they knew we had to dispose of the evidence, or we'd face his wrath. We never expected them to go up in flames so quickly."

At that, Mr. Moffit banged on the table, setting his plate and silverware clanging. Evelyn shot her siblings and parents a pleading look, and they leapt into action, capturing Mr. Payne's attention in another conversation while the others turned their attention away from Mr. Moffit.

"I do not think that story is as humorous as you believe it to be, Mr. Moffit," said Evelyn, nudging the food on her plate with her fork. "It may have only been a lark for you, but Mr. Payne paid dearly for it."

Shaking his head, Mr. Moffit sighed. "It is a shame he bore the brunt of our stupidity, but what good would it have done if we had stepped forward? There was no need for us all to suffer."

Evelyn's grip on her knife and fork tightened, and she forced herself not to scowl, holding onto a calm tone with the last shreds of her patience. "At the very least, you should treat his sacrifice with honor rather than laughing at it. He remained silent and protected you."

"He is the best of men and a good friend."

Bless her soul, Marian leaned over from Mr. Moffit's other side and asked him about his trip from London, which he was quite eager to recount in all its glory, turning what was a rather uninteresting few days into a long and rambling tale that painted him both as the hero in his own mind and a fool in everyone else's.

Leaning back, Evelyn glanced around Mr. Moffit and gave Marian a silent look of gratitude, and her sister-in-law smiled, hiding it behind a sip from her glass.

Evelyn hazarded a look at Mr. Payne. Thankfully, he was engaged in conversation with Mama, leaving her free to study his profile. It was clear Mr. Moffit was an old friend, and from how Mr. Payne had introduced him, she guessed the fellow might even be his closest. That distinction had given Evelyn certain expectations, but after only a few words exchanged, she was flummoxed by the relationship.

Mr. Moffit was a Ninny of the highest order, and Mr. Payne did not seem the sort to suffer such buffoonery. Of course, when they'd first met, Mr. Payne had been hiding amongst their ranks, so it ought not to have been such a surprise. Evelyn's brow furrowed as she considered that, but she could not comprehend why he suffered their company. Perhaps loyalty bound him and Mr. Moffit together.

Yet that did not explain why they maintained such a close relationship. A friendship would be understandable, but why did Mr. Payne insist on surrounding himself with such vacuous people? One ought not to be judged by one's friends, but the people with whom one chose to associate said something about a person. So, why did Mr. Payne pass his time amongst those he didn't seem to like?

Evelyn's gaze drifted along his profile, following the sweep of his nose. Oh, Mr. Payne. Her heart felt all twisted up and frayed at the edges; she needed to get herself under control. Somehow.

But as she considered him, Evelyn stilled, sensing something amiss with him. Mr. Payne hid it well, but there was no hiding the tension at the corner of his lips and eyes. The tightness in his shoulders. While she had caused him enough frustration and heartache over the past few days, there was something more to it. Evelyn couldn't say what for certain, but instinct had her considering all the other possible sources. Mr. Moffit certainly featured high on her list of problems, but she didn't think Mr. Payne's unease involved him.

Evelyn's thoughts were so caught up in speculation that she hardly noticed as the plates and dishes were removed, leaving behind only the table decorations. The Christmas pudding was brought forward on a silver platter, a great sprig of holly sticking out of the top as the smell of spices and brandy filled the room. It was placed before Papa, and the room stilled while they watched with bated breath as it was set ablaze. Flames swept across the cake, lighting the brown in waves of flickering blue as the gathering applauded.

Then Papa's voice rang out with "We Wish You a Merry Christmas." They all joined in, singing through the verses as the flames died down, though her brothers bellowed the line, "We won't go until we get some" with extra gusto as the cake was sliced and served up.

Though everyone was poised to dig in, Mama gave each of them a narrowed look until the last slice was passed around and everyone had their plate. With a nod, she set loose the dogs, and they fell upon their cake with determination, picking through it with their forks. Mama and Papa insisted on savoring it, but their grown children poked and prodded their pieces, searching for the charms that may lie within.

Miles laughed, holding up a silver trinket. "The coin!"

The revelation elicited groans from his brothers, though George scoffed as Marian's slice revealed a tiny baby. Working together, George distracted Miles long enough for her to swap their baubles.

"No, the pudding has promised me wealth for the coming year," said Miles, forcing the baby back on his brother.

"We are not having another child so soon," said Marian in a firm tone that brooked no argument.

"And you think he should instead?" asked Mama with a shake of her head, though her eyes lit with laughter as the other trinkets were discovered. Jests and laughter abounded as the finders had their futures predicted by the infallible Christmas pudding.

But Evelyn couldn't pry her gaze from the thimble nestled among the bits of her cake.

It was silly. This was a dessert, not a prophet, and its ability to divine what was to come for the next year was naught but a bit of holiday cheer, not a true portent. Yet, of all the symbols, she had received the thimble.

Lifting a bite to her lips, she tried to pretend the trinket wasn't there, but the warm spice and fruit tasted bitter on her tongue.

"Did you find one, Evelyn?" asked Bridget, stretching to see from across the table.

There was little point in hiding the fact, for they all knew how many charms there were, and all the others were accounted for, yet Evelyn couldn't bring herself to speak.

Mr. Moffit snatched it from its hiding place and held it aloft. "The thimble. Your pudding has quite the sense of humor, for it gave Mr. Payne the button, and myself the ring."

Turning to his friend, he winked. "I ought to trade with you, for of the two of us, I doubt you will end the year as a bachelor, and I am determined to do just that. But I suppose it is of no use as the pudding has decreed Miss Finch is to remain a spinster for another twelve months."

As quick as they were to tease, even her siblings avoided anything too blunt. Hints were one thing, but Mr. Moffit's bold insinuation had Evelyn's face flaming as red as holly berries. Her family's gazes were fixed on them, unable to do more than stare—some with their forks hanging halfway in their mouths.

The similarity of this scene struck Evelyn, drawing her thoughts back to a time when an even more irritating man had shamed her in a similar fashion. But where Mr. Townsend had intended to embarrass, Mr. Moffit was merely a fool. And he was the dear friend of her beau. Calling upon her strength and equanimity, Evelyn held onto her strained smile even as a biting retort came to her thoughts.

"What makes you think the button condemns me to bachelorhood?" asked Mr. Payne with a light air. "The trinkets often hold more than one meaning, after all."

Mr. Moffit laughed. "Ah. And what do you believe it is predicting?"

"That I am going to be blessed with a new wardrobe."

That drew chuckles from every corner of the table, and even Evelyn managed a proper smile at that.

But Mr. Moffit continued, "However—"

"Mr. Finch," interrupted Mr. Payne, turning his gaze to Miles. "I understand you are quite the cardsharp."

Mr. Moffit's gaze gleamed, and he latched onto that diversion as quickly as a child abandons an old toy in favor of a new one. The conversation shifted, and though the heaviness lingered in the air, it eased, allowing Evelyn to breathe once more.

Her gaze lifted from her plate and found Mr. Payne watching her, those hazel eyes gleaming in the candlelight as his brows pulled low. The question etched into his expression conveyed his meaning as clearly as any words, and Evelyn heard it echoing in her thoughts, his low voice humming through her. Her lips turned up, and she gave him a reassuring nod: Mr. Moffit was an irritant, but he had done no true damage.

Their eyes locked for several heartbeats, and Evelyn's chest expanded, the warmth in his gaze flowing through her and settling into her bones like when she returned from a midwinter walk in the woods and curled up with a cup of tea, holding it close so that the heat radiated through her hands; then that delicious moment when it was raised to her lips, the cold fleeing as the liquid slipped past her lips and down her throat, leaving her flushed.

Someone called for Mr. Payne, but they had to repeat themselves before the man in question finally broke her gaze and turned his attention to the interruption. Air rushed into Evelyn's lungs, filling her to bursting as her eyes dropped to her plate, drifting towards the thimble Mr. Moffit had abandoned on the edge.

Clarity seized hold of her thoughts, clearing away all the jumble of emotions and monologues and leaving behind only one certainty. It had been buried beneath the fears, the what ifs, the inferences, crushed beneath that great weight. Always there, yet unseen. Lost in the chaos. But at that moment, Evelyn saw the truth for what it was—she had to explain herself to Mr. Payne or she was going to lose him.

The jumbled mess surged back into place, burying her in an avalanche of feelings. Her insides twisted and wrenched as invisible insects skittered along her skin. Her muscles seized, holding her in place as everything within her tensed at the realization. It all slammed into her at once, threatening to overpower her and drag her back into that pit of misery.

But that quick glimpse of truth allowed her to break through the chaos and cling to that certainty amidst the torrent. Denial tried to pry her fingers free, but Evelyn held firm, for no matter how she longed to justify her silence, she knew it would guarantee the trinket's portent of doom. Now that fate had handed her a different path, Evelyn was not willing to embrace spinsterhood.

That thimble was not her future.

Chapter 26

They say loyalty was a virtue, and while Gideon normally espoused that belief, at present he cursed the wretched sentiment for pushing him to extend Charles the invitation tonight. Of course, his friend hadn't given him much of a choice, for Charles had been determined to meet Miss Finch. But that was merely an excuse. Gideon ought to have put up a fight; at the very least, he ought to have switched places with Charles at the table.

Thank the heavens that the Finch family didn't stand on ceremony at such a time, for when dinner was finished, everyone went together into the drawing room, and the moment the gentlemen rose, Gideon wove through the crowd to Miss Finch's side, stepping between her and Charles, who seemed determined to monopolize the entirety of her time.

"Worried I'm going to make off with her?" asked Charles with a grin that had Gideon squeezing his fist.

This was his friend. His oldest and dearest, in fact. Yet after being forced to watch Charles tease and torment Miss Finch for the entirety of the meal, Gideon was at his breaking point. Impulse thrashed and pushed against his better sense, begging to be released.

"Mr. Moffit," said Mr. Miles Finch, sliding into their group as they entered the drawing room. "Might I persuade you to settle a dispute between my brother and me? As you have far more knowledge of London than either of us, you must know which are the best clubs in Town."

Straightening his jacket, Charles followed after the gentleman without a backward glance, though Miss Finch's brother gave Gideon a subtle wink before leaving the pair of them be. Gideon motioned Miss Finch towards a chair as the others all gathered about in little conversations, but she shook her head, wandering towards the farthest corner before taking a seat hidden there.

"I fear I need a moment," she said with a sigh.

Gideon sat beside her and grimaced. "I apologize for Mr. Moffit. He doesn't think before he speaks, and he adores teasing."

Miss Finch's brow quirked upward. "So does my family, but there is a vast difference between someone who seeks humor in the foibles of life and one who revels in others' discomfort."

"I am sorry he made you uncomfortable." Gideon sighed, and Miss Finch straightened, studying him with a furrowed brow.

"I am not concerned about myself, Mr. Payne. It is you, I cannot bear to see mocked. I cannot comprehend why you count him a dear friend."

Gideon opened his mouth, though no ready words sprang to his lips. Closing it again, he considered that. "I do not have many, and he is the only one who has stuck by me through thick and thin. Charles can be grating at times, but I am in no position to turn him away."

Biting on her lips, Miss Finch's brows twisted closer together, her thoughts puzzling through some great mystery, yet no explanation was forthcoming. Then her gaze broke from him, dropping to her lap as she shifted in her seat.

"And how are you faring?" she asked.

"Well enough," Gideon replied, giving the answer that was

expected.

But Miss Finch's dark gaze drifted up to him, studying him from the corner of her eyes. "You seem out of sorts tonight."

Gideon stiffened, his heart thumping, though he couldn't say if he was more touched or terrified that she had noticed, for both feelings were present in equal measure. With Father's conversation fresh in his thoughts, he could think of little else, but the oath binding his tongue would not allow him to unburden his soul. Not that he wished to admit the truth surrounding his birth while things between them were on such tenuous footing.

Yet years of unspoken worries and frustrations piled up, filling his chest to bursting, begging to be let out. Keeping them hidden away had been a necessity and then habit, but with Miss Finch's gaze settled on him, Gideon longed to voice them and allow someone to help him bear this burden. But an honorable man did not break his word, and his oath rang through his thoughts, binding him to silence once more.

Gideon gave her what he hoped was a reassuring smile, though the tightness of Miss Finch's lips told him he had failed. "I am sorry to have missed your performance today."

Miss Finch smiled, her cheeks coloring a pretty shade of red, her face ducking away. "You've heard us practice enough times. You didn't miss a thing."

"I fear our choir was quite inferior," he said, relaxing into his chair. "I kept comparing the two, and ours fell short. If Father hadn't been determined to attend, or if our services hadn't been at the same time, I would've liked to attend yours. See the choir in all your glory."

Gideon's breath stilled as he realized this was the easiest conversation they'd shared in several days. Miss Finch did not look strung as taut, ready to snap. Neither did she look at ease, but he wouldn't look the gift horse in the mouth, as they were wont to say. He simply needed to tread carefully.

"You are too kind, Mr. Payne. We did our best." Her words were halting and a little unsteady, but they were there all the same.

Slowly, Miss Finch described the morning's services, reveling in the successes and mourning the failures. But all the while, her fingers fiddled with something in her lap. Gideon tried to focus on the conversation, but his gaze darted down to it as she rolled it through her hands. A glint of silver caught his eye, and when silence fell again, he couldn't help but bring up the Christmas pudding disaster once more.

"I do apologize on Mr. Moffit's behalf," he said. "I wouldn't have brought him had I known he would make you so uneasy."

Her brows rose, and her gaze met his once more. "There is no need for you to apologize for his behavior. Others with far more power and skill have tried to discompose me. I am not afraid of your Mr. Moffit."

Gideon nodded at the thimble in her lap, a faint smile on his lips. "I am quite envious of your bauble, Miss Finch."

Fitting it on the tip of her finger, she raised the charm. "You wish to be a spinster for the coming year?"

"Many say it predicts domestic bliss," he replied. "I would be quite happy to have a bit of magic ensuring I am happy with my home and family."

The corner of her lips turned upward as she lowered her hand to her lap. "That does sound lovely, Mr. Payne. If only it were possible to ensure such a thing, but I fear the Christmas trinket has no such power."

Though she spoke lightly, there was a heaviness to Miss Finch's tone that matched the hint of sadness in her eyes, and Gideon's hands itched to reach out for her. Instead, he plucked the silver button from his waistcoat pocket and held it up.

"Do not say such a thing! This button has promised me a wardrobe, and it had best keep its promise."

Miss Finch broke into a grin, a laugh on her lips. A few heads turned their way, but the Finches quickly turned their attention back, though Gideon spied a few pleased smiles pointed in their direction.

"I love seeing you so happy," he said. "I've missed it of late."

Gracious, she looked lovely in the candlelight. Gideon

didn't think there was a single light that wouldn't favor her, but tonight, Miss Finch wore a gown of deepest green, which complemented her glowing hair, making both brighter for being together. Those burning locks were gathered up in a mass of curls, with a few sprigs of holly in it for good measure, and Gideon wondered if her hair was as soft as it looked. Would those curls wind around his fingers or spring with a little tug?

Gideon didn't understand the arbitrary nature of fashion, for the more he saw Miss Finch, the more convinced he was that her freckles only enhanced her beauty.

Her gaze fell to their hands, and Gideon wasn't sure when he'd taken hold of hers. Miss Finch stilled, staring as he allowed his fingers to do as they'd wished for so long, skimming across her skin in a whisper of a touch. So often, their hands were encased in leather or silk, but in this intimate family setting, there were no such strictures, and her soft warmth sent a flutter through him, connecting him to her with that barest of contacts.

"Miss Finch," he whispered, and her gaze jerked up to meet his, her eyes wide as she sucked in deep breaths, her chest rising and falling in quick succession. For a long moment, the lady sat there like a startled statue before shooting to her feet.

"Excuse me a moment, please," she murmured before fleeing the drawing room in a whirl of silk.

Chapter 27

R ubbing her forehead, Evelyn paced the corridor outside
the drawing room. Her lungs heaved, sucking in great
breaths, yet it didn't feel like enough. Had the air grown
thinner? With her free hand, she flapped at her face, but it felt
as though lava flowed through her veins.

Just a moment. That was all she needed. And a bit of air.

With quick steps, she scurried into the entryway, hurrying
to the front door and throwing it open. A winter breeze hit her,
its frigid touch doing little to cool the flush of her skin. Filling
her lungs, Evelyn forced her breaths to still, and though her
heartbeat slowed, its pulse grew stronger, thumping against her
ribs.

Was she determined to ruin even a little tender moment?
Silly, feckless girl! Just say the words. Just speak out. An explanation of any sort must be better than rushing out of the room
as though it were on fire.

Footsteps echoed somewhere close, and Evelyn shut the
front door. A giant stairway sprouted from the center of the entryway, sweeping up and splitting to wrap around in both directions. Creeping into its shadow, she leaned against the wall beneath and covered her face. Evelyn's shoulders hunched, a

litany of curses aimed inwards as she replayed that delicious moment again and again in her thoughts.

"Miss Finch?"

Evelyn stilled at the sound of his voice, all gentle and cautious like when one approached a startled animal. Dropping her hands, she saw Mr. Payne standing at the base of the stairs, and though he deserved to be irritated or angry at her behavior, the gentleman simply stood there, his brows drawn together as he studied her, his eyes full of concern.

"Have I done something to upset you?"

Dropping her head, Evelyn covered her face. Of all the things he could've said, that question drove deep into her heart. Mr. Payne was so good and kind and did not deserve to be yanked back and forth by her ridiculous behavior.

Tell him. Tell him. Tell him. Her heart beat out that refrain, demanding she speak, and Evelyn felt it in the air around her, pressing down as she thought back to her revelation at dinner. It grew in strength, forcing her to acknowledge that not only did she need to be honest with him, but she could not put it off a moment longer.

"No, you haven't upset me." Evelyn winced as the words shot out of her with more force than she'd meant to give them. Her feet needed to move, so she pushed away from the wall and paced the length of the entry as Mr. Payne stared at her. "Yes, you have, but not really. Not you. No."

Rubbing at her forehead, Evelyn tried to bring order to her thoughts, but this was not a conversation she'd ever thought to have. Courting was supposed to be simple. Lady and gentleman met. Their feelings grew. They married. Nowhere did any of her stories include a moment where the heroine fell to pieces because she didn't know the first thing about courting.

Evelyn stopped, whirling around to face him. "I do not know how to do this."

"Do what, exactly?"

Waving her hands between them, she stopped herself just short of shouting. "This."

Mr. Payne rocked back on his heels, his cheeks puffing out as he studied her. Evelyn's lungs heaved as her eyes pleaded with him to understand, for she wasn't certain she knew what more to say.

"Do you mean 'this?'" He mimicked her hand movement. "As in courting?"

Evelyn's shoulders fell, her chin trembling as she held his gaze and nodded.

Blinking, Mr. Payne nodded, his expression showing little as he considered that. "Do you mean courting me, specifically? Or in general?" When Evelyn had no quick response to that, he added, "Because if it is I who is objectionable—"

"No." Evelyn shook her head in a jerky movement. "It is not you. I..."

Her head fell, and she covered her face once more. She had read of cases of spontaneous combustion, and though she had not understood the science, Evelyn felt it now; her body was so flushed that she was certain to go up in flames. But as much as she longed to escape into the cold outside, she held her ground.

Lowering her hands, she straightened her shoulders and forced herself to meet Mr. Payne's gaze; he stood just feet from her, his muscles tight and his gaze so full of concern that Evelyn nearly fell to pieces once more.

"I may be a grown woman with nearly three decades to my name, but I have never been courted by anyone." Though she tried to hold onto the last of her strength, her words were little more than a whisper. "I have been out in society for nearly half my life, and no man has ever shown a modicum of interest in me as a woman."

Evelyn rubbed at her forehead, kneading the growing tension between her brows. "Courting sounds like a simple thing, but the truth is I am terrified. For once, I have someone who sees me in such a light, and I am certain I will ruin it. One day I will say or do something to turn your feelings against me, and I will have to return once more to that cold solitude."

Clearing her throat, she closed her eyes. "I try to behave as

I always do, but there are these voices in my head, whispering and warning about every word, every action, convincing me that I've done something wrong. There is hardly a person outside of my own family who enjoys my company for more than an hour or two, so how am I ever going to keep such a wonderful man interested?"

She sucked in a deep breath, letting it out in a slow gust, and faced him once more, shoulders back and head held high. "If this ruins your opinion of me, then so be it. I know that trying to act as though nothing is amiss is only making things worse, and so I lay my fear before you in all its wretched, broken glory. I do not know how not to be afraid of losing you."

Strength came in many forms. Most people only acknowledged the sort that faced down troubles without flinching, battled with an enemy, and risked life and limb for the cause of the just, but Gideon had long ago learned that true courage was not the lack of fears but the overcoming of them. And Miss Finch's quivering confession, which laid bare all she wished to keep hidden, was perhaps the bravest thing he'd ever witnessed.

Heavens, Gideon wished there was some way to show her his thoughts, for he was certain she would not believe them otherwise. But at that moment, he was certain that if either of them ought to worry about killing this beautiful thing growing between them, it was him.

"...such a wonderful man..." Miss Finch was perhaps the only person in this world who viewed him in that light and spoke of him as though his presence alone bestowed an immeasurable blessing.

And she stood, awaiting his pronouncement.

Sifting through his thoughts, Gideon weighed each word carefully, praying hard that he would settle on the right ones. "There is nothing you can say or do to drive me away, Miss Finch."

Absolutes were rarely proved true. The world was too full

of grays to use such black-and-white terms like "always" or "never." But Gideon felt deep in his heart that his statement was true. Though they had known each other only a short time, Miss Finch had opened up the whole of her soul to him; no doubt there would be disagreements and conflicts, but Evelyn Finch's heart was everything he wanted, and he wouldn't surrender it easily.

"You say that now, Mr. Payne—"

But he shook his head. "My feelings are not so fickle, Miss Finch. I see you, and I like every bit of it."

With each word, Gideon drew closer, and though her chin trembled, she remained in place as he inched nearer. Eyes wide, Miss Finch watched him, her muscles quivering as her skirts wrapped around his legs. Her perfume filled his nose, all flowers and springtime mingled with the Christmas spices that hung in the air, and Gideon reveled in it, for it was the scent of home—perhaps the only true one he'd ever had.

Holding her gaze, he brushed his fingers against her hands, which were clenched at her sides, teasing and coaxing until they entwined with his. Then he looked up, drawing her gaze to the sprig of mistletoe hanging in the doorway above them. And when he faced her once more, her eyes were wider than before.

Gideon leaned closer, moving with care so she would not bolt. His lips hovered before hers, close enough that he felt every sharp breath, and he waited. Miss Finch didn't blink. Didn't move. Frozen in place, she stood there with her pleading eyes, though he wasn't certain if she was begging him to close the distance or to back away.

"Trust me, Miss Finch," he whispered.

Her eyelashes fluttered as a sheen of tears gathered. "I don't know if I can trust anyone like that, Mr. Payne."

Chapter 28

Not everyone felt things as she did. Some lived in a muted world, experiencing it while remaining mostly untouched. However, like her mother and so many in her family, Evelyn's heart was like a cacophony, filling her with such feelings that at times it was difficult to contain them all. Hurts and happinesses were all magnified, reverberating through her long after the moment had passed.

Yet Evelyn felt as though she'd lived surrounded by cotton, and now, Mr. Payne had peeled it away, opening her up to a world filled with so much more. Fear, giddiness, disbelief, hope. All were heightened and coursed through her, making every nerve spark at once. It was beyond her control, and she reveled in every beautiful and painful detail.

Mr. Payne waited there, his gaze inviting. But Evelyn couldn't move. She didn't want to. Not yet. Her gaze studied every detail of his face. Those flecks of green in his hazel eyes. The tiny twist of his lips. The feel of his fingers caressing hers. Every word he'd spoken. She wanted to remember it all.

And then she kissed him.

Thoughts crashed into her mind like a derailed train, bringing with it every fear and doubt she'd ever conjured (along with many more), and her mind fixated on what she may or may not be doing wrong. Her muscles tightened, and she couldn't even say with any certainty what Mr. Payne's lips felt like for hers were puckered tight.

What ought she to do? Where to put her hands? Evelyn sensed she should do something more than touch her lips to his, but she could not surmise exactly what that was with so many thoughts warring for attention.

Heat (and not the good sort) swept through her, settling into her cheeks as she pulled back, her gaze refusing to meet his as she jerked backward. Wretched was too harsh a descriptor for that buss, but pleasant was far too generous. Disappointing. Evelyn was not so naive as to think this was Mr. Payne's first, but she was certain this must be his worst.

Evelyn stepped farther away, but when she tugged at her hand, he did not release it. Her gaze fell to their interlocked fingers and followed the length of his arm, settling on his face once more for no more than a heartbeat before she dropped her gaze to the floor.

"I apologize," she mumbled, stumbling over her words as she tried again to put more distance between them. "That was not—I hadn't expected—I wanted to—"

But when she retreated another step, Mr. Payne moved in, his hand dropping hers as his arms encircled her, pulling her flush to him.

"I will admit that wasn't all I'd hoped it to be," he said with a hint of a smile in his tone, but it fled as his voice lowered. "But Evelyn, I will not surrender so easily."

She stilled at the sound of her Christian name, and her eyes met his of their own volition. His right hand drifted up, caressing the edge of her jaw, and his touches grounded her in the here and now, even while they set her nerves sizzling and snapping.

"Clear your mind," he murmured, his lips so close that they brushed hers.

Evelyn tried to speak, but her voice came out in a breathy

whisper. "It is not that simple."

Mr. Payne huffed, a small little puff of air that held just a hint of humor in it. "Perhaps you can start by breathing."

"I am." But even as she said that her head swam, growing lighter. He took in a deep breath, urging her to follow, and it was only then that she realized she had been holding hers. After a long, slow breath or two, the dizziness eased away.

"I don't know how you expect me to relax at such a moment." Evelyn attempted a light tone, but she felt more like scowling than laughing at her ridiculousness.

Taking her hand in his, he lifted it to his chest, resting it against his heart. Even through the layers of fabric, Evelyn felt the pulse quicken beneath her fingers. When she met his eyes once more, Mr. Payne gave her a tender smile.

"Nerves are understandable," he said with a rueful smile. "I feel ready to fly apart if you distance yourself again. Please, stay with me."

And with that declaration, Mr. Payne captured her lips. His hands rubbed her back, easing her muscles when they tensed. Evelyn's mind roared to life once more, but his low words cut through the tumult, reminding her to breathe. That sure, certain tone wrapped around her like a shield, allowing her to focus on the here and now.

Like a dance, he led the way, and though her hands trembled and her heart stuttered at her stumbles, with each tender touch, Evelyn relaxed. They moved together as though feeling their way through the unknown steps, and thoughts faded until she simply reveled in the moment. The pressure in her chest did not ease, but it shifted into something warm and joyous, filling her with strength rather than stealing it away.

Evelyn wanted it to last forever, but when they did part, she found a whole new level of joy, her heart expanding until it filled the whole of her as she basked in the tenderness glowing in his gaze.

"I love you, Gideon," she whispered. Where only five minutes ago, such a confession would've sent her into another rambling mess, Evelyn knew those words were true, and they could not be contained.

In times such as these, a man ought to be suave. Debonaire. Collected and charming. He certainly ought not to stare at his lady love with wide eyes and a gaping mouth.

Evelyn Finch loved him. It defied logic, for Gideon knew there was no reasonable explanation as to why such a lady loved him so dearly. Yet there was no denying the sincerity with which she'd spoken the words; they rang out in the silent entryway like the church bells ringing in the new year with all its hopes and possibilities. Those words had been absent in his life for many years, and hearing them from her lips was like a blacksmith's billows in his heart.

Gideon knew he ought to say something—anything—but he didn't trust himself to speak. His throat tightened, holding back the explosion in his chest as Evelyn stared at him with those bright and beautiful eyes. What could he say to such a confession? He was no poet to describe how his heart expanded beyond the confines of his ribs, filling the whole of him. Her trust and faith brought tears to his eyes, humbling him as nothing else could.

And so he showed her, seizing her lips in a kiss that burned with all the feelings swirling inside, threatening to consume the both of them. For all that Evelyn thought herself awkward, she followed every prompt, every movement, matching it with her own heartfelt touches. It was a perfect blending, bringing the two of them together until it felt as though they were only one heart and one soul.

His Evelyn.

When he finally freed her lips, there was a laugh curling their edges and a spark in her eyes that echoed the giddiness that vibrated off her.

"Oh, Gideon..." she whispered, her words trailing off. Then, with a halting chuckle, Evelyn threw her arms around his neck, pulling close and snuggling into his hold. Her lips tickled his neck as she murmured, "I am sorry for tormenting you so. I wish I had some better explanation—"

"Hush," he said, his hands rubbing along her back. But Evelyn insisted on pulling away, stealing away all the warmth in the room, leaving only the heat from her hand joined in his.

Wiping her eyes with the other, she shook her head. "You've been so patient and kind with me as I've dithered, vacillating between raving and running away."

Reaching into his jacket pocket, Gideon pulled out a bedraggled sprig. Holding it up, he smiled. "Though you said your sister uses mistletoe liberally in the decorations, I didn't want to risk it."

Her smile blossomed as Evelyn studied the plant. "You came prepared, did you?"

"I came with a lot of hope in my heart," he said, though the sudden flood of warmth dropped his voice to a low murmur.

Evelyn's gaze darted to his, her lips trembling as a sheen gathered in her eyes. Drawing her arms up around his neck, she settled into his embrace once more.

"If you believe the trinkets are prophetic, do you believe in Stir-up Sunday wishes as well?" she asked, though Gideon struggled to focus on her words as her fingers traced patterns along the back of his neck.

He cleared his throat. "I am not familiar with that tradition."

"It's said that when you stir the Christmas pudding, whatever wish you think will come true." Evelyn paused, and her eyes were bright, her lips trembling. "Every year I have wished for someone who would love me as I loved them, and every year passed with no sign of it. This was the last year I was ever going to allow myself that wish—"

Evelyn's voice broke as tears gathered. "And then you appeared, sweeping into my life like magic."

It wasn't fate or fantasy that had put him in her path, and

though the realization sent a shiver down his spine, Gideon batted it away: he would not steal her magic moment away. How they had arrived at this moment was a mere detail, no different than if they'd been introduced by a friend or been thrown together during a dinner party by an enterprising hostess. If anything, Gideon was grateful for her father's interference, for he hadn't been searching for love; like the crafty hunter it was, love had stolen up behind him, taking him by surprise.

But was it right to keep it from her? It may be only a detail, but a secret was a secret.

Gideon's thoughts vanished when Evelyn pressed another kiss to his lips, as sweet and chaste as their first, yet infinitely more enjoyable.

"What are you doing, Aunt Evelyn?"

The child's voice snapped them out of their reverie, and Evelyn stiffened, her face reddening as her wide eyes held his. But she didn't jerk away. With a laughing grimace, she stepped out of his arms to stand beside him, though she held fast to his hand as she beamed at her niece.

"I was showing Mr. Payne our mistletoe," said Evelyn, pointing up at the cluster of leaves. The child's eyes followed the action and then fell to the sprig in Gideon's hand.

"Grandmama asked me to find you."

Gideon chuckled (though it sounded more disappointed than merry), and Evelyn slanted him a commiserating look. Their time alone had been noted and was at an end.

Before the child could ask more of the questions knocking about her head, Evelyn asked, "Are you and the other children joining us for some games?"

Gemma nodded, her curls bouncing as she snatched Evelyn's free hand in hers, tugging her down the hall. "Mama said we can come down for a few minutes..."

And so she led her aunt along, describing all the possible games they might play. As Evelyn did not release her hold on Gideon's hand, he followed after the pair, and Evelyn glanced over her shoulder, her eyes filled with that same contentment and laughter that seemed ever-present in the lady.

There was a hint of a promise in her gaze, and Gideon hoped the Finches had more mistletoe hidden around the house. Tucking his sprig back into his pocket, he held it in reserve. Just in case.

Their little train stepped into the drawing room, and Gemma bounced over to her mama and announced with a loud voice, "Aunt Evelyn was showing Mr. Payne the mistletoe!"

Chapter 29

Despite years of dreaming and hoping, Evelyn hadn't believed courting was magical. Not truly. Life and love were not perfect things, so one could not expect perfection—even when swept up in the whirl of romance. But years of being overlooked had her wishing for the fantasy despite knowing reality was unlikely to match expectations.

And she'd been correct: reality was far better.

No matter how hard she'd tried (and Evelyn had spent quite a lot of time doing so), she hadn't captured the wonder steeped in an embrace or the power of an admiring look. Or seeing Gideon smile and laugh, knowing she had inspired such joy in him. That was true magic.

The three days leading to Christmas had been agony, but the three days since had been even more blissful. Evelyn's cheeks heated whenever she recalled that awkward conversation in the hall, but it was impossible to hold onto her embarrassment when it had led to such joy. Evelyn felt like she was walking about on her tip-toes, barely keeping her feet on the ground, and the feeling was only enhanced when she entered the assembly rooms to find the Wolvertons had transformed the drab space into something far grander than Bentmoor deserved.

The town was lucky to have any public spaces at its disposal. If not for the assembly rooms, the Wolvertons would be forced to give up their Christmas ball or crush everyone into their tiny drawing room; Evelyn doubted they'd choose the former and forfeit the title of finest hosts in Bentmoor to the Meechams or the Wrigleys or the Doddingtons. Or heaven forfend, some upstart would take advantage of the hole in the social calendar. Evelyn didn't understand that sort of competition, but she enjoyed the result.

As the Wolvertons were forced to let the rooms for the evening, they compensated by decorating them until they were unrecognizable. The usually plain walls were adorned with wreaths and garlands, the red holly berries looking all the brighter amongst the varying shades of dark green. At the far end, the musicians' platform had been reinvented; the usual green drapery that framed their seats had been replaced with a rich red, mimicking the holly berries and contrasting nicely with the green of the walls. Even the musicians themselves were decadently dressed with matching livery that looked more befitting of a ducal estate.

There was more food, music, and entertainment than necessary, though the guests were doing their best to consume it all. Yet Evelyn remained fixed in place, taking up a position near the door. Not so close as to be obvious, but with a clear view of everyone who entered.

If only Gideon would arrive. Evelyn made a valiant attempt to clear her mind of all the dire circumstances that might have kept him from coming, but there was little she could do to stop the odd thought creeping in as the minutes ticked by. Likely he was occupied with business or his father—not overturned in a carriage and crushed beneath its wheels or paying call on some other young lady—but habits were difficult to break, and all Evelyn could do was bat away the worries as soon as they arrived, allowing them no room in her thoughts.

"I am certain he will arrive soon," said Mama with a silent laugh in her tone. Drawing up beside her daughter, she laced Evelyn's arm through hers and patted it.

"I know." A movement at the doorway had Evelyn's gaze snapping to the figure.

Not Gideon.

She sighed.

And Mama laughed, squeezing her daughter's arm. "I am so happy for you, my darling. You two seem well suited."

Those words filled Evelyn to the brim, coursing through her with wild abandon until she was buzzing with an energy unlike anything she had felt before. Powerful and electrifying. She took a deep breath, struggling to contain it all before it made her do something silly like singing a grand aria or skipping about. She may be grinning like a fool, but she had some decorum. A modicum, at least.

"I am happy, Mama. He is so wonderful." Her voice cracked, and she batted her eyes, for she was not about to burst into joyful tears.

"I had my reservations about him at first, but I think he's far better than his reputation led me to believe," said Mama. "And your father trusts him."

"Whom do I trust?" Papa's question had them turning around as he drew up next to his wife as she released Evelyn and took hold of his arm. Giving Mama a quick wink (which Evelyn pretended not to see), he turned his attention back to his question.

"Mr. Payne," said Mama.

"That bounder didn't bother to speak with me first before sweeping my daughter off her feet," said Papa with a mock scowl. When Mama elbowed him, he smiled. "Mr. Payne is a good man."

"He is the best of men." Evelyn drew in a deep breath, trying to keep all the feelings swirling through her from bursting out as she added, "He is so much better than people understand. Honorable and kind. Willing to sacrifice his happiness for others. And so patient. I do believe Gideon has a never-ending supply of it."

Her parents stiffened, her father barking out a sharp, "Pardon?"

Evelyn's cheeks burned bright, and she winced. "I meant Mr. Payne, of course. A slip of the tongue."

Mama's brows were raised as high as they could go and remained there for several heartbeats before she shook her head with a sigh. Releasing Papa's arm, she drew close, bussing Evelyn on the cheek.

"I am happy for you, my dear girl. You deserve someone who sees how wonderful you are."

Blinking rapidly, Evelyn tried to keep her vision from blurring, but with her heart already brimming, it was difficult to keep it from spilling over. And then Papa cleared his throat, pointing her attention to the door. Evelyn spun, and her gaze met Gideon's, those hazel eyes brightening as his smile broadened. His attention did not waver from her as he crossed the room, ignoring the throng as he made his way directly to her side.

"Good evening, Mr. Payne," she whispered.

"Miss Finch." His tone was warm and rich, reminding her of stolen kisses and tender caresses.

"Good heavens," muttered Papa.

Evelyn blushed deep, the flush of heat sweeping through her.

"Leave them be," replied Mama, giving him another elbow to the ribs.

"Were we ever so—"

But Papa stopped when Mama gave him a narrowed look. "According to Great Aunt Imogene, we were much worse. So, hush."

Turning to Gideon, Mama stepped forward, greeting him with a buss on the cheek as though he were already one of her sons-in-law, which made Evelyn blush all the deeper.

"Is your father willing to part with you on Sunday?" Mama asked when she stepped away.

He hid it well, but Evelyn wondered if Gideon knew how much his jaw tensed whenever someone mentioned his father. Stepping closer, she slid her arm through his, her hand resting on his forearm.

Some of the tightness eased, and Gideon nodded.

"Excellent," said Mama with a grin. "I understand you are fond of galantine turkey."

Gideon's brows rose. "I am."

"Then I will make certain it is on the menu," she replied with a sharp nod.

"Might we have a chestnut pudding, too?" asked Papa with all the eagerness of a child.

"I will add it, as well." Mama huffed, patting his arm. Then tugging Papa away, she gave Evelyn and Gideon a nod in farewell. "Enjoy yourselves."

Her father glanced over his shoulder at them, his gaze dropping to Evelyn's hold on Gideon's arm, but Mama murmured something, drawing his attention away.

Pulling free of Evelyn, Gideon stood before her, smoothing his lapels and preening like a peacock. Granted, he was a handsome sight and deserved closer inspection; his tailcoat was a rich green, which was quite in keeping with the holiday decorations, but it had the added effect of highlighting his hazel eyes. Beneath it, he wore the waistcoat his mother had made him, and the color matched the stitched vines perfectly.

Evelyn cocked her head to the side, lost in her perusal, until he said, "Do you like my new tailcoat? As you can see, the Christmas pudding was quite correct in its predictions."

"It is quite fine, sir," she said with a laugh. "The color goes quite nicely with your waistcoat."

Gideon's fingers drifted to the stitching. "No doubt there would be people here scandalized that I would wear the same piece twice in such a short time, but I thought it fitting."

"I like it, and as it makes you happy, it doesn't matter what anyone else thinks."

A laugh rang out, jolting her as Mr. Moffit invaded their conversation, draping his arm around Gideon's shoulders.

"If anyone in Town heard such a thing, Miss Finch, they would die of shock," he said with a smirk.

Evelyn forced herself to relax despite Mr. Moffit's grating voice. In one hand, he held a glass that was already half empty, and her gaze darted to it with a frown.

"I am certain they would, Mr. Moffit, but as I do not care what Town thinks, it doesn't bother me."

"You are a lady with a strong opinion," said Mr. Moffit with more than a hint of derision in his tone.

"Charles." Gideon's sharp tone and narrowed gaze had the gentleman straightening, his hands raised in supplication.

"I meant nothing by it. It just reminded me of something the fellows say about strong-minded women—"

"I understand Mrs. Wolverton has some card tables set up in the next room," said Gideon with a hard smile. Mr. Moffit's eyes gleamed as he straightened and went off in search of the promised entertainment. Evelyn watched the man go, wondering yet again why Gideon had a friend who seemed disinterested in anything but his own pleasure.

"I apologize for my tardiness," said Gideon, offering up his arm to her.

Taking his arm, Evelyn smiled as they wandered along the edge of the room. "I assumed you had just cause."

She met his gaze, and her breath caught at the sight of his heart shining in that mix of brown and green. Gratitude, adoration, and several other warm sentiments blended into what Evelyn could only classify as pleasure. Unmitigated and unrestrained. Fire coursed through her veins as Gideon's eyes flicked to her lips, her cheeks heating at the spark of wickedness that promised a tender embrace was forthcoming—as soon as privacy allowed it.

Unfortunately, that was unlikely to happen tonight. Evelyn sighed.

Gideon's lips twitched, his gaze aglow with a laugh before it faded. "I fear my father took a turn for the worse."

She pulled him to a stop, her brow furrowed. "Is there anything I can do for either of you? You needn't be here tonight—"

He held up a staying hand. "He is well looked after and doesn't want me 'underfoot.'"

Gideon's tone made it clear the final words were a direct quote, and Evelyn hid away the scowl that threatened to shove its way to the surface. Though she hadn't made his acquaintance yet, Evelyn did not care to meet Mr. Winslow Payne. Gideon never spoke a cross word about him, but the snippets he shared did not speak highly of the man. As things were progressing, she supposed she would eventually be forced to engage with her beau's father, but that was a battle for another day. Perhaps by then, she would have the fortitude to hold her tongue when faced with the man who seemed only to criticize and overlook his son. Perhaps.

Evelyn shoved aside her feelings for the father and focused on the son, nodding as Gideon spoke of the latest downturn, relaying all the physicians had said about his father's deterioration. His brow furrowed, his gaze full of such pain that Evelyn could not comprehend. Like Mr. Moffit, Mr. Winslow Payne did not seem worthy of Gideon's affection.

Though honesty had done much to heal the breach between them, Evelyn was not foolish enough to think telling him so would help matters. The wrong message, delivered in the wrong manner or at the wrong time, might harm more than heal.

"You are a good son, Gideon Payne," she said with a gentle smile.

He sighed, shaking his head. "It is only right. I owe him so very much."

Evelyn stiffened, her brows pulling together as she studied him. Gideon's words had sounded more than merely fervent. She couldn't give his tone a proper label, but there was an edge that sounded almost desperate. Determined? Either way, his statement settled into her stomach like a chunk of ice.

Gideon's gaze fell to her wrist. "You have a dance card tonight?"

Her insides wriggled as she tried to think of what to say about the previous subject, but Gideon's expression lightened as he met her gaze once more, and Evelyn embraced his diversion. Even if it made her cheeks pinken.

Good gracious, was she going to constantly blush around him?

Lifting her wrist, she displayed the card and the two spaces with names filled in beside them. "It seems I require one tonight. They say Innocents' Day is unlucky, but it has brought me nothing but good fortune."

Evelyn huffed and dropped her arm. "I don't know what has gotten into the gentlemen tonight, but it seems you have some competition for my attention."

Gideon arched a brow. "Then I must secure my dances before they are all stolen away."

"Two dance partners shan't occupy the whole of my evening. There is no need to fear."

"I shan't risk it," he replied, snatching the card and pencil. Gideon's gaze fell to the spot next to the dinner dance, and then rose to meet her eyes. She didn't need to speak the words aloud, for they were written in her face and shone in her eyes. Though the other gentlemen had expressed polite interest in it, Evelyn wouldn't allow anyone else's name in that space.

With a flourish, Gideon put his name in the space next to it. And then another. His eyes laughed as he met her gaze, turning the pencil towards a third. As much as she longed for him to occupy them all, Evelyn shook her head.

"My parents have been very encouraging—do not try their patience," she warned with a laugh. "They may not think kindly if you give rise to rumors of an engagement."

Gideon sighed, his shoulders slumping in exaggerated despair. "I suppose I shall have to content myself with two."

Taking his arm once more, they continued their turn about the room.

"I might have to burn your dance card," he muttered, and Evelyn laughed, clutching him even tighter.

Chapter 30

If one were able to set aside scandal and speculation, Gideon knew most people thought him even-tempered. Restrained. Amongst his friends in the army, he'd been considered bland. But at present, he felt liable to burst from all the sentiments burbling within him—though he doubted anyone else saw the war raging within.

As Gideon wanted to smile and scowl in equal measure, he settled on a neutral expression while he watched Evelyn flit across the ballroom. Hands tucked behind him, he tried to relax, but his gaze darted to Mr. Durrant. The fellow's hands rested at a respectful height, never drifting where they ought not to be or holding her too close. Gideon couldn't help but watch the fellow, ensuring he treated Evelyn with respect; far too many gentlemen only played the part, sneaking little touches and comments here and there while testing a lady's boundaries for weaknesses.

Sanity demanded he stop watching her, but Gideon's eyes couldn't fight her pull. Evelyn's gown shimmered in the candlelight; the shiny silk twisted around her bodice and flowed to her feet like a cascade of molten gold. The color complemented her fiery hair, and the dusting of freckles along her arms and décolletage winked as the edges of her gloves and gown shifted with every movement. Though most of her gowns muted her natural shine, allowing her to hide away, tonight she drew the eye.

No wonder the gentlemen were taking notice.

Of course, it didn't help that her father had been entirely accurate in his poor assessment of bachelors. Though many fellows teased Gideon about being snared by the Finch spinster (something that made him wish he were as dissolute as the rumors claimed, for then he might give in to the impulse to plant them a facer), several had made inquiries that were pointed enough to make it clear they were curious about the lady who had captured the fancy of the notorious Gideon Payne.

Interest was piqued. Unfortunately for them, he was not going to surrender his place at her side so easily. Gideon supposed he deserved this irritation for his part in Mr. Finch's scheme.

Mr. Durrant and Evelyn spun about, passing along the edge of the dance, and her gaze caught Gideon's, watching him as long as she could before the polka had them skipping along to the other side of the room. Just before she drew out of sight, Gideon winked at her, earning him a blush.

Sighing, he searched for a clock, but there was no indication of how much longer the dance had left. It was his fault for dancing with her right after he arrived; now that the supper dance had passed, he had no recourse but to watch from the edge as Evelyn was swept into another man's arms.

"She is a sweet girl."

Gideon jerked, his gaze swinging to his right to find Mrs. Little standing alongside him, watching the dancers. His brows rose, and though the matron did not look at him, she clarified, "Miss Finch."

But that was not the question he'd been thinking. The subject of Mrs. Little's conversation had been clear; the fact that it was directed towards him had not.

"I've known the Finches for years and have watched her grow from such an open and caring child into a lady who hides from others because she fears how they will treat her." Mrs. Little's brows pulled low, her gaze filling with concern as Evelyn swept by once more. "Miss Finch deserves better than that."

Turning, Mrs. Little faced him, her gaze boring into his as she studied him with narrowed eyes. Gideon didn't know what to do or say, so he simply stood there, his brows fixed high upon his forehead—frozen as the seconds ticked away. And when a smile lightened her gaze, he felt like he could breathe again.

"I believe Mr. and Mrs. Finch are right about you, Mr. Payne," she said with a nod. "Have you met the Hinshaws?"

Gideon cocked his head, trying to grasp the sudden shift in conversation and the friendly manner in which Mrs. Little took his arm, leading him away from the dancers. Struggling for words, he didn't know what to say to that, for the Hinshaws had not been inclined to chat when he'd attempted to approach them before.

So, he settled on a partial truth. "Only in passing."

"They are good people for a gentleman in your position to know," she said, guiding him along without asking him if he wished to know them (not that he would've turned down her offer). "Mrs. Hinshaw is very active in local charities, and it's rumored that Mr. Hinshaw will be standing for office this election. They may be young, but they are already quite influential. An approval from them will open doors to you, Mr. Payne."

...

Life was a strange thing. Continuing in one fashion with such determined regularity that it became impossible to envision another mode of living. Then it changed course, sending one off in an altogether foreign direction. Unexpected. Unpredictable. And usually unsettling. But at times—those blessed few—it was magnificent. Miraculous. And utterly marvelous.

Evelyn didn't know what to do with her abundance, other than laugh at herself for thinking of five dance partners in such terms, but paupers clung to every farthing and pence.

How did the others stand up for every set? Evelyn glanced at the dance floor, seeing Miss Hawker sweep by with as much vigor as she'd had in the first dance, despite hardly sitting long enough to catch her breath.

But that was neither here nor there. Evelyn's eyes drifted across the sea of faces, looking for one gentleman in particular. Having completed the requisite steps that continued after the dance, she had accepted a drink, exchanged a few pleasantries, and bid her latest partner *adieu*. And now, she was free to do as she pleased.

Catching sight of Gideon, Evelyn didn't bother with feigning indifference, gently meandering along until her path crossed his; she strode through the crowd, making a direct line to his side. A fretful voice in her head warned her that she was being far too brazen, but Evelyn batted it aside like a gnat, giving it no more thought. As Gideon was not being circumspect in his attentions, she felt free to do the same; coquetry was a game she refused to play.

Though he didn't look in her direction, when she drew near, Gideon raised his arm in invitation, and Evelyn took it without hesitation, even while the display drew the gazes of everyone else in the circle. Mrs. Tomkins slid a smile at Evelyn as she stood at her husband's side, her arm weaving through his in much the same fashion.

The gentlemen debated the merits of various investments, and Mrs. Tomkins sent her a commiserating look, but Evelyn couldn't share in it. True, listening to Mr. Norwich ramble on about profits and yields made her long to scamper away, but seeing Gideon alight with pleasure at the conversation had her snuggling closer.

Thinking back to their first meeting, Evelyn compared that quiet and withdrawn man with the one who now stood amongst a group, speaking with the same determination and energy as the others. Gideon would never flit about the ballroom—she didn't know if she would ever care to see him do so—but seeing him appreciated and acknowledged warmed her through. His standing in society was shifting, and Evelyn couldn't think of a more deserving man.

"Call on us next Tuesday to discuss some of the finer points," said Mr. Norwich, extending a hand to Gideon. "If your calculations prove correct, I am certain we can do business together."

Mr. Tomkins nodded. "Good to see a banker who is more circumspect in his promises. I find mine is always promising me the wealth of Solomon, and I cannot bear to give my money to someone whose eyes are bigger than his stomach. Doesn't bode well."

His wife tugged on his arm, nodding towards another section of the room, and he followed her prompting with a quick word of farewell to the others. The shift in the group caused it to dissipate, as was often the case, with Mr. Norwich and Mr. Biddlesby echoing promises to speak with Gideon at a later date.

Evelyn held onto her demure smile, looking for all the world calm and collected, though she felt like clapping her hands and laughing. And when they stood alone, Gideon beamed, looking ready to do the same.

"That was brilliant," she whispered.

"I cannot believe it," he replied, his eyes burning bright. "And that is not the first conversation I've had tonight. It is a miracle, Evelyn."

"You are a brilliant and talented man, Gideon, and it is time the others see it as well."

Reality nipped at Evelyn as she spied another group not ten feet away, watching Gideon with narrowed looks and snickering whispers. When she frowned, his gaze followed hers, and he turned her away.

"Pay them no heed. Having anyone speak to me is a miracle, and I will not allow anyone to dim the joy of this evening."

Gideon paused, his brow furrowing. "I fear some of your hope and cheerfulness has infected me."

Evelyn nudged him. "You are not a sour man."

But that earned her a truly contemplative look, his gaze holding hers as he studied her. "But neither was I happy. Or even content. At best, I was resigned."

Though Gideon did not speak the words, he didn't have to. They hung in the air between them, his eyes echoing them until they seeped into Evelyn's heart. *"Until you..."*

His free hand rose to rest atop Evelyn's, his fingers brushing hers with gentle touches that did dangerous things to her pulse. They could be standing in the middle of an empty field or a choked London street, for all she knew; Gideon had the power to make it all fade from existence, erasing time and everything else that bound them to this earthly realm.

"You two are going to cause a stir," said Mr. Moffit with a laugh as he bumped into Gideon before draping an arm about his shoulders. With a heavy sigh, Gideon cast off his friend's hold, but Mr. Moffit wasn't so easily moved. Despite swaying on his feet.

Evelyn forced herself not to grimace, though her smile teetered dangerously towards it. This was Gideon's friend. Incomprehensible though it may be, the man she loved cared about this fool, and she wasn't going to cause a rift between them.

"I'm happy for you, Gideon" murmured Mr. Moffit, his eyelids drooping heavily as he leaned more of his weight on his friend. Evelyn had no choice but to let go of his arm and step away, though a happy spark skittered in her heart when Gideon frowned at that.

"Your father should consider taking a position as a matchmaker, Miss Finch." Mr. Moffit blinked and laughed at his own comment, drawing others' attention.

"Quiet, Charles," said Gideon with another telling sigh. "You're inebriated and causing a scene."

"Nonsense," he replied with a wave of his hand. Turning to face Evelyn, Mr. Moffit shook his finger in her direction. "I had my doubts about you, my dear—how awful must a woman be if her father has to bribe a man to court her—but you seem nice enough. A bit strange and not that fetching—"

"Charles!" Gideon scowled, barking at his friend with such sharpness that a bit of sense returned to Mr. Moffit's bleary gaze. "Return home and get some rest. You are done for to-night."

Giving himself a shake, Mr. Moffit straightened and managed to remain so. "Miss Johnson promised me a dance."

And with that, the fellow wandered off in search of his dance partner. The poor young lady. As much as Evelyn enjoyed dancing, she would gladly sit out if the gentleman reeked of spirits and stumbled about, spouting nonsense.

Gideon turned to face her, his brows pulled low as his eyes burned with fury. "I apologize, Evelyn. What he said—"

"Think nothing of it," she said with a shake of her head. "I do not think him handsome, so what does it matter if he thinks me plain?"

Evelyn sent him a saucy smile, hoping the jest might set him at ease again, but Gideon stood there for a long moment, watching her. Mr. Moffit may have leveled some egregious sins against her beau and her father, but they were nonsense. Merely the ravings of an intoxicated man, who was ridiculous at the best of times.

She knew Gideon. Trusted him.

But then his gaze darted away from her, and he shifted in place, tucking his hands behind him. Gideon tried to hide it, but Evelyn felt it lurking beneath his attempt at nonchalance.

She stepped away, her eyes lowering, unable to focus on him or anything else around them.

Sifting through the past few minutes, Evelyn searched for any sign that she was reading too much into his silence. Heaven knew she was capable of inferring much, but her heart pulsed in her chest, thumping painfully as her thoughts veered towards that which she did not wish to think of at that moment. Their first meeting sped through her mind, and Evelyn threw out a dozen different explanations for the odd interaction. There were so many to choose from that did not include some grand collusion between him and her father.

But still, Gideon remained mute while Mr. Moffit's words bounced about her thoughts, growing in strength the more she considered them. Had she truly thought a gentleman had swept into her life, falling for her charms so quickly? A mere fortnight after she'd rejected any hope for courtship?

And confessed it to her father?

Magic, indeed.

Evelyn's insides clenched, and a quiet voice buried deep in her heart frantically whispered to her. Could she not merely pretend? Embrace the fantasy for now? It may not be true, but it was the closest thing she would ever receive to love and admiration, so why not forget Mr. Moffit's words and take Gideon by the arm once more?

That silly voice painted such a picture for her, luring her starving heart in with a feast filled with delectable treats she could find nowhere else. She needn't go hungry anymore. What did it matter that the meal was made of pasteboard and stuffed with sawdust? It was better than sitting at an empty table. Surely, feigned love was better than none at all. And perhaps— just perhaps—it might become something real.

A cold wind blew through her, chasing away those warm images, and though Evelyn's throat tightened around the words and her tongue cemented to her dry mouth, she forced the question that needed asking.

"Was he speaking the truth, Gideon?"

With a long and heavy breath, his shoulders slumped. "I know how it must seem, but though things began on the wrong foot—" He paused. "I was hesitant at first, but you must understand—" Another pause. "Your father wanted my help. I was being kind—not that spending time with you is charity—simply that I wanted to help you—and myself—I—"

Gideon's words jerked here and there, his brows pulling

tight together as he stumbled around an explanation, but Evelyn's thoughts seized, unable to grasp the direction her life had taken. Mere moments ago, she had believed losing Gideon would cause her heart to shatter into a million pieces, never to be mended again.

But she'd been wrong.

One had to have a heart for that to happen, and Evelyn couldn't feel it there anymore. No pain. No sorrow. There was nothing inside her. Standing there, she was a husk. Empty and alone.

Chapter 31

Words flew from Gideon's lips, struggling to find the right ones. Evelyn's gaze was unfocused, her expression slackening as she stood there, listening without hearing.

"How we met is merely a detail." Gideon forced himself to breathe and continued to speak, uncertain of what he said but knowing he had to explain. He was not proud of the mercenary motives that had forced them together, but everything since had been real. His feelings were as true as any that had grown from a natural meeting of two souls.

"I was mercenary before, but not now. I like you." Gideon grimaced at that insipid statement, but his tongue tripped over his words. If only she would rail against him or weep. Not that he desired either reaction, but seeing her standing there as though carved from ice sent a chill through him as no other sight could.

"I liked you as well, Mr. Payne."

His heart shuddered at her use of the past tense and his surname, and Gideon shook his head. "No, you do not understand—"

"Please excuse me. I need to sit for a moment." Evelyn didn't blink. Didn't look at him. Her words were stilted and eerily calm, but Gideon felt the anguish lurking beneath them.

"Please, Evelyn," he said, grabbing her arm as she turned to leave. "Allow me to explain."

Her gaze fell to his hand and slowly rose to meet his eyes. All her usual warmth and glow were snuffed out like a candle at the end of its wick. "Leave me be."

Gideon dropped his hand, and she turned on her heel, striding through the crowd with her head held high. And without a backward glance.

...

The sitting room was little more than a cupboard with a few chairs scattered about, providing just enough space to allow a lady or two to fix a ripped hem or torn flounce. As gowns had grown sturdier since the gauzy fashions of their parents, fewer ladies required such a space, and taking a turn outside was far more refreshing than hiding away in this musty place, so there was no one to disturb Evelyn. Though the faint sound of laughter, chatter, and music whispered in the space, it was quiet enough to suit her purpose.

Evelyn shuddered at the prospect of venturing out of her sanctuary, but the sentiment was a faint approximation of what she knew she ought to feel. Blinking, she stared at the red walls and the paint flaking and peeling up in the corners; there was no need to waste funds on covering this solitary space with silk. Had they ever bothered to refresh the paint? Or was the room merely sitting in this forgotten corner, ignored and overlooked as it slowly fell to ruin?

"There is nothing you can say or do to drive me away, Miss Finch." Gideon's—Mr. Payne's—words had played through her thoughts constantly for the past few days, and now Evelyn saw them for what they truly were. Of course, he would not be

driven away. No matter how ridiculous she was, Mr. Gideon Payne would not surrender his opportunity to step into Bentmoor society.

This new image of Mr. Payne seemed so foreign. So utterly impossible. No matter how Evelyn tried to reconcile it, she couldn't accredit his confession to the man she'd come to know. Had Papa paid him per kiss, or had that merely been an amusing diversion until the assignment concluded?

After being bombarded with emotions over the past sennight, Evelyn felt nothing. Not a shiver of dread or twist of anguish. At the very least, she ought to be overcome by the betrayal. But the bands that had wound so tightly around her heart of late had snapped, and there was nothing left for her to feel.

With no clock to mark the passage of time, she was only faintly aware of the notes tripping along like the dancers in the ballroom. She didn't know how long she sat there, staring into nothing. It felt as though she had always been there, hidden away from the others.

The turn of the doorknob jerked Evelyn's gaze towards it to find Mama peeking through.

"There you are. Mr. Payne said you required my assistance—" But she paused on the threshold, her red brows pulling together. "What has happened, dearest?"

Evelyn opened her mouth, though she didn't know what she might say. Mama quickly shut the door and came to her side, taking the chair beside her.

"Have you and Mr. Payne quarreled? It does happen even in the best of courtships, and it is no reason to fret."

"We weren't courting. Not truly."

The words fell heavy in the silence that followed. Evelyn let them settle in her heart, the weight breaking through the numbness that had seized hold of her.

"Mr. Payne was only playing the part because Papa bribed him to."

Mama stiffened, her brows rising. "I cannot believe it. Surely, it's a misunderstanding—"

"Mr. Payne told me so himself." Evelyn's lungs jerked, her breaths stuttering and shaking as her heart fluttered to life once more, releasing the dam of emotions and flooding her all at once. Her hands flew to her mouth to cover the sob that burst out as she folded in on herself, and when Mama's arms drew around her, Evelyn shook free, unable to bear the sympathetic touch.

This was her fault! Though Papa and Mr. Payne shared a portion of the blame, it was her heart that had run headlong into loving him. Declared it, even. She struggled against the pain in her chest that threatened to suffocate her as Mr. Payne's voice played in her mind. All those lovely things, yet never once had "love" left his lips. Gideon—Mr. Payne!—had never confessed any greater sentiment than affection. Evelyn wasn't so naive as to believe gentlemen treated kisses with any weight, yet the moment he'd pressed his lips to hers, she'd professed her love for him.

She stiffened, as reality beat down on her like torrential rain. Even that sin she couldn't lay on his shoulders, for it was she who had kissed him! Throwing herself at yet another man.

Lungs heaving, Evelyn wanted to crumble into dust and scatter to the winds. The world waited outside that door, and she would have to face her folly again and again. It had been some four years since Mr. Townsend's tutelage had trained her to guard her heart, and she had learned nothing, rushing headlong into loving the first man to look in her direction.

Was there a greater fool than Evelyn Finch?

Pacing the corridor, Gideon cursed himself with every footstep, the words growing ever more colorful the longer he waited there, lurking just out of sight and sound. The rest of the guests frolicked about the assembly rooms, unaware of the heartbreak unfolding in this quiet corner, and Gideon searched for any-thing he might do to fix the mess he'd made. But beyond fright-ening off a few ladies wandering towards Evelyn's sanctuary, there was nothing.

The image of Evelyn walking away from him haunted his thoughts as he paced outside her door. Evelyn—that bright and happy spirit—stood there, frozen and silent. Unable to look at him or anyone else...Gideon swallowed, his muscles tensing as his head swam.

Forcing his lungs to work, he tried to hold onto the tattered remnants of his self-control. This was not beyond all hope. He simply needed to explain himself. That was all. Gideon played out the speech he would give her, sifting the words about until they were perfect. Then she would forgive him. Surely, this hur-dle was not insurmountable.

The door opened, and Gideon spun in place to see Mrs. Finch shutting the door behind her.

"How is she?"

But that question earned him a hard look before Mrs. Finch hurried down the hall. "You and my husband manipulated her, and you dare to ask if she is well? Men are fools."

Following close on her heels, Gideon said, "Please, I need to speak to her."

His eyes glanced behind him to Evelyn's hiding place, and though Mrs. Finch's gaze was turned away from him, she snapped, "Don't you dare, Mr. Payne."

The doorway to the main room was just ahead, and before Mrs. Finch stepped into the ring of light streaming from the opening, she faced him.

"Now is not the time for you to talk to her." Mrs. Finch's eyes flashed with a challenge, as though daring him to cross her, and though he was a fool of the highest order, he wasn't about to make that misstep.

"What can I do? I beg you."

Mrs. Finch sighed and shook her head. "There is nothing you can do but go about your business at present. People are going to notice our early departure, so do not give them any more fodder for gossip."

Gideon nodded, his heart sinking as his gaze turned down the hall, as though that longing and hope might make her appear. As much as it pained him, the only assistance he could provide was to follow Mrs. Finch's orders, and so, Gideon bowed and disappeared into the crowd. It took all his playacting skills to maintain the easy facade as he mingled amongst the guests, and he prayed no one could see the anguish lurking beneath his false calm.

Tucking her arm through her mother's, Evelyn clung to it for strength. Smiling was beyond her capabilities, but she managed apathy. As long as no one met her gaze.

Mama complained loudly of a megrim and the frustration of cutting the festivities short, even going so far as to ask Evelyn's forgiveness for the inconvenience. The act nearly brought forth a new bout of tears. The reason behind their early departure didn't matter, but her mother quickly shouldered the attention (both at present and in the future as people were bound to ask later).

Evelyn couldn't bear to look around in case she might spy him, but her traitorous gaze darted a few glances around her. Mr. Payne was not in sight, but she felt his gaze on her. She couldn't explain the feeling; she simply knew he was nearby, watching.

Thankfully, they were bundled into the carriage in a trice, and Mama tucked a lap blanket around Evelyn as they settled. Papa followed, mumbling something about ladies ordering him about for unknown reasons, and Evelyn dropped her gaze to the floor, unable to face him.

Papa stilled and straightened as the carriage rolled away. "I was only jesting. What has happened?"

Tears pricked Evelyn's eyes anew, and she forced them away. Not again. There was time enough for such things when she was safely ensconced in the privacy of her bedchamber, and she could not bear to do so now—not even in front of her parents. One ought to be allowed to lick one's wounds in private.

"What do you think has happened, Lewis?" asked Mama, leaning forward. "Deceit nearly tore us apart when we were courting, yet you asked Mr. Payne to lie worse than I ever did? Did you truly think it would help your daughter?"

Papa perched on the edge of his seat, and Evelyn felt his gaze on her. "I don't know what you mean, Felicity. Tell me what I am supposed to have done."

Turning her face to the window, Evelyn hid her cringe and took deep breaths to hold onto her equilibrium while Mama outlined the whole wretched affair.

"Courting? I never said a word to Mr. Payne about courting," said Papa, a panicked edge to his tone. "I would never do such a thing!"

Evelyn's gaze snapped to his and found his eyes, just a shade lighter than hers, begging her to believe him. "You didn't?"

"Not in the slightest." Then with a sigh, he scooted down the seat so he sat opposite her, taking Evelyn's hands in his. "I was worried about you, my dear girl."

Papa took a long moment before he spoke again, his gaze warming despite a sad smile pulling at his lips. "I was worried you were turning into what I once was: resigned and giving up on a better future simply because life dealt you a rum hand. You've always struggled in society, and it pains me to see it. I know how hard it can be to venture out on your own, and most of your siblings are married and occupied with their families, and your bachelor brothers do not see the problem nor do they make the best companions. I simply wanted to find a friend for you to help you feel more at ease in society."

Evelyn groaned, covering her face. "I cannot make one on my own, so you bribed someone?"

The silence that followed was evidence enough, and she longed to leap through the carriage door, plunge into the snowbanks, and hide from everything and everyone in the world.

"Mr. Gideon Payne is a good man who has been mistreated by his father and society. I thought it would be mutually beneficial for you two to venture out into society together. That is all," said Papa.

Mama huffed. "Lewis, you asked a young man to escort your daughter to social functions. Did you not think he might infer you meant for him to court Evelyn?"

With a wince, Papa sighed once more. "I thought it more appropriate than seeking out a young lady in private conversation. And how would I even accomplish that? Pay call on her at home with her mama listening in? It didn't occur to me that Mr. Payne would interpret it as anything more than friendship."

Shaking his head, Papa turned his gaze to Evelyn. "I didn't mean for this to happen. I simply didn't want you to give up hope and surrender yourself to a life of solitude. You are such a gem, and I merely wanted to help you shine."

Evelyn's chin trembled, her vision blurring as she clutched the lap blanket. "You may not have meant any harm, Papa, but you hurt me greatly. Even if Mr. Payne had not overstepped, I told you what I was feeling and what I desired, and you refused to listen."

"I only—"

"Do you not understand, Papa?" Evelyn held his gaze, willing him to understand. To see. She had thought that of her parents, he would comprehend her struggle. Her heart surged to the forefront, beating against its confines as the roil of emotions from the past hour swept over her.

"I cannot do this anymore!" she cried. "Hope destroys my heart again and again. Every evening I spend secluded in the corner, every failed ball, every time I see someone and think, 'Perhaps this time will be different!' It is killing me slowly. If I cannot dim that wretched hope, I will cut it free. I cannot allow it fester any longer."

Shifting over, Papa squeezed beside her, the three of them crushing close as he wrapped his arms around her. A flood rushed through Evelyn, spilling out as tears overtook her words, sweeping them into nothing. Papa held her close, and they rocked together with the sway of the carriage, his voice low as he begged her forgiveness.

But that was the trouble. Evelyn didn't know if she had enough heart left to do so.

Chapter 32

Linden Place was a terrible sanctuary, but as Hamilton's was not only closed at this hour but tainted by the business with Mr. Finch, Gideon had no other choice. There was no peace to be found at present, so his father's house was as good a sanctuary as any.

Gideon's knees twinged as he turned on his heel, striding the eight steps it took to reach his bedchamber door. His joints hadn't bothered him at first, but after pacing for the past few hours, they were protesting the frequent turns. Sitting on the bed, Gideon allowed them and his spinning head a rest before returning to his previous march. If it were summertime, he'd easily find a field in which to tromp, but at present, this was his only recourse.

Sleep certainly wasn't possible. No matter how he attempted to convince himself that he had a plan in place, Gideon's thoughts wouldn't calm enough to allow him a rest, and he hopped to his feet once more.

Seeing Evelyn whisked away by her parents filled his chest with pain as real as any he'd felt, twisting in like a hot knife. She had made a good show of it, but Evelyn looked like a shade of the person she was. A specter. And he had done that to her.

Not intentionally, no, but that didn't ease his conscience any. Again, he recalled everything that had happened from the moment that horrid Mr. Finch sat in the coffee shop. Surely, their deception was only a detail. Since almost the beginning, his pursuit of Evelyn hadn't been about social clout or redemption. It had been about her.

But no matter how Gideon clutched that justification close, it slipped through his fingers the moment he recalled Evelyn's expression when she'd discovered the truth. The lie was no small thing to her, and it had eviscerated that dear lady's heart, destroying not only it but the trust she'd given him so freely. Evelyn Finch was one of the only people to have ever judged him solely on his behavior, and he'd now proven himself a cad and a bounder.

Gideon slumped onto the bed, his legs unable to hold him upright any longer. Leaning forward, he rubbed at his face, but no amount of scrubbing would clean his conscience.

The clock on the side table chimed the hour, and though it was unreasonably early for visits, the Finches' estate was still some distance away; by the time he arrived, it would be within a forgivable hour. If only just. Darting to the door, Gideon hurried down the steps.

"Boy? Boy!" Father's bark drew him to a stop as he passed the doorway, and when Gideon peeked inside, he found a pair of dark eyes glaring back at him. "Must you stomp about all night? I require rest, and I couldn't get a moment's peace with that constant noise."

A cough racked his body, emphasizing Father's complaint with each wheezing, rattling breath. Nurse Johnson stirred herself long enough to help him with a cup of tea, though Father's lungs couldn't calm long enough to take a sip. Gideon stepped closer, offering his inner strength if nothing else (or what little he had at present), and Father narrowed his eyes as he struggled for breath. Once his coughing fit was finished, his nurse eased him back against the pillows, and Father panted, his arms lying limp beside him.

"You look awful," Father wheezed, his chest heaving with each word. Gideon tried not to scoff, for that was the very definition of hypocritical; the fellow looked as lively as death.

"I didn't get any sleep last night."

"I know." Those two words held as much censure as any lecture Father could've given, and Gideon forced himself not to hang his head.

"I didn't mean to disturb your sleep, but I had a terrible evening—"

"Did the Finch girl finally throw you over?" Father's right brow twitched as though he meant to arch it, and Gideon held back the scowl at the sneer inherent in the man's tone. Breathing through the pain tightening his chest—from his father's words and the truth lying beneath them—Gideon refused to accept this new shift in his world as fact. He would win Evelyn back again. He would.

Teeth grinding together, he tried to hold firm to that conviction and ignore the fire sparking in his chest as he looked at the frail man lying in bed, hardly able to do more than sling insults at his "son." Casting his thoughts back to Christmas morning, he drew his epiphany close, holding it up like a shield. Winslow Payne had given him everything, and Gideon couldn't demand his love and respect as well.

"I am not surprised," muttered Father, the mirth dying from his expression. "She is too good for you."

Those words doused Gideon like a bucket of water, for what defense could he give against the truth? In quick succession, he categorized his strengths and weaknesses and knew the latter far outweighed the former. He may be legitimate according to the letter of the law, but in truth, he was a baseborn child, granted a surname and protection solely through the mercy of his mother's husband.

And though circumstances landed him as society's outcast, the truth rang in Gideon's heart. All but a few found him lacking, so why did he believe himself something more?

Shoulders drooping, he nodded as Father finally waved

him away. As he was certain to make a nuisance of himself in his bedchamber, Gideon wandered to the parlor and dropped on the sofa. Leaning his head back, he stared up at the ceiling and its bright, unblemished white.

"You are far too serious for such an early hour." Charles stumbled over his words as readily as his feet when he staggered into the room, a bottle clutched in one hand.

"It isn't early." Gideon watched the fellow drop onto the sofa opposite, aware that he ought to be furious—and he was, in an abstract manner. If he could muster the energy, he would be properly furious, but Gideon's strength had fled him, leaving him as weak and unmoving as his father upstairs.

Charles chuckled and lifted the bottle to his lips. When nothing came out, he shook it, examined the glass, and then dropped it to the ground. Luckily, it hit the carpet with a dull thud and rolled a bit before striking the hardwood floor.

"Has someone died?" asked Charles when he finally looked at Gideon. Then with another laugh, he added with a hopeful look, "Did your dear father finally pop off?"

"Quiet."

The fellow straightened at the growl in Gideon's voice and then gave an uneven chuckle. "It's your Miss Finch, isn't it?"

"Charles."

"That is it. I know you told me that in confidence, and per-haps I ought to have kept my mouth shut, but she was bound to discover it one day." Charles huffed and shook his head. "You needn't look so sour, Gideon Payne. Miss Finch is as plain as the day is long. You can do far better—"

"Don't." The word was hard and cold, infused with the ice that had frozen his heart. Gideon held Charles's gaze, as un-bending as his tone, and his friend's eyes widened, a hint of so-briety returning. "You caused enough trouble last night, Charles. Do not say another word, or you will regret it."

His friend held up his hands in surrender. "As you wish. I do not understand why you are bothered. Courtship leads to matrimony, and the whole mess sounds like rum business, but if you are serious about your Miss Finch, then stop wallowing and win her back."

Gideon's throat tightened, his muscles going slack again as his head fell back against the sofa. "There is no hope of that. She doesn't wish to see or hear from me. I even sent a note of apology the moment I arrived home last night, but she returned it unopened. I've ruined everything."

Despite the stench of alcohol wafting around him and the bleary tinge to his gaze, Charles studied him with a narrowed look, and Gideon squirmed beneath that regard. "That sounds like your father talking."

Silence was the only answer Gideon could give.

Charles huffed, straightening. "Hang him, Gideon! Do not let that sour bag of bones keep you from what you want. Go find Miss Finch and make things right."

Gideon opened his mouth, but before he could say a word, Charles was already waving off his concerns.

"Ladies adore a bit of courting drama. It's all part of the process," he said with a deep yawn, his eyelids drooping. "You've upset her, and she'll shed a few tears and complain to her mama, her sisters, and every other female. Then little Miss Finch will calm, and you'll visit her with something sparkly or a fist of flowers or some other nonsense, and she'll fall into your arms in a trice."

Then, prostrating himself on the sofa, Charles mumbled into the cushions, "Though I doubt you'll need even that. A woman with her prospects wouldn't dare turn any gentleman away—"

"Do not speak of her like that—" But a low snore cut short Gideon's protests. He stared at his friend and sighed. There was no more conversation to be gotten from him; not that Charles was a font of wisdom unless the subject was spirits or gambling.

Yet Gideon felt those words melt some of the ice in his heart. His worthiness of Evelyn Finch was not in question—it was an indisputable fact that he was not nor ever would be—but if she had given her heart to him once, perhaps he might win it again. Having worked with figures and funds for years now, Gideon was well aware that not every investment paid off equally. Unworthy ventures often surprised people, paying back far greater than anyone predicted.

He couldn't allow this opportunity to pass.

...

Plans were well and good, but despite having rehearsed it all in his head, Gideon was at a loss when the footman slammed the door in his face. What did one do when a hefty bribe didn't earn him entry? If the equivalent of a year's wage didn't soften the fellow's heart, there was no hope of getting past him. Either the Finches paid their servants handsomely, or they'd earned the utter loyalty of their servants. Both of which spoke highly of the family and did nothing to help Gideon's cause.

Stepping backward, Gideon stared up at the house. The hodgepodge of architectural styles and stones was more pronounced on closer inspection, but it was the windows that held his attention. Was that the edges of a dress? A flash of red hair?

The front door opened once more, and Gideon grinned for the briefest moment before Miss Finch's eldest brother emerged, a hard glint in his eye. Instinct had Gideon stumbling backward a step, as the clenched fists made it clear what Mr. George Finch intended to do, but he forced his feet to remain in place as the fellow barreled forward until they were nearly nose-to-nose.

Mr. Finch's arm cocked back, his other grabbing Gideon by the lapels. "I warned you not to hurt Evelyn."

Holding up his hands in surrender, Gideon awaited the sensation of knuckles connecting with his cheek, but Mr. Finch's fist hung in the air for several long moments before he released his hold, dropping his arm with a sigh and a shake of his head.

"Go away, Mr. Payne. You are not wanted here."

"Please, I must speak to her," said Gideon as the other gentleman turned on his heel and stalked back to the house. "I didn't mean to hurt her. I care for her."

Mr. Finch scoffed. "You haven't hurt her. You've destroyed her. Broken something deep inside her."

The front door swung open again, and Gideon's gaze darted to the opening, his heart lifting at the sight of skirts. He nearly called out to her but stopped as his attacker's wife emerged and stormed down the steps, looking twice as murderous as her husband.

Oh, good heavens. Gideon was in for a pummeling.

"What do you think you are doing, George?"

Mr. Finch straightened and glared at Gideon. "I am sending him away, and if he is as intelligent as he claims to be, he'll stay away."

Placing her hands on her hips, young Mrs. Finch glared at her husband. "And what right do you have to judge another man's blundering? Need I remind you how much heartache you caused me before and during our courtship?"

Mr. Finch's shoulders dropped. "But, Marian—"

"No! I'm sure the pair of them will continue to make a muck of things, but it is not your place to interfere. Evelyn's had enough of her family's bungling. Let them be!" The command in her tone brooked no refusal, and both gentlemen blinked at her for several silent seconds.

"I..." But Mr. Finch's words died as his wife narrowed her gaze on him.

"Go inside," she said, pointing at the front door. "See to your sister. Dealing with her beau is her right, not yours."

With a heavy sigh, Mr. Finch nodded and turned to the front door, though he gave Gideon a hard glare from over his shoulder as he stepped through the doorway. But before Gideon could make a plea to his savior in petticoats, the avenging angel turned on him, her eyes blazing.

"Go, Mr. Payne."

"Please, let me inside. I need to make things right with

her—"

"On your timetable, I see," she replied with a cold tone and an arched brow. "Never mind that Evelyn ought to have time to lick her wounds and sort out her own heart before you come barging in to say what you wish to say."

Gideon's mouth hung open, his words evaporating beneath the lady's withering glare. It was clear why her husband had done as bidden with his tail tucked between his legs; Mrs. Finch's determination was as hard as steel, demanding obedience. And it was aided by the fact that she was entirely correct.

"Why must men make such a mess of courting?" she muttered. Then, turning as though speaking to the universe itself, the lady huffed, her voice rising with each word, "They claim women are fickle and tightly strung, but all we want is honesty and for you to see what is standing right in front of you!"

Straightening, Mrs. Marian Finch closed her eyes and took in a deep breath. Once composed again, she turned to meet Gideon's gaze, and though not warm, precisely, her expression held none of the fury that had burned there moments ago.

"If you wish to make things right, Mr. Payne, then leave her be, for now. Give her time, and then return to state your case." She paused, her eyes narrowed once more. "But only if you come bearing apologies and not excuses."

Gideon's shoulders slumped, and he nodded as Mrs. Finch spun on her heel and marched back to the front door. His sleigh sat just behind him, and Gideon turned to face the groom, who stood there, pretending he hadn't witnessed the entire thing, though the sympathetic grimace stated otherwise.

Snow smacked the back of Gideon's head, knocking his hat clear off, the sloppy mess dripping into the nooks and crannies of his collar, and he spun around to find Mrs. Finch wiping off her hand before she slammed the door behind her.

Chapter 33

O nly a fool ignored sound advice, and despite recent evidence to the contrary, Gideon strove to avoid that unfortunate label (imperfect though he may be). And Mrs. Marian Finch's counsel had certainly been of the sound sort. However, even a will of iron bent with enough heat and pressure, and justification had pitted his, eating away at it like rust.

Two days was quite a length of time. Perhaps not in normal circumstances, but Gideon couldn't bear to let a third sun set without taking a proper step towards repentance.

Farleigh Manor loomed above him, and his breath stilled as he studied the thick front door, hoping and praying he'd cross that threshold. But the moment the door opened, the footman swung it shut once more, and Gideon hardly had time enough to throw himself in the path, taking the full brunt of the wood against his shoulder.

The footman brought back the door to give the intruder another firm smack, and Gideon rushed to say, "I'm here to speak with Mr. Lewis Finch."

With narrowed eyes, the servant paused and frowned. "The family aren't at home."

Gideon held up his hands in surrender. "I give you my word

I am not here to disturb Miss Finch. You may sneak me in and out if need be, but I came to speak to her father."

When the door opened no further, Gideon sighed and reached into his pocket to retrieve the wad of bills the fellow had turned down during his previous attempt. "I would greatly appreciate it."

The footman didn't count it. He didn't need to, for there was enough heft for the fellow to know it was a substantial sum. The servant stuffed it into his pocket with another scowl and motioned Gideon inside. Holding a finger to his lips, he led Gideon through the entry and up the stairs, the pair sneaking along like thieves in the night, not making a bit of noise until the servant knocked at a closed door. At the prompt, he opened it and stepped through.

"Mr. Gideon Payne to see you, sir."

That earned him a rather unflattering oath. Then silence.

Gideon stood just out of sight, waiting for some sign, but it was several drawn-out moments before the footman emerged and nodded at him to enter. Gideon didn't need to be told twice. Hurrying forward, he stepped through the doorway and found Mr. Finch sitting at the expansive desk situated at the center of the room, surrounded by an array of dark wood shelves and leather-bound books. The gentleman held his gaze, those unblinking eyes boring into his heart as Gideon stepped forward, sweeping into a bow.

"I apologize for intruding, Mr. Finch."

That was met by silence. The gentleman still did not blink. Did not move. Sitting there like a statue, he studied Gideon, his lips turned down as though his merit had been judged and found wanting. Not that Gideon could blame him.

"I wish to offer my sincerest apologies for what has occurred," said Gideon. "Firstly, I was indiscreet and shared private information with someone incapable of keeping it secret. I keep replaying the moment, wishing I could keep Mr. Moffit from speaking out. But no matter how our courtship began, my affection was true. From almost the beginning. I swear it. I do not regret a single moment of what passed between us, other than the unfortunate circumstance in which we met. I care for her. I do. That was not feigned."

Gideon winced, struggling with the words that had come so easily in the past few days. All his practiced speeches and carefully thought-out statements crumbled to dust as he faced her father. This was no abstract fear that had his pulse racing, a fine mist of sweat wetting his shirt; he was losing his Evelyn.

"I had your permission to court her once. Might I have it again?" Gideon dabbed at his forehead while his words tripped over themselves. "I know I have lost your faith, but I am willing to do whatever I can to repair it..."

That wonderful Christmas night when they had first kissed—had it been less than a sennight ago?—Evelyn had been convinced it was she who would ruin it all. But Gideon had been correct. It was he who had driven them into the ditch, both literally and metaphorically, and with each word, he grew more frantic.

He was babbling. He knew it. But Gideon couldn't quite stop himself. If he could get the right words out, it would heal everything, but the ones that came to his mind were not aiding his cause. And so, he rambled on for minutes. Or had it been hours? Gideon couldn't know for certain, though his heart felt ready to beat free of his chest. Squeezing his eyes shut, he dropped his head, forcing his lips to close.

Silence fell, and he refused to squirm. Or at least, he tried.

"I never asked you to court my daughter," said Mr. Finch in a cold tone.

Gideon's head shot up, his brows knitting tight together. "But—"

Mr. Finch held up a silencing hand. "I realize now that our first conversation might've been misleading, and I take responsibility for that. But you should know I hadn't intended you to insert yourself so fully into her life. I cannot say I am happy you would court a lady under false pretenses, but I understand why you accepted my offer."

Eyes widening, Gideon stared off at nothing, his thoughts struggling to see that conversation in the coffee house as Mr. Finch described it. He couldn't say whether or not this realization made the situation better or worse, but he supposed it made little difference for Evelyn had been wounded either way.

Quiet descended again as Mr. Finch narrowed his eyes, his expression dimming. "And if you've come here seeking my approval because you believe it will be easier than approaching her directly, you are sadly mistaken."

"I hadn't—"

But another hard look from Mr. Finch had Gideon closing his mouth once more. The apology was sincere, and Gideon had needed to speak with him on this subject, but he couldn't deny there was some truth to Mr. Finch's assertion.

"My forgiveness will be the harder one to gain, Mr. Payne, for my daughter is quick to forgive. Too quick, I fear."

Gideon's brows rose at that. "Your daughter's kindness and faith in others are gifts."

"They are," he replied with a sad smile that softened his features. "Like her mother, Evelyn is full of hope and optimism, but her heart is far more tender than Mrs. Finch's. It doesn't take much abuse for it to break. My daughter will forgive you, make herself vulnerable once more, and if you are not careful, she will be damaged beyond repair."

"I wish I could promise never to cause her pain, but clearly, I am inept." Gideon gave him a sad smile. "But I give you my word I will never purposefully do so. She is precious to me, and I will do everything I can to secure her good opinion once more."

That was met by another long, hard silence as Mr. Finch studied him.

"I understand your hesitancy, sir. If the roles were reversed, I do not know if I would be sympathetic or forgiving. But all I am asking is the opportunity to try again," Gideon said, his throat tightening. "I am not the sort to beg, but I will prostrate myself, if need be, simply to speak to her once more. I miss her dearly."

Clearing his throat, Gideon allowed his gaze to drift from the man before him, his thoughts turning through all that had happened. "You once said society had judged her unfairly, and I know that to be true, for she is magnificent. And she truest friend I've ever had..."

His voice faltered, and he swallowed past the lump, struggling to meet Mr. Finch's gaze once more. But the hardness in that man's gaze had eased, and though his lips were twisted in a frown, Mr. Finch's eyes were filled with understanding.

"As I have meddled enough in my daughter's life, I shan't do so again, Mr. Payne. If she wishes to speak to you, it is her decision, and I will not stand in the way of it." Mr. Finch nodded towards the door, waving him out.

But Gideon remained in place. Swallowing, he fought against the instincts that wanted him to drop his gaze. "Am I forgiven?"

Mr. Finch sighed. "Until Evelyn smiles once more, I cannot forgive either of us."

Gideon nodded, understanding the sentiment entirely, though he wasn't certain his guilt would ease even then. Not that he regretted the circumstances that had drawn her into his life, for he doubted their paths would've crossed otherwise. But knowing he had caused her such anguish, intentionally or not, was a weight that could not be so easily cast aside.

Mr. Finch waved him away, and Gideon bowed. Opening the study door, he stepped into the hall and found Evelyn standing there, her gaze fixed on him.

Chapter 34

Gideon's thoughts were so full of Evelyn that she seemed like a mirage, conjured from his fevered imagination. Yet there she was, watching him. Her dark eyes held not the joy he longed to see, but Gideon counted it a victory that they weren't glaring at him in disgust or anguish. She merely studied him, her brows drawn close together.

With his hand still clutching the study doorknob, he remained fixed in place, afraid to move. To even breathe. The whole of him stilled, his heart not risking a single beat as she held his gaze.

Had this been three days ago, Gideon would've taken the opportunity to steal a kiss. His lips knew how perfectly hers felt against his. The tickle of her breath against his skin. The feel of her wrapped in his arms. Even with her father sitting just feet from them, he would've risked being caught for the pleasure of a few tender touches.

Gideon longed to close the distance and pull her tight; his instincts felt certain that a demonstration of his feelings would be far more efficient than convincing her with words. Especially when she looked so alluring with the afternoon light filling the window at her back, illuminating the mass of curls pinned atop her head. But he forced his feet and hands to recall why that was a terrible idea.

One way or another, he had to earn her forgiveness and trust.

A wealth of platitudes and proverbs warned against eavesdropping, but the authors of such sentiments underestimated curiosity's pull. It was impossible to hear one's name spoken in muted tones and not stop to listen. For good or bad, it was better to know what was being said. And when one heard the man she loved speaking behind closed doors, one couldn't help but put one's ear to the wood.

Evelyn wished she were stronger. After everything that had passed, she should've continued on her way. But the anguish in Mr. Payne's tone was too alluring.

"...I am not the sort to beg, but I will prostrate myself, if need be, simply to speak to her once more. I miss her dearly." Gideon cleared his throat, his voice straining as he added, "You once said society had judged her unfairly, and I know that to be true, for she is magnificent. And the truest friend I've ever had..."

All those emotions she'd tucked away surged to the forefront, warring against the ones that had pestered her for days now and heaping on more for good measure. Between the restless nights, listless days, and the war raging within, Evelyn's head throbbed, beating in time with her heart.

How could one word bring such joy and pain? "Friend" was not a terrible label; Evelyn had thought of him in much the same terms. But having allowed herself to think of him as so much more, Evelyn couldn't bear to hear that cold description on lips that had kissed her so tenderly.

And now, the gentleman in question stood before her, frozen in place, staring at her.

"Good afternoon," he murmured.

Evelyn forced herself to remain calm, and she waited until

she was certain her words could come out clear and even. "Good afternoon."

"Did you receive my flowers?"

Dropping her gaze, Evelyn nodded as her hands clenched. "They were lovely."

And they were, though she felt like growling at herself. Despite all that had passed, she had everything in hand to press them the moment they were beyond saving. Her silly, romantic heart insisted on keeping a memory of those blissful days. Those lies.

"And my letters?"

Evelyn nodded, though her insides twisted as she recalled just how many times she'd read his words.

"Please allow me to say how very sorry I am." Drawing closer, Gideon reached for her, though he stopped short and his hands fell away. "I never meant to hurt you, and I would never have accepted this ridiculous arrangement if I had thought it would end as it has. I may have had mercenary motives at first, but I truly believed it was mutually beneficial. Otherwise, I wouldn't have—"

Gideon sighed and scratched at the back of his head. The movement drew her gaze, and Evelyn met his eyes; dark skin ringed them, and a bone-deep weariness seeped from those hazel depths, matching her own fatigued soul.

Tripping over his words, he heaped on more and more apologies, one atop the other, burying her beneath his sorrows until her heart creaked from the weight of it all. Time was a powerful thing, and as the present faded into the past, the passage of days twisted what had happened into something altogether new. With it, Evelyn saw what had happened in different lights, gaining clarity that was lacking the last time he stood before her.

Swallowing, Gideon paused, his voice quivering as his gaze fell from hers. "I know I do not deserve your forgiveness, but I cannot surrender if there is any hope that I might win it."

Could she hold this against him? Having witnessed the shift

in his fortunes of late, Evelyn couldn't blame him for accepting her father's foolhardy plan. Mutually beneficial was the precise word for it. And as much as she wanted to rage against the lies he'd spouted and the hopes he'd revived, she couldn't hate him for it.

For one beautiful moment in time, she had felt desirable. Adored. Evelyn had known the touch of a man. Felt his lips against hers. Reveled in the whispered tendernesses. Gideon had played the part well.

Mr. Payne. She really ought not to allow herself such liberties. Not anymore. One did not think of a man in such intimate terms.

"I am not angry with you," she said, the words loosening a knot in her chest. Of course, there were plenty of others still there, but at least she could let go of that one. Whatever else may have happened, Evelyn was certain Mr. Payne had meant no harm.

No, all her fury was directed precisely where it ought to be—on herself. Once more, Evelyn Finch had allowed her flights of fancy to take hold, building what was into something far grander than reality. Rushing headlong into love without thinking. Not waiting to see if Mr. Payne truly returned her feelings or was worthy of them. Simply falling for the fantasy because she wanted so desperately for it to be true.

What was he guilty of? Romancing a spinster for a few weeks? Allowing her to live out her dreams? Mr. Payne had never declared himself or given any promises. Besides stating that they were courting, he'd done little to encourage her. It was Evelyn who had sprung the term "love" upon them. It was she who had pushed him to drive her about constantly. It was she who had built a few kisses into something more meaningful.

Mr. Payne's tired eyes met hers, and though they begged, something in his gaze seemed to have surrendered all hope of it. And despite the falseness rife in their courtship, Evelyn didn't think his present desperation had anything to do with the mercenary motivations that had pushed him to first seek her out. Despite everything, he wasn't such a good actor that he could feign that anguished pleading in his gaze.

"I cannot say I forgive you yet, but I do understand why you..." She couldn't even say the words. There was no reason to, for her meaning was clear.

"I have missed you," whispered Mr. Payne. "Might we begin again? Start anew? Please give me another chance."

It would take a heart much harder than hers to cast aside those earnest words, and after so many written petitions and flowers flooding her home over the last few days, Evelyn had little strength left to fight his determination. But for all the many things he'd spoken and written, she couldn't help but wish he'd speak the one she longed to hear—the one she'd imagined spoken so many times but had never heard.

Even now, he spoke of friendship, admiration, even affection of a sort, but not love.

To start anew. After having been given a taste of courtship, could she return to the beginning? Treat Mr. Payne as a friend? Forget how delicious he smelled and the way her heart stuttered at the feel of his hands entwined with hers?

"Would you accompany me to the Campbells' skating party?" he asked.

But Evelyn's thoughts weren't on the question at hand. They drifted to the what-may-bes. It was easy enough to imagine what would happen if she said no. It was a life she had lived for so long that she saw it all in vivid clarity. The past few weeks had given her a taste of something new.

Mr. Payne may not be the sort of companion she desired, but what good did it do to pin one's heart on false hopes? Evelyn had accepted that truth once before, and it was time to return to it. Better to let go of the poisonous dreams that filled her head and heart with foolish notions of love. Here stood someone longing for her company. Someone entertaining. Guaranteed to make each outing and party interesting, if nothing else.

Perhaps it was flirting with disaster, but Evelyn wasn't ready to return to her solitary existence. If Mr. Payne wanted a friend, she couldn't turn him away. Not when her resolve was so weak. Surely, a companion was better than nothing.

Evelyn nodded, and Mr. Payne stared at her.

"Yes?" he asked.

"Yes." The word was both sour and sweet on her tongue, as was the way her heart thumped at the smile stretching across his face.

"I promise you shan't regret it—"

But Papa's study door opened, and he peered out, his brows furrowing at the sight of the two of them standing in the hall. His gaze fell to their hands, which had somehow entwined during their discussion. Evelyn stared at them, wishing she knew when and how that had happened, and cursing the pang in her heart when Mr. Payne dropped hers like a hot coal.

"Are you still here, Mr. Payne?" asked Papa with a narrowed look that darted between the two of them.

"I was just leaving, sir." And with that, the gentleman bowed over her hand and scurried away, though the image of his warm smile lingered in her thoughts.

"You shan't regret it," he called one final time.

But Evelyn suspected that was one promise Mr. Payne couldn't keep.

Chapter 35

E velyn adored Christmas, and not solely because of the holidays themselves, but because of the extra pageantry that accompanied every event. Any other winter's day might feature skating or parlor games, during those twelve delightful days of Christmas, hosts and hostesses went to great lengths to provide an experience that lingered long after the candles faded.

Though pleased her parents did not get swept up in the hubbub, Evelyn enjoyed the fruits of others' labor, and the Campbells had certainly been busy.

Harley Lake was by no means a large body of water, though it was the grandest offering their tiny corner of Devon had to offer. Despite that drawback, once the ice froze through, it provided endless entertainment for all the locals as they zipped across its hardened surface, even using the adjacent Little Leigh River as a sort of winter road.

Though the area was not forested, tufts of trees dotted the edge of the water, their branches hanging low beneath the weight of the snow. With so many people using the lake in the winter, the ice had long ago been cleared, but the Campbells had gone to extra lengths and cleared any drifts creeping across it. Most of Bentmoor's and Oakham's society had come to Harley Lake today, and the air was thick with the music and good cheer as people availed themselves of the Campbells' generosity.

A rainbow of Chinese lanterns hung along the edge of the lake, ready to be lit when the sun sank beneath the horizon, and Evelyn had heard whispers of a fireworks display to come.

Those not skilled enough to skate were pushed about on sleds, their laughter ringing out as they raced across the ice. And those of a more daring temperament attempted to dance across the ice to the strains of the quadrille band. Though Evelyn didn't know how the poor musicians kept their instruments in tune or their naked fingers warm.

The clear skies meant colder temperatures, but the added beauty of the sunlight was well worth it, and the Campbells had bonfires around the edge of the lake, providing a refuge from the cold. Evelyn was bundled up tight, wrapped in so many layers of wool that she didn't feel the nip. Gliding around, she circled Mr. Payne, and he gave her a mock scowl as he slowly shuffled along with his arms held wide to keep his balance.

Even if she'd wished to hold a grudge, Mr. Payne made it impossible, sliding back into her life for the past three days as though they'd never been apart with only the occasional apology, bouquet, ribbon, or trinket to show just how determined he was to remain in her good books. Drifting along the ice, they fell into habits that felt familiar and old, despite having met Mr. Payne only a month ago. The conversation zipped along as easily as her skates across the ice, though it helped that he was being even more solicitous than usual, quick to fetch her anything her heart desired.

But some friends were like that. Even if they were different in superficial aspects, they shared the same heart, easing into each other's lives as though they had always been there. And when memories of their courtship threatened to emerge, Evelyn batted them away. Surely, this was enough. Having Mr. Payne as a friend was better than not having him at all.

"Aunt Evelyn!" called Gemma, clutching her brother and the sled as their father pushed them along. Bridget and the younger children were nowhere to be seen, though Evelyn was certain they were here amidst the chaos. She waved as they passed, and the children's laughter rang out as they urged their papa to go faster.

Metal scraped ice, and a foot flew upward, drawing her attention as Mr. Payne struck the ice with a thud. Nudging herself over, she slid to a stop beside him, staring down as he winced. Perhaps she wasn't as charitable as she believed, for she did derive the smallest bit of pleasure from watching him fall again and again.

"You should've told me you don't know how to skate," she said with a laugh, holding out a hand to him.

Waving her off, Mr. Payne shifted to his knees and pushed upwards, his skates slipping and sliding beneath him. "I know how to skate. It's simply been a few years."

Evelyn watched him with narrowed eyes. "How many?"

"Twenty or so," he muttered.

"And were you exceptionally proficient at that time?" she asked, knowing full well the answer.

Mr. Payne's silence said it all. Offering up her arm to him, she led him along, wobbling slowly as they wove between the others.

"I am glad to see you aren't too prideful to accept my assistance," she said with a smile, which he matched.

"Any pride I might've had was knocked loose after the first dozen falls." Mr. Payne's eyes were fixed on the ice at his feet, his blades shuffling along.

The quadrille band ended their song and began a new one, shifting from the tunes of the ballroom to Christmas carols. Songs of new beginnings, festive moments, grand miracles, and the like filled the air, and Evelyn embraced the moment, singing along. Mr. Payne glanced at her, his eyes bright and merry. A few passersby stared as well, but she waved their surprise aside: there was hardly a more fitting time to sing such joyful songs.

Then Mr. Payne's feet slipped out from beneath him, sending him careening to the ground. His hold on her arm jerked her off balance, taking Evelyn with him. Despite her best efforts, her elbow landed hard in his middle, and Mr. Payne let out a pained grunt as they tangled up together.

Evelyn laughed. She couldn't help herself. And the lumpy bed beneath her began to rumble as well, making her bob as Mr. Payne gave in to the mirth.

"You are a menace, sir," she said as others stopped to help them up. Though Mr. Payne had taken the brunt of the fall, Evelyn's knee throbbed as she brushed away the snow clinging to her skirts and jacket.

"Perhaps we'd best rest a moment," he said, motioning to where the refreshments sat, waiting to be enjoyed.

With a nod, she held fast to him once more as they shuffled towards the makeshift stalls. Their blades cut into the snow when they stepped from the ice, giving them a touch more stability than before—but only just. Servants had pots of water boiling on the bonfires, and an array of tea and coffee brewed and ready for the cream and sugar. Stripping off her mittens, Evelyn took hold of a cup, breathing in the mix of spices and berries that had been added to the mixture.

"Heavenly," she murmured as she took a sip.

Mr. Payne hazarded a glance at her before turning his gaze back to his drink, studying the surface as he blew on the piping hot brew. "I am terrified to broach that taboo subject, but I realized that despite so many other apologies I've offered, I haven't said how truly sorry I am for Charles's behavior. He ought to do it himself, but I am afraid to allow him anywhere near you again. One never knows what will come out of his mouth."

Straightening, Mr. Payne met her gaze with a frown. "The situation was terrible enough, but having him blurt it out in that fashion is wretched. I am sorry for putting you through that."

"You cannot control your friends." With the skates still firmly attached to their boots, it was impossible to walk much, but Evelyn took his arm and led him towards a quiet patch away from the crowds gathered at the bonfires.

Again and again, she found herself wondering why a man like Mr. Payne put up with a lout like Mr. Moffit. The pairing made no sense, and the mystery of it bothered her—not just because of its oddity but because of how often Mr. Payne suffered at Mr. Moffit's hand. It was not cruelty, per se, but carelessness could hurt just as much, and she doubted Charles Moffit cared about anything beyond his own desires.

Evelyn tucked that thought away. And stopped. Without the expectation of courtship, what did it matter? Not that she wished to risk an argument with Mr. Payne, but what good was a friend who could not accept her as she was? Of course, the same could be said of a beau, but that was another thought for another time and entirely inapplicable to this situation.

And before cowardice could get the better of her, she blurted out, "Why are you friends with Mr. Moffit?"

"I know he may not seem it, but he's a good sort. He's quite kind to me."

"Is he?"

Mr. Payne cocked his head to the side, a bit of a smirk on his lips. "Of course he is."

Evelyn blinked at that, considering his tone, expression, and words, and realized a horrible truth—Mr. Payne truly believed it. More heartbreaking was that he seemed to think such an inferior friendship was acceptable. The more Evelyn came to know Mr. Payne's history, the lonelier it sounded. Though she had thought herself solitary and friendless, she had a father who adored her. A mother still amongst the living. Siblings who fought for her. If the past few days had taught her anything, it was how much her family prized her.

Mr. Payne had never known what true friendship was, taking whatever scraps of affection were tossed to him, and Evelyn's heart ached at the thought.

"You deserve better than the likes of him," she said.

With a laugh, Mr. Payne shook his head. "You speak as though he's wretched, but he's not that terrible."

She didn't know which idea to confront first—that the fellow wasn't terrible or that Mr. Payne thought "not that terrible" was an acceptable descriptor for his closest friend.

"Do you honestly enjoy him? I have seen you two in public, and I would swear his boorish behavior embarrasses you. I can see it every time you are together."

Mr. Payne shifted in place, glancing around at the other skaters. "No one is perfect."

"But your minds and tastes are so dissimilar. I do not understand what binds you together."

Opening his mouth, the gentleman considered that, but no answer was forthcoming. And so, Evelyn pressed on.

"Even if that were not the case, Mr. Moffit does not treat you well," she said with a shake of her head, her brows pinching together. "He only shows interest in you when he's bored or wants something from you. That is not a true friend in any sense of the word."

Mr. Payne's mouth continued to hang open, but Evelyn took his hand in hers, giving it a kind squeeze, and added, "You deserve so much better than that."

"No, I do not."

The answer flew from his lips with such certainty that Gideon surprised even himself. Perhaps he wouldn't have noticed just how vehemently he felt the words if Evelyn were not standing before him, staring at him with a furrowed brow. But she was. And he felt like squirming beneath her regard. His ankles wiggled as he shifted in place; the skates lashed to his boots were causing him no end of trouble.

Feigning a smile, he waved an airy hand as though this were all a bit of nonsense, and adopted Evelyn's usual levity. "The entire goal of society is to keep climbing higher up the ranks, which requires one to surround oneself with one's betters."

Then he added with a wink, "It is the reason I spend so much time with you."

"No." Sharp and unyielding, the command rang out between them like a shot. Evelyn scowled, her muscles tightening as she stared him down.

Gideon felt like groaning. He'd intended to be flirty, and he certainly hadn't meant to draw a parallel to the unpleasantness that had nearly driven a permanent wedge between them, but he'd stepped into a verbal fox trap, and he felt like gnawing off his leg to get free of it.

"Miss Finch, I—"

"Do not speak of yourself in such a manner." Evelyn shook her head, her fingers clutching the cup in her hands. "You do not deserve censure—especially from yourself—and I will not stand by and listen to anyone—even yourself—denigrate or demean you."

The vehemence of her words held Gideon in place, blinking at the certainty with which she spoke.

"A friend may tease and jest but never mocks, and family never harp or belittle." Tears gathered in her eyes, though Evelyn batted them away. "If they do, they are not true friends or family. You do not deserve to be treated like a bank account or a burden. No one deserves to be demeaned and abused, especially not someone so loyal and good."

Unblinking, she met his gaze as though willing him to believe her, and Gideon cast his thoughts back through the years, seeing them as she did. His home was nothing like the Finches', and Gideon's heart ached for the affection that permeated their family. Imperfect they may be, but that did not diminish the joy and love that bound them together by something more than blood and surname.

He looked at the lady before him, filled with righteous anger on his behalf, ready to defend him even from his own demons, and despite all her assurances, Gideon didn't understand how he had earned Evelyn's affection and loyalty. No matter what she said, he didn't deserve her. No man did. But her fervor almost made him feel like he did. Almost.

All he could do was thank the heavens she'd given him another opportunity to win her heart. This courtship would be entirely different.

Reaching forward, Gideon took her free hand in his. "You humble me, Miss Finch."

Her expression relaxed, a half-smile forming on her lips. "That was not meant to humble. It was meant to inspire."

"And all it has done is prove I do not deserve you."

Even with the chill winter and the vigor of the skating air pinking her cheeks, Evelyn flushed a vibrant red, and she shifted in place and lifted the teacup to her lips. Gideon's thumb brushed across her knuckles, and she froze, mid-sip. Her gaze darted to their hands and back to his eyes, her brows pinching together.

Gideon studied her, and she studied him right back, though he couldn't discern anything from her blank expression. But neither did he release his hold of her hand. It may be too public a place for any true show of affection, but a touch of hands was not improper, either, for a pair in their situation. Yet still, Evelyn stared at him as she lowered the teacup.

Despite his good sense warning him that he was rushing things, Gideon couldn't help but recall all the tender embraces they'd shared. His blood thrummed with the memories, and he couldn't allow this perfect moment to pass. Lifting her hand, he held her gaze as he brought his lips to her knuckles.

"What are you doing?" Evelyn gasped.

Her eyes widened, and she yanked her hand free with such force that she flew backward. With the skates anchoring her in the snow, her feet remained planted where they were, and Evelyn had no place to go but down. Gideon's eyes widened, his brain shouting that he ought to do something, but it had disconnected from his body, leaving him unable to do anything but watch as she tumbled to the packed snow.

Chapter 36

Gideon fought to remain upright himself as he struggled against the skates and the snow, and Evelyn lay there, her arms flung wide as she winced.

"I think I broke..." she mumbled, and Gideon dropped down beside her, his heart pounding as he searched her for injuries, "...the teacup."

With a groan, she turned her head to the side, where the pieces lay scattered, surrounded by steaming splatters of tea. Someone called to them, but Gideon waved off their offers of assistance as he helped her to her feet. Clinging to his arm, Evelyn stared at him, her brows knitted together as she searched his expression.

"I apologize if I am rushing things," he said, helping her to her feet. "But I cannot seem to help myself around you."

"Pardon?" she asked, her face scrunching even further.

Gideon cocked his head to the side, matching her look of surprise and confusion. He remained close, his arms about her until she was steady once more, lingering just a moment longer as he tried to sort out this puzzle. But it didn't take him long to recognize the signs. He'd seen them before.

"For goodness' sake!" he muttered with a heavy sigh. The ridiculous skates made it impossible to pace, so Gideon scrubbed at his face, though it didn't wipe away the weariness of being in this position again. Straightening, he faced her once more and affected a rueful smile.

"I cannot believe I must say this again—for the second time—my dear Miss Finch, but I feel it my duty to inform you we are courting."

Evelyn shook her head. "You asked to be my friend, nothing more."

"I would think I would know if we were courting."

"And I wouldn't?"

Gideon huffed. "As this is the second time I've had to bring it to your attention, you are hardly a reliable source. You overheard my conversation with your father, so why would you believe I desire only friendship?"

"You told my father I was a dear friend," she said with a frown. "And you asked me to start again, and we began as friends. And despite my having thrown myself at you many times during our 'courtship,' you've never spoken of anything stronger than affection—"

"Enough," he begged, with hands raised in surrender. Groaning, Gideon scrubbed his face again. Was there no end to his idiocy? The situation was so ridiculous that he felt like laughing if it weren't so tragic. Here he was, hoping to claim her as his sweetheart, and she thought him only interested in companionship. Would neither of them learn from their mistakes?

With a huffing laugh, Gideon straightened, digging his skate blades into the snow. Thank goodness they had stopped moving, for he would be certain to make an even bigger fool of himself explaining this while on the ice.

The time for tip-toeing was gone. It had passed weeks ago. Though Gideon had thought his actions quite clear enough, they were not to Evelyn, and he was done with misunderstandings.

Stepping closer, he held her gaze. Though some part of him wanted to look away, Gideon wouldn't allow himself to hide those vulnerable pieces of his heart that shivered and shuddered over what her reaction might be, whispering to him that this lady was beyond his reach and ought not to be coveted. Instead, he let his feelings shine through, showing her just how much this moment mattered to him.

"Had you heard the whole of my conversation with your father, you would know how wrong you are. But as we both seem inept at the courting ritual, I am going to tell you now without hesitation or reservation that I adore you, Evelyn Finch."

His throat tightened, and Gideon swallowed past it, forcing his voice to remain firm. "From almost the very beginning, I've desired you not as a friend—though I do count you as my dearest one—but as a man desires a woman. My feelings were never feigned."

Evelyn stared at him as though she could not comprehend this, and he wondered if they were bound to repeat the previous cycle. As entertaining as her awkward and stilted conversation could be at times, he didn't like seeing her so uncomfortable and discomposed.

"I have not spoken of love before because the word isn't found in my repertoire," he added. "I have so little experience with it, but I had hoped my behavior made my feelings clear."

Taking his hand in hers once more, Gideon raised it to his lips, pressing a kiss to her knuckles. "From the first days of our acquaintance, I have wanted to be at your side because I cherish every minute with you. I adore your honesty and that brightness of hope that burns within you. I adore your ability to make me smile even in the worst of moments. I adore the faith you have in me, though I have done little to earn it. If you wish for only friendship, I will take it. But please tell me I have not made such an infernal muck of things you cannot return my love."

The air was gone. Evelyn was certain of it, for though her lungs worked as they ought, she couldn't breathe. Her head spun, though she couldn't tell if it was from giddiness or shock.

Mr. Payne wanted to court her and seemed ready to expire should she reject him. Evelyn's heart bubbled forth with all sorts of answers to give, mostly sentimental dribble that professed her undying love for the gentleman while throwing herself into his arms. And kisses. Yes, lots and lots of kisses. If not for the awkward skates on her feet, she would already be there, ignoring the onlookers to revel in the feel of his touch. Her heart leapt in her chest, pressing against her ribs as though it could carry her forward.

But she kept her feet firmly planted.

Evelyn clenched her hands, hoping to get some warmth back in them, but the cold seeped through her. The world seemed a chaotic thing, spinning around her as she tried to grasp onto some bit of calm, but the skating party continued, full of laughter and music and utterly unaware of Evelyn and Mr. Gideon Payne. She could hardly think with such noise ringing in her ears, and the sun above burned into her eyes, blinding her.

And Mr. Payne stood there, his expression so bright and yearning. But it fell as the silence stretched on. She wanted to say something, but she didn't know what to say. And so she told him.

"I do not know what to say, Mr. Payne."

"You do not trust me," he murmured, his gaze falling to the ground. "I do not blame you, Miss Finch. You are the only person who has shown me such unwavering faith, and it breaks my heart to know that I have broken it."

Evelyn shook her head and frowned, struggling to explain something she did not fully comprehend herself. "I will admit, it is difficult to believe you care for me in such a fashion. I have grown far too used to being overlooked to believe it without reservation."

With a huff, she swung her arms wide. "How do I know you aren't simply here because your manly vanity cannot give up the hunt? Your feelings may not be so deep, only sparking to life at the thought of losing your quarry. That happens often enough."

Mr. Payne snorted, though he tried to cover his huffing laugh, and Evelyn stepped away with a scowl, though he moved closer.

"Do not mock me."

"I am not," he said, holding up his hands in surrender. "But I find it exceptionally humorous that you would think anything about this courtship has puffed up my vanity. Having to convince a lady *twice* that I'm courting her has eviscerated any remnants of my fragile ego."

Evelyn couldn't meet his eyes, yet neither could she concede the fact. "I know too well how easy it is for men to see the sport in courting."

"Does this have anything to do with the bounder who toyed with your heart?"

Stiffening, her gaze shot up to meet his. "Pardon?"

Mr. Payne grimaced and held up a placating hand. "Your brother, George, mentioned you had a rough go of it with another man."

Wincing, Evelyn rubbed at her forehead. "And what did my dear brother say?"

"Only that you had been hurt by someone else."

Unable to hold still a moment longer, she turned towards the lake and stepped onto the ice, gliding forward. With a few quick pushes, she shot out, allowing the breeze to cool her warm cheeks. Despite her family knowing much of her history with Mr. Townsend, no one truly knew the breadth of her mistake and foolishness. She kept it buried deep in her heart, away from any prying eyes that might discover how silly she'd been.

To love a man after only a few weeks. Only a fool did such a thing. Even years later, Evelyn could not think back on that time without a shudder. And she had now done so a second time.

Spinning in place, she turned back to see Mr. Payne shuffling along after her. She swung back, coming to his side and circling him.

"There is little to say on the subject," she finally said, settling on the barest of facts. "Mr. Townsend came to visit a distant cousin, and while he was here, he paid me some attention, which was remarked upon. In the end, it had only been a way to ease his boredom."

Arms held wide for balance, Mr. Payne paused and studied her. "I think there is far more to the story."

Evelyn's throat tightened, her gaze falling to her feet as they circled him once more. "It was nothing. Truly."

Mr. Payne's hand shot out, grabbing hers and pulling her to a stop before him. "You cannot hide the pain from me, Miss Finch. I see it in every stuttering word, every tearful look. If you do not wish to speak of it, then say so. I will not force a confidence. But do not prevaricate and pretend."

"I—" Evelyn didn't know what she was going to say, for her throat fairly strangled the word before she'd formed it. Mr. Payne simply stood there, without judgment or condemnation, demanding nothing from her, and Evelyn couldn't help but think of a time not long ago when he had laid his past bare.

Squeezing her eyes shut, she took his arm as they skated forward. Slowly, she started the tale, beginning with the first meeting, which had seemed so providential, and each moment she'd shared with Mr. Townsend. Every word of encouragement others had given her. The hopes she'd fostered, made all the stronger by the blatant preference Mr. Townsend demonstrated repeatedly. She gave Mr. Payne the whole truth, hiding not a single bit of her crushed heart.

Evelyn sighed, shaking her head as they slowly drifted about the lake. "I thought we were in love. He flitted into my life, seeming like an answer from heaven, and he was only interested in me because my overt adoration fanned his ego. When he grew bored of the game, he ignored me. The moment I did the same, his interest was piqued again, and he'd throw just enough affection to raise my hopes once more. And fool that I was, I forgave him again and again."

Mr. Payne held firm to her, his hands squeezing hers as they clung to each other.

"When I finally broke with him entirely and refused to be baited any longer, he attacked," she whispered, her voice trembling. "In front of others, he mocked me, laughing at the fact that I had thrown myself at him, laying bare my shame to ease his wounded pride. The only comfort I have is that at the moment, I was able to conduct myself with dignity and turn his accusation on its head. I had been circumspect in displaying my feelings, and when viewed from an outsider's perspective, it was he who had done all the chasing. However, we both knew the truth."

The more Evelyn spoke, the more she felt the truth burning in her heart—Mr. Payne was not Mr. Townsend. With each detail, he stood there, silently listening. The hard expression and concerned gaze held not a shred of exasperation or disappointment, not condemning her for her folly but looking ready to take up the fight on her behalf.

"I am not Mr. Townsend," he said.

"I know," she whispered.

A few raised voices drew attention towards the far end of the lake, but nothing of substance could be heard above the quadrille band, and it was forgotten as quickly as it came—leaving Evelyn with no distraction from the hard truth rife in her confession.

Evelyn's heart could not be trusted: it threw itself into loving anyone who deigned to show her the slightest kindness. Her conduct with Mr. Townsend and Mr. Payne was proof enough of that. To say nothing of the lengthy list of gentlemen she'd pined for from afar simply because they'd smiled at her. Her heart wasn't searching for the right man. Any would do.

Her stomach sank at the prospect. As much as she felt her feelings were good and true, how could she trust them? Were they genuine or merely born of desperation, preferring any modicum of love to being a spinster?

"I realize you are nothing like Mr. Townsend. I do," she said, turning back to the subject at hand as they slowly glided along. "But I cannot trust myself. I am repeating my past mistakes, throwing myself wholeheartedly into loving someone simply because he's kind to me. I was never witless enough to tell that man my feelings, but what does it say about my faculties that I declared my undying love to you after only three days of courting?"

"It shows you have excessively good taste," came the quick reply, a faint smile on his lips.

Wiping at her eyes, Evelyn gave a halting chuckle. "It does, does it?"

"Absolutely," he said with a sharp nod. "And I will remind you that we were courting for a good fortnight before any declaration was given. Not three days. You may not have realized I was your beau, but that doesn't make it any less true."

That earned him another huff, but Evelyn sobered as she met his eyes. "Three days or three weeks. Does it make a difference? It's hardly enough time to know someone, and I do not know if what I feel is real or merely a desire for it to be so."

Puffing out his cheeks with a heavy breath, Mr. Payne nodded. "I understand—"

"Mr. Payne!"

The voice was distant enough that they could not tell from whence it came, but the pair stiffened, searching it out. The crowd along the ice rippled as the call was carried along, and Mr. Payne's hold on her tightened.

A young boy slid forward, ducking between the skaters as his boots slipped along the ice. "Mr. Gideon Payne!"

Raising his hand in answer, Mr. Payne motioned for him, and the lad scrambled forward, nearly losing his feet more than once. "I was sent to fetch you, sir. The doctor says you're needed at home. Your pa's in a bad way."

Evelyn's gaze shot to Mr. Payne's, but he merely nodded and tossed the boy a coin, who snatched it and scurried towards the cakes and biscuits for yet another reward. And the man at her side made no other move to leave.

"Oh, Gideon," she said, his name slipping from her lips without bidding, and his gaze met hers.

Turning to stand before her, his eyes never wavered, his attention fully fixed on her. "I understand your reticence, Miss Finch—"

"Now is not the time for this," she murmured, waving him off, but Mr. Payne shook his head.

"I will not let things stand as they are," he said, threading his fingers through hers. "I cannot argue about what you do or do not feel. It is your heart to decipher. But as long as there is hope I might secure your affection, I shan't cry defeat. You are worth the wait."

Evelyn's vision blurred, her chin trembling at that sweet declaration. It resonated through her like the booming of the church bells. Pressing one more kiss to her knuckles, Mr. Payne turned away and scoured the crowd.

"Mr. Landry!" he called, and when her brother-in-law stopped, his children began squealing, rocking back and forth to make the sleigh go once more. "I've received word that my father is ill, and I am needed at home. I fear I shan't be able to escort dear Miss Finch home—"

"Don't fret, Mr. Payne. I shall make sure she arrives safely there." Then with a frown, Robin added, "I hope this business with your father isn't serious."

Mr. Payne gave the usual platitudes, but Evelyn saw the weight settling on his shoulders, for they both knew the truth. Mr. Winslow Payne would not send for his son unless it was dire. Mr. Payne stepped away, but Evelyn snatched his hand, giving it one more squeeze, and he turned to face her again. His gaze held hers, lingering over her face as though memorizing each detail.

Holding her hand to his chest, Mr. Payne leaned forward and lowered his voice. "Whether it is three weeks, three months, or three years, I know my heart, and it belongs to you. I love you without question or doubt, and I will wait as long as it takes for you to decide."

Tears gathered in Evelyn's eyes, and she opened her mouth, unsure of what to say to such a declaration, but Mr. Payne merely gave her that wry smile of his and bowed before turning on his heel and skating off to his sleigh.

Chapter 37

I t was impossible to keep from thinking about certain subjects. Sooner or later, the taboo topic tip-toed its way back into one's consciousness, worrying the hapless mind. The more one told oneself that one shouldn't think about it, the more strength the subject was given, making it all the more difficult to ignore. And now that Farleigh Manor was silent for the night, Evelyn had nothing to keep her thoughts in check.

She was not thinking about Mr. Gideon Payne. Definitely not. Nor was she contemplating the elder Mr. Payne's well-being, for she knew no better than she had this afternoon whether he was failing or on the mend. Sucking in a deep breath, Evelyn let it out in a heavy sigh, unable to fight the pull of either topic.

How did one trust one's heart when it was so fickle? So easily swayed? So quick to blind itself to danger?

Forgiving Gideon had been a simple thing, especially once the full context of the situation was revealed. The majority of their time together had not been driven by his misunderstanding, nor had he meant any harm in it. Forgiving herself was the greater task.

Slowly, Evelyn wandered the house, her feet choosing her path while her thoughts fixed on him, but she paused at the light spilling from the parlor door. With the family only just retiring for the night, the Christmas tree was still lit. The shadows danced in the room, flitting about with every flicker of the flames. The children and adults had stripped away many of the trinkets and candies, leaving the branches mostly bare, though Evelyn still thought it quite lovely, all golden and glowing.

Moving to the sofa, she sat before it and leaned heavily against the arm while her thoughts churned. The house was empty now that her siblings had fled to their homes and beds, so she heard footsteps echoing in the hall long before they stopped at the parlor door.

Mama poked her head into the room. "Oh, there you are. You'd best go to bed so the servants can snuff the candles."

Evelyn nodded, her gaze fixed on the beacon of golden light.

"Dearest?" Mama slid onto the sofa beside her. Those red brows that matched Evelyn's were twisted together. "What is the matter?"

Instinct told her to deny everything, but Evelyn held the impulse in check. Sitting alone in her thoughts had proven useless, and she needed advice desperately.

"I—" She paused, her lips and brow pinching as she tried to sort through her wording. "How did you know you were truly in love?" With brows raised, Mama cocked her head to one side, so Evelyn continued, her gaze turning to the floor, "How do I know if what I'm feeling is real?"

Evelyn sighed, shaking her head and shifting in her seat. "I want so much to be in love. To have someone who looks at me as Mr. Payne does, but how do I know if it is true or if I am simply convincing myself of it because he is the only beau I've ever had? What if I am so desperate for it to be genuine that I overlook faults and flaws that could ruin our future simply because he is the only one seeking my affection?"

Huffing, Mama drew closer, leaning against the sofa as they stared at the tree lights. "You are so like your father in many ways. So quick to doubt yourself, yet with so many gifts at your fingertips. Despite your doubts, you are a good judge of character."

"I hardly think myself a good judge after what has occurred with Mr. Townsend and countless others," murmured Evelyn. "How can I trust my heart when it didn't see the signs of danger?"

"Didn't it?" asked Mama with an arched brow. "Or did you simply ignore its warnings?"

Brows pulled low, Evelyn considered that.

"But any more than that, I cannot say. I have no answer for you, sweetling. The best I can tell you is to ask yourself, 'Why do I love Mr. Payne?' If you can answer that truthfully, then you have no reason to fear."

With a sigh, Evelyn shook her head. "You and Papa have waxed poetic about that question many times before, but even knowing that, it did not help me guard against Mr. Townsend."

"You may have heard it, but you weren't honest with your answer before. I heard you speak of your feelings for Mr. Townsend, and they never drifted beyond surface attractions and generic statements," replied Mama. "Ask yourself why you care about Mr. Payne, and do not lie or skim over the truth. You will find your answer readily enough."

Mama paused. "Not that you need to bind yourself to him this very minute. There is time enough to sort all this out."

"If I am not mistaken, you and Papa were engaged in about the same amount of time—"

"It was two months. Nearly three," replied Mama with a narrowed look. "Far different than only one."

Evelyn merely raised her brows in response, which earned her an affronted huff.

Then leaning in to kiss her forehead, Mama whispered, "Do not fret, my dearest. You will sort it out. I have faith in you."

And with that, Mama left Evelyn to her thoughts.

...

Vigils were such morbid things. Perhaps it would be different if Gideon cared about the outcome, but having studied his father's ashen face for hours now, he could say without a doubt that he felt little for the man who had raised him.

Gideon supposed he ought to feel guilty for that; a twinge of the feeling did bother him from time to time, but it was difficult to maintain when this estrangement between them was not his doing. Even now, he couldn't entirely understand why Father had sent for him. Other than lurking about the house, Gideon had done little, and the man hadn't welcomed him at his bedside. Even now, the only reason his presence was deemed necessary was because the physician and nurse were sleeping, and someone needed to keep watch over Mr. Winslow Payne.

And wait for him to die.

Matters weren't helped by the conversation he'd abandoned to be here. Gideon had already spent an inordinate amount of time thinking about that cad, Mr. Townsend. Flexing his hands, he cracked his knuckles, longing to drive them into that smug fool's face. Despite having spent so many years in the army, Gideon wasn't particularly skilled in fisticuffs, but he was quite willing to get some practice on the blackguard's nose.

His insides twisted as he recalled the anguish in Evelyn's gaze as she laid bare her worries. Surely, a courtship ought to bring the pair joy, yet so much of theirs had been filled with tears and terror. But despite the itching along his spine and the way his heart batted about like a leaf on the wind, just the thought of being allowed to sit at her side sent a bolt of electricity skittering through him. Those quiet, seemingly unimportant moments as they laughed and talked filled him with such peace and contentment that whatever else may come, Gideon knew it was worth the battle.

Evelyn was worth it all.

However, considering her turmoil and the questionable future that lay ahead was a useless endeavor. It lurked in the back of his mind, cropping up at random moments, but had not the power to distract him from this silent vigil. No, it was another moment that occupied Gideon's thoughts, capturing his attention back to it again and again when all other subjects could not distract. Having recalled it dozens of times now, there was little to be gained from doing so again, but that didn't stop the memory from playing in his head.

When Evelyn had said he deserved better than the poor treatment he received, his reaction had been so instant, so certain, and so visceral, as though everything within him rebelled at her claim. Had his reaction been any less, he wouldn't have given it a second thought, but it was impossible to ignore such a strong response. And without Evelyn's beautiful example, perhaps he wouldn't have seen it.

Was Charles a good friend? Was there even a single instance in which the fellow had done something truly kind for him? They laughed and made themselves merry together, but it was always on Charles's terms. Even now, when Gideon could use a friend at his side, the fellow was off chasing his drink and barmaids. Casting his thoughts through the years, Gideon recalled all his friends, and none of them compared to what he'd experienced with Evelyn and the Finches.

It was as though the color had been leached from his life, and Gideon had grown used to the shades of gray. Now, Evelyn had swept in with a great, big paintbrush, filling his world with a rainbow of colors. Did he deserve such beauty?

And did he have any right to judge Charles for not being a perfect friend? Loyalty was not reserved for only those who behaved precisely as one wished. For good or ill, Charles had been there at Gideon's side. Imperfect though he may be, that did not mean he was a terrible friend.

The festive merriment of that afternoon had been replaced with a weighty silence broken only by his father's labored breathing. His lungs rattled and wheezed, fighting for every breath, while Gideon sat and waited. Father's breaths stuttered and paused, and Gideon leaned forward in his chair, his brows pulled low as his own lungs stilled. The silence drew out, pressing down on him as the seconds ticked by.

"Father?" Reaching forward, Gideon grabbed the man's hand, but Father gasped and jerked away. His muscles tightened, his body shaking to life once more. His father's eyes opened wide with a wild gleam as he twisted in bed. Standing, Gideon stood over him, unsure of what to do, but the man relaxed once more, his breath hissing as he settled into the pillows.

"Josephine," murmured Father, his eyes roaming the room as though searching for her. "Forgive me."

Gideon tried to calm him, but there was little he could do as his father's gaze sought her; no good would come from telling his father's fevered mind that his wife could not attend to him.

Though Gideon had not seen much action during his time in the army, no soldier was free from it, and the vacant look his father leveled on him reminded Gideon of the expressions he'd seen on his comrades' faces before the light left their eyes completely. As though they recognized what was to come and had not the fight left to hold on another minute.

Taking his father's hand in his, Gideon stared at the prone figure, certain that foremost amongst all the conflicting feelings plaguing him at present was regret that things had not been different between them.

"Gideon."

His eyes snapped to his father's, and he found a spark had returned to them. A racking cough seized hold, and Father struggled for breath before Gideon stood to help him take some broth.

"Let it be," he said, waving his son away with a scowl.

But Gideon ignored the command, reaching for the bowl sitting on the side table. "You need to keep up your strength."

"There is little point in that, boy." Father's chest heaved as he struggled to speak. When he lifted a tremulous hand and pointed at the seat, Gideon took it once more. "My time is short. I know it. You know it. That charlatan of a physician knows it. I shan't be long for this world."

Gideon didn't know what to say to that, for a denial felt insincere.

"I need to tell you—" Coughs ripped through Father again, and Gideon was forced to simply watch as the man fought through it, refusing any aid from his son (what little there was to give). When Father's lungs cleared again, he panted, his brows knit tightly together as his gaze pleaded with Gideon. "I cannot leave this world with a guilty conscience. I must tell you the truth or damn myself forever."

Brows rising, Gideon tried to brush that away, but Father only grew more agitated, fighting off both his son and his coughs.

"My wife—my dear, sweet Josephine—was never unfaithful."

Chapter 38

Gideon straightened and leaned back in his chair, but before he could say a word, Father continued, rushing through the words as he stared up at the canopy above his bed.

"I cannot allow you to believe that her sin brought you into this world, for it was mine." Father's voice trembled, and his brows furrowed. "When my wife discovered my folly, she demanded we keep you. We couldn't have children, and she longed for one. I had failed her already; I couldn't deny her that. But I should've known better. A child born in such filth and lies was bound to be a slave to his baser needs, just like his poor fool of a father."

Sitting stiffly in his seat, Gideon tried to comprehend his father's confession, knowing full well what each word meant but unable to fit them within his view of the world. They sat there, his father's labored breaths breaking the silence as Gideon tried to grasp what was happening.

"Who...?" He could hardly form the question, and that single word hung there, his thought unfinished.

Father waved it away as though the detail was of little consequence. "One of our maids. She was just so young and pretty.

I couldn't help myself. She bewitched me. But she couldn't afford to keep you, so Josephine took the girl across the country to wait out her confinement."

His tone was so dismissive, reciting the tale as though the details of his son's birth were of little consequence. Gideon's throat tingled, and the scant dinner he'd eaten churned in his stomach; he fought for his breath, struggling against the pain that shot through him as his sluggish thoughts began to grasp what his father was saying.

"I cannot face my dear Josephine again knowing I allowed you to think she'd behaved in such an abhorrent manner," said Father, his words blurring together as his eyelids drooped. "I never imagined you knew the truth concerning your birth nor that you'd leap to such a ludicrous conclusion."

Gideon stared at his father's chest as it moved up and down; he knew he ought to say something, though he knew not what that should be.

"Where is my mother?"

Father's eyes opened once more, and his gaze drifted towards his son, showing nothing more than bone-deep weariness. "Couldn't very well have her under our roof again. Josephine found her a new situation, and that was that."

"What was her name?"

"Not important," replied Father, his lids drooping once more. Forcing them back open, he reached for Gideon's hand, gripping it with far more strength than one in his position should have. "Give me your word you will not tell a soul."

The exertion set him coughing again, but Father's gaze held fast, his eyes begging for the words. But Gideon couldn't speak. His father shook as he fought for breath, gasping out broken words. "I am a good man, but I am frail and weak like any other."

Gideon opened his mouth to speak, but Father added, "My sins are my own. Do not make them fodder for gossip. Please do not darken my name."

That familiar refrain had Gideon's teeth clicking together

as he bit down, his jaw creaking from the strain.

"If not for me, then do it for yourself," Father whispered with a frenzied glint in his eye. Snatching Gideon's hand in his own, he clung to his son. "Protect your reputation, boy. What would your Miss Finch say if she were to discover the truth? Do you think she would rejoice at the thought of marrying the natural son of a maid? A bastard. A baseborn child. There is no kind word for one such as yourself. No woman would wish to bind herself to such taint. If you care about her, you'll keep silent."

The door opened behind him, and Nurse Johnson bustled in, her mobcap askew as she grumbled about needing sleep. Coming to Father's bedside, she forced some medicines down his throat and shooed Gideon from his seat, plopping herself in his place. She crossed her arms and sighed as Father's muscles slackened, his gaze growing unfocused as he continued to murmur.

"Forgive me, Josephine..."

Father's plaintive words followed Gideon as he backed out of the doorway, his gaze never leaving the figure sprawled in the bed, struggling for each breath.

"You're letting in a draft!" barked Nurse Johnson, throwing him a scowl over her shoulder before she reached for her teacup, adding a hefty dose from a flask before she guzzled it down.

Shutting the door, Gideon stood in the empty hall. The first morning rays shone through the window on the landing above, giving him the barest light by which to see—not that it did any good, for Gideon couldn't focus on the world around him. He stared at the door, barely noticing the chill in the air; in winter, they were always cold, but at this time of the morning, it was frigid enough that he could nearly see his breath.

It had been nearly two decades since he'd discovered the "truth" of his parentage. Coming to the realization had taken more than a mere rumor whispered in his ear. Time and much pondering had led him to it, allowing him to adjust to the ever-changing world around him. But this was not a scenario Gideon had ever thought would occur, and it had been dropped on him with all the care of a flying cannonball.

Not that it was easier to believe Josephine Payne capable of such weakness of character and loose morals, but between her and the man who clung to goodness and virtue like a vice, she was the more likely candidate. Gideon couldn't begin to understand it.

The world had turned on its head, and like an hourglass, everything inside him rushed out, leaving behind an unfeeling void, as though his soul had disconnected from his body, leaving him there, living and breathing but hollow. Though that was not entirely correct, either. So many sentiments burbled beneath the surface, waiting to spring forth, but though Gideon sensed them there, he could not identify what he felt.

Feet moving of their own accord, he stared off ahead, his eyes searching for some answer that would not come. They carried him away, searching for the closest thing to a sanctuary he had in Linden Place.

Josephine Payne was not his mother. The lady whose smile had seemed so like his was merely a surrogate. And the woman who had given him life was out in the world somewhere, living her life completely separate from the child she bore. The man dying downstairs had sired him and then raised him against his will.

Gideon's stomach clenched, and he focused long enough to see Charles's bedchamber door just beyond his own. He knocked, hardly waiting for more than a second or two before repeating the sound. And again. And again.

"What is it?" asked Charles as the door swung open. His friend still wore his clothes, his shirt billowing out of the top of his trousers and his hair sticking up every which way.

"I need to speak with you."

Charles sighed, his shoulders slumping. "Can it not wait until morning? I only just made it to bed, and I am ready to collapse at any moment."

Gideon stiffened, his brow furrowing. "It is already morning, Charles. And I wouldn't be waking you if it weren't important."

"I'm certain it's dire, but unless the house is burning down at this very moment, I don't see why I cannot be allowed a few hours' rest before we tackle this serious subject. I cannot face difficult conversations on no sleep." Charles rubbed his face, his words muffled.

Gideon's insides twisted at the thought of returning to his empty bedchamber, the silence only broken by the sounds of his father's last breaths echoing through the halls.

"Please, Charles—"

But his friend waved him away, turning back to the bed. "Give me a few hours, and then I will be ready to listen to all your woes."

The door swung shut, reverberating through the hall, and Gideon stared at the unyielding wood. Evelyn's words rang in his mind, telling him he deserved better, reminding him of all the times he'd aided Charles, only to have his friend turn a blind eye when Gideon needed his friendship the most.

Shaking his head, Gideon turned away from those thoughts, hurrying down the stairs and past his father's bedchamber. With a few orders, he sent the sleepy servants scurrying to fetch his things and his horse, vaguely aware that he was sending them into a dither when they were just stirring for the day's work. He would give them a peace offering later, but now, he had not the capacity to fret about such things.

Soon, he was on his mount, determined to do something to work this out of his system. Tortoise fairly shivered with delight, having not been allowed such indulgences while his master had been so occupied of late. They wandered about the wintery landscape, not knowing where to go. The sun rose above the horizon, lighting the ice crystals that had formed on the trees and hedgerows, making them sparkle in the early morning rays.

Turning towards a long stretch of land that was clear

enough that they needn't worry about ice or holes, Gideon gave the stallion its head, and Tortoise sped forward. Proving precisely why he'd earned this jest of a moniker, the horse barreled forward, and it took all of Gideon's skill to keep the beast under control. Gideon's legs burned as he hovered in the saddle, sitting light above his horse's back. He knew better than to push the beast for too long, but they both needed the moment to stretch their muscles and embrace the rush of wind.

They crested a hill, and Gideon sat down, pulling Tortoise to a stop, their breaths heaving in great puffs of vapor, swirling out into the chilly air. Rubbing a hand along the horse's neck, Gideon gazed out at the rolling hills, dotted with trees, and spied a familiar sight.

He stiffened and stared; Farleigh Manor was some eight miles from Linden Place, and though Tortoise was a strong mount, even he could not gallop such a distance. But Gideon wasn't entirely surprised. Not truly. He may not have consciously chosen a path that led him here, but Evelyn had been in his thoughts, spurring him on.

She was in there, bundled up against the cold. Perhaps by the fire, enjoying a leisurely breakfast. Having left his pocket watch at home, Gideon didn't know the time, but the height of the sun warned it was too early to pay a call on anyone. Yet he knew Evelyn wouldn't begrudge it, and where there was no peace to be found at home or with his friend, Gideon knew he would find it at her side.

His Evelyn.

"If not for me, then do it for yourself..." Father's warning rang in his thoughts, and Tortoise pranced in place as Gideon tugged on the reins. With a low, soothing sound, he rubbed the beast's neck, offering up a soft apology.

His father was a fool. A bitter, stubborn man, incapable of true love. What did he know of Evelyn's feelings or capacity for understanding? She wouldn't hold him responsible for something beyond his control. She wouldn't. She would not.

But a chill settled into his bones, seizing hold of him with an unyielding grip that no amount of assurances could loosen. Dreams were well and good, but reason wouldn't allow Gideon to lie to himself. Logic could not be ignored.

Illegitimate. Baseborn. Bastard. Father had been correct: there were no kind descriptions for children born out of wedlock. That fact alone forced Gideon to accept the truth. Breeding and bloodlines were everything, and no one willingly bound themselves to inferior stock. Evelyn eschewed convention at times, but even men of the cloth condemned such unlucky children as sinners—tainted by the sin and the fallen souls who conceived them.

Yet she called to him with promises of peace and comfort. A haven. A refuge. His wound was deep and festering, and his usual sanctuaries had not the healing balm Gideon required. To sit, even for a quarter of an hour, with Evelyn would bind it up and staunch the bleeding.

And Tortoise ought to rest before the trip back. That excuse was genuine enough that Gideon nudged his mount forward, though if it had been a lie of the highest order, he couldn't have turned away from her. As a lad, he'd waded through such troubles on his own, but knowing she was there, willing and able to aid him, he couldn't bring himself to forge on entirely alone.

He needn't tell her a thing. He only needed to be near her company. That was enough.

Chapter 39

Arriving at the stables, Gideon gave Tortoise into the care of the grooms and marched to the house. He didn't know what to say, though he tried to cobble together an explanation for the early hour. The footman admitted him, leading Gideon through the hallways. The household was only just stirring in earnest with the servants bustling about their chores as the family moved through their morning routines.

Opening the door to the parlor, the footman ushered him in to find Evelyn seated on the sofa; the light from the window behind caught her like a beacon while the deep blue of her morning gown complemented the coppery brightness of her hair. Her brows twisted together, her gaze studying him as she rose to greet him. The sight of her filled him to the brim, but it was the clear concern written on her face that had him hurrying across the room.

Not bothering with propriety or any other nonsense, Gideon scooped her into his arms, clutching her close. She let out a tiny squeak, and he forced his hold to loosen. A heartbeat passed, and Evelyn drew her arms around him, clinging to him as though holding his broken pieces together. Gideon burrowed into her embrace, not caring if anyone witnessed the tender moment. He needed her comfort and love.

Gideon clung to her, knowing that when he let go, he would have to face the world again. She said not a word, simply giving her support without question. Everything that had happened of late gathered in his chest, pressing into a tight ball that threatened to strangle him, and his breath shuddered.

Evelyn only held him tighter.

"Your father?" Her quiet question rang through the room.

Letting out a sharp huff, Gideon shook his head. "Dead for all I know, but I couldn't stay there one moment longer. I had to leave." He drew back just enough to see her. "I had to see you."

"What happened?"

Evelyn pulled him towards the sofa, but for all that he'd spent a couple of hours working out his physical frustrations atop Tortoise, Gideon's body thrummed with energy, forcing him to pace the length of the room. The Finches' parlor was not unlike any number he'd seen—of decent size, with a smattering of furniture, but otherwise a prime pacing location. Taking advantage of the space, Gideon marched while Evelyn returned to her seat, her eyes tracking him back and forth.

"What is the matter?" she echoed, her worried tone reaching deep into his heart. But how could he answer it?

Scrubbing at his face, Gideon tried to sort through what to say, but the weight of years pressed down on him, holding his tongue firmly in place. What woman would accept a baseborn child like him as her beau? What family would wish for him to court their precious daughter? The answers were easy enough—there were none.

Leaning against the mantle, he stared at the fire burning low in the grate. Then, drawing in a breath, Gideon straightened his shoulders and held fast to the knowledge that he had borne this in silence for years and would continue to do so. No good would come from revealing this secret.

"It is simply difficult to be around him," he said, letting out a heavy sigh.

That was met by a long silence before Evelyn finally spoke.

"There is something more than that," she said, the worry thick in her voice. "What is it?"

"It has been a trying night. That is all."

Then Gideon turned to face her.

Evelyn's eyes met his, and it wasn't concern that shone brightest in her gaze. This dear lady, who had stepped beyond her fears to share her heart, watched him with veiled pain, and that one look threw Gideon back to those frightening days when he'd lost her. Those phantom fears bubbled up, seizing his heart in their cold grasp.

He'd come so close to losing her once because he'd kept the truth from her. Evelyn was already slowly giving him back her trust, and Gideon knew—positively knew—it would not survive a second blow. Tenuous and fragile as it was.

"If you care about her, you'll keep silent," his father had warned, but the truth was that if he loved her, Gideon had to speak.

Bile rose in his throat, his stomach clenching and rebelling, though there was nothing inside it. Hands cold and clammy, he straightened his jacket and shifted in place.

Despite facing down enemies in battle, meeting sword against sword, Gideon had never felt fear's touch so deep in his heart. He shuddered at the possibility of what this honesty might cost him, but if he wanted her trust, he must give it in return. And if there was anyone worthy of such faith, it was her.

If only his tongue would work.

Gideon swallowed, trying to ease the tension in his throat, but it was no use.

"I gave my word I would not speak of this," he said, thinking back to that wretched promise his father had extracted weeks ago. "But I need to tell you the truth."

Frowning, Evelyn took a seat on the sofa. "If it will ease your guilt, I promise not to speak of it to another—"

Gideon held up a hand. "There is no need to assure me, for I know you will not."

Pausing, he sighed, scrubbing at his face once more.

"It is unfair of someone to thrust their secret upon you and expect you to bear it alone when it is troubling you so," said Evelyn.

"It is my secret as well."

"Then all the more reason that they shouldn't hold you to such a promise. If it is yours, you are free to do with it as you wish, and they ought not to bind your tongue when it is causing such anguish."

Despite everything, Gideon almost felt like chuckling at that logic, but it came out in a weak huff.

Shaking his head, he whispered, "You will think the worst of me."

He couldn't bring himself to look at her. With his back turned, Gideon listened to the silence that followed it, and his fears surged up, scratching at him. Pulling him towards the door. Whispering of all that he would lose. But he could not bear it any longer. He had to tell her—for his sake as much as hers.

"I am not who you think I am," he whispered. "I—"

Shaking his head, he pinched the bridge of his nose.

"Tell me, Gideon. Please." Evelyn's quiet words rang out in the silence, and he met her eyes once more. Despite wishing to flee from that unflinching gaze, the sight of her calmly waiting loosened the knot in his chest.

"My life is a lie."

Beginning with snippets of his childhood, he described his home and family. Gideon paced to and fro, unable to look at her as he detailed the whole of the story, ending with the revelation his father had dropped on his lap that very morning. The pressure in his chest pushed out the whole story, bringing with it far more than he'd intended to say, laying out the whole of his past for Evelyn to see.

Common belief held that men did not need to speak of their troubles, working them out in some physical fashion instead. A man never admitted weakness or showed vulnerability, and only women required a listening ear. But Evelyn knew differently.

True, her father and brothers did not vocalize their troubles as often or voluminously as the ladyfolk, but that didn't mean they never required such comfort. Many a weary day was followed by a long conversation with their wife, mother, or sister, detailing the frustrations found in every life. And Evelyn had seen a tear or two from each of them when those trials grew too much to bear.

And Gideon Payne bore quite a burden—one great enough that even he did not realize the full extent.

Violence and its effects were easy to identify, but words were a weapon of another sort that cut all the deeper and left wounds no one but the victim could see. No physician rushed forward to staunch the bleeding and bind the wound. More often, the injured was told to ignore the bruises and cuts marring their heart. Forgive and forget, as they say. As though the feelings that accompanied that betrayal were mere inconveniences—the emotional equivalent of a papercut, rather than the gaping gash it was.

Evelyn's eyes filled with tears for the poor boy despised by his sire, the young man mistreated by his peers, and the gentleman judged by those who did not know him. Rising to her feet, she took him in her arms, holding him tightly to her, wishing that might stitch the broken bits of his soul back together.

Though their journeys in life were entirely different, Evelyn saw the shared pain that bound them. How easy it was to gain one's value from others, allowing their opinions to sway one's own. To view oneself as lesser simply because shortsighted peopled deemed one unworthy of proper affection and admiration.

And so much of Gideon's burden had been placed there by someone who ought to have loved and protected him. In her darkest moments, when the world seemed pitted against her, Evelyn had her family to cling to. He had no one.

Except her.

"Please tell me I have not lost your good opinion," he whispered.

Chapter 40

Evelyn jerked away, and Gideon's brows twisted together, his eyes wide and pleading.

"I know it is a shock, but I couldn't keep it quiet any longer," he said. "Not when I have already given so many reasons to distrust me."

Though Evelyn could not blame him for thinking that of others—so many placed a high value on bloodlines, after all—but did he think her so petty? But it was clear from the rapid stream of pleading that he expected her to turn him away.

"It is shocking, to be certain, but if it has altered my opinion at all, it would only be to raise it," she said, wiping her eyes.

Gideon huffed, shaking his head. "Do not give me platitudes, please—"

"It is not platitudes," she said.

"But it's in the bloodline, isn't it?" He shook his head, his gaze falling to her ground. "My father was forever reminding me not to darken our family's name and fretting over any behavior he viewed as lascivious. I thought it was because he believed I owed him some great debt for having accepted me into his home, but in truth, he believed me tainted by his lusts and sins."

"Your father is a fool," she said, forcing Gideon to meet her eyes. "I am well aware of how many believe such ridiculous lies, but why is it that bad seeds spring from good people? It is rare to find a family—no matter how virtuous and good—without one wayward child or grandchild. And there are good who spring from bad, turning their backs on the teachings of their parents to forge a new, virtuous path. People simply spout such nonsense to feed their vanity with the superiority of their breeding and to blame others for the poor circumstances they were born into. Never mind that we are all thinking, feeling creatures who have a will of our own, capable of making our own choices!"

Gideon's eyes fell once more, and he shook his head. "But what does it say about me that my father hates the sight of me? Before, it made sense. What man wouldn't hate the product of his wife's liaison? But now..."

Grasping his hands, Evelyn forced her voice to remain calm. Though her heart pulsed with a thrum of emotions, begging to be let free, the person who deserved a tongue lashing was not the man standing before her.

"It says that your father is a petty, small-minded man. Too afraid to accept his mistakes, so he turns his anger on a poor, defenseless child who did not ask to be brought into the world in such a fashion." Evelyn prayed as hard as she ever had, begging for any divine influence that would help him to see the truth of her words. "Your father couldn't love himself after what he'd done, so he punished the physical manifestation of his weakness. It was his sin, and you were made to bear the brunt of it."

Pressure built in her chest, spilling out in her tears; the strength of it pressed against her ribs, begging to be let loose as she thought of that odious Winslow Payne and all she longed to say to him.

"How dare he do such a thing! You do not deserve such treatment, Gideon! You do not!" Gritting her teeth, she shook her head, struggling against the pain tearing at her heart. "I only wish I could make you see just how wonderful you are. You do not deserve to feel worthless and small because of his actions, and I hate your father for making you believe you deserve to be censured and belittled instead of treasured!"

Gideon's brows rose, a halfhearted chuckle on his lips, though his smile was more sad than amused. "With such a show of faith, I almost believe it."

"But it's not just I who believes in you, Gideon." Evelyn's eyes held his, longing for him to see the truth, and the shadow of doubt she found there made her heart shudder. "Did my father ever tell you why he approached you?"

Hardly waiting for him to shake his head, she continued, "Papa had a strained relationship with his father as well—not as difficult as yours, but I know Papa suffered for it, struggling with many of the demons you now battle. Though our families did not run in the same circles, he was aware of yours. So many think your father is a pillar of the community and an upstanding man of faith, but Papa saw how Winslow Payne treated you. More importantly, he saw what you did with it."

Evelyn wished for better words. Something more poetic. Something with the strength of her convictions. Even now, she heard her father's voice as he had explained the details behind their deception, and she scoured those memories for anything that might be of use.

"True, Papa knew you were more likely to accept because it would be in your best interest, but so much of why he chose you was that he admires you. You've been mistreated by someone who ought to have cherished you, and rather than allowing it to make you bitter and angry, you are kind and gracious."

Gideon opened his mouth, but Evelyn clutched his hands tighter, willing him to listen. "And if we are going to measure your value by your parents' affections, what does it say that both your mothers loved you so?"

"Both?"

Evelyn nodded. "We may know little about your natural mother, but he said she couldn't afford to keep you—not that she didn't want you. Imagine how difficult it must've been for her to give you up; it may have been the sensible choice, but logic doesn't often prevail in such situations. I am certain she saw how much your mother wanted you and would take good care of you, and I can think of no greater love than that of a natural mother choosing her child's future over her desire to keep her child by her side."

Before Gideon could say a word, Evelyn sped forward. "And the lady who raised you as if you were her own? Josephine Payne was put in an awful situation. For years, she hoped for a child, longing for that blessing. That in and of itself must've been agony, but then, she discovered your father had betrayed her, chasing after a bit of muslin while claiming to love her. And in her home—her sanctuary!"

Evelyn's voice quivered, the emotions surging anew as she pictured what it must've been like for Mrs. Payne, and her heart ached for that poor lady.

"But she turned that tragedy into a blessing," whispered Evelyn, struggling to get the words out as her throat tightened. "Your father would've tossed you into the gutter rather than acknowledge his sin to the world, but your mother embraced the child born from that misalliance. You were a reminder of his infidelity as much to her as you were to him, but she loved you still. What does that say about you, Gideon?"

Her thumbs brushed along the backs of his hands; a tear rolled down her cheek, but she would not release him to wipe it away. "This news has thrown your world into chaos, but it is a gift, for it has allowed you to see your mothers' unwavering and unconditional love."

Gideon dropped his head, and Evelyn prayed as she had never prayed before that her words had helped and not hurt. That he might feel the truth of her convictions. That he would know he was worthy of every good thing.

"Thank you," he whispered.

Leaning close, she pulled him into her arms again and closed her eyes, resting her head in the crook of his neck. Despite the tears staining her cheeks, she delighted in the feel of him near. The strength of his trust filled her, warming her like a bonfire on a cold winter's night.

When they leaned away once more, Evelyn stared into his eyes, which shone with a spark of hope. Fleeting it may be, but the sight was so rare that she reveled in it.

"I love you." Evelyn didn't know the words were coming until they were spoken, yet neither could she wish them unspoken, for they were true. She knew it. Whatever doubts she may have harbored died the moment this man stood before her, terrified of losing her yet needing to speak the truth. How could she have not known this was love? Certainly, there was no man as worthy of such a sentiment as Gideon Payne.

Yet he stood there, rigid and staring at her, which was not at all what Evelyn wanted at that moment.

Gideon blinked as her hands grabbed his face, holding him close as her lips pressed to his, and he wasn't certain if she was real or some figment of his imagination manifested in the real world. He could hardly think, his thoughts shifting sluggishly from what had been to what was now happening. And then his arms drew her flush, thrilling in the affection she so freely gave.

Then her lips were gone, and she was babbling as Gideon's mind struggled to alter course once more. His arms remained fixed around her, and her words spilled forth as tears gathered in her eyes, and all he could do was stare as she bumbled about like a bee on the breeze. Lifting his hand, he pressed it to her mouth, forcing her words to still long enough for him to sort through what was happening. Her brows rose, though there was a hint of chagrin in her eyes, and when he released her, she gave a watery chuckle.

"My tongue is getting away from me again," she said with a shake of her head. Then Evelyn's smile turned into more of a frown as she sighed. "Forgive me for being so fickle. You've been so patient, and I keep causing you heartache, doubting everything that is before me. You do not deserve that. You are wonderful and splendid, and I do not know why I haven't been able to see what is right in front of me—"

Gideon chose his lips instead of his fingers this time, pressing a kiss to hers. Drawing it out, he poured his heart into that touch, not stopping until she relaxed once more.

"I love you, Gideon Payne," she whispered. "I love you because though you are cynical at times, you are not cold or unfeeling. I love that you refuse to be callous and bitter, though you have every right to be. You care deeply and love truly. And you give your all to whatever task is at hand. I love that you see me—the whole me. And that, though you find me ridiculous at times, you never mock me."

Her words flowed through him, wrapping tight around his heart and filling him as nothing ever had. Gideon had never imagined just how powerful such a sentiment could be, but it seeped into every inch of him, making him over into something new. Though she'd tried to use other loving examples to prove his worthiness, it was her heart that served as the strongest evidence of his goodness.

"You are far more amusing than you think," he said with a half-smile, his lips brushing hers.

Evelyn huffed a laugh, shaking her head as tears spilled down her cheeks. "I love that despite everything that has happened to you, you are honorable to the core, willing to sacrifice your happiness to help others. And when I am spinning about in a dither, you help me to find my footing once more. Even though I have caused you no end of irritations and megrims, you are endlessly patient with me and my fickle heart."

"You are worth waiting for, Evelyn Finch." Truth rang in those words, warming him through. He loved her, unequivocally and irrevocably.

"I always knew that when I fell in love, I would fall quickly," she murmured, her eyes blazing with joy despite the furrow in her brow. "And it terrifies me that it might all go away. That I might be mistaken or that our feelings will change—"

"You needn't explain fear to me, Evelyn Finch," he whispered, his eyes tracing the lines of her face, longing to memorize every detail. "For the first time in far too long, I have someone in my life who cares for me. Who thinks of me as something more than the rumors and suppositions would have her believe. And the thought of losing you terrifies me to my very soul."

Swallowing past the lump that had taken up residence in his throat, Gideon pressed a gentle kiss to her lips, which gave him time to gather the words he needed to say.

"Because I love you, Evelyn Finch. I love that you see the world with such unbridled optimism, refusing to bend when others try to break you. I love that you are all sweetness and light and do not hide your heart, as I have for so long. I love that you see me as no one else does, and I will no longer allow my fears to keep me from you."

Evelyn nodded, her breaths hitching. "And neither will I."

How she loved this man.

Her past doubts pricked at her, making it impossible to relax entirely, despite the warmth spreading through her. Even as Evelyn batted away fears warning that she would do something to ruin this, her faith in this man steadied her, bolstering her heart. How could she have doubted him or her feelings? The more she knew him, the more she admired him, yet she had distrusted both him and herself at every turn.

No amount of batting her lashes cleared her vision; his face blurred, and Evelyn sniffled, struggling to keep the tears locked away. The last thing she needed was to turn into a watering pot again. She had embarrassed herself enough of late—

"Enough," Gideon whispered, a light censure in his tone as he gave her a rueful smile. "I can hear your thoughts churning, and your worries are working themselves into a dither. Stop whatever it is you are thinking, Evelyn. Both of us have made a muck of things, and it does no good to wallow in the past."

He pressed a quick kiss to her lips and added in a low voice,

"And never be ashamed of feeling things so strongly. It is one of the things I admire about you. Laugh, cry, sing. You do it all without reservation, and I would not have it any other way."

That was good, for Evelyn was certain she couldn't keep the tears at bay this time. Only by the barest bit of control did she keep herself from falling completely to pieces at such a sweet statement. Heavens, Gideon certainly knew how to compliment a lady.

Leading him to the sofa, Evelyn sidled up beside him, drawing Gideon's arm around her shoulders. With so many weighty words shared, her heart was wrung out, leaving her spent.

"My past truly doesn't bother you?" His question reached right into Evelyn's heart; his tone was full of such innocent hope, like a child begging for a bedtime song to chase away the monsters in the shadows.

"Not in the slightest." Snuggling closer, she rested her head against his shoulder in a manner that felt so natural. "Would you tell me more about your mother?"

Gideon's head lowered, his hold on her hand tightening a fraction as he cleared his throat. "She loved anything that bloomed, and she was as giddy to receive a bouquet of bedraggled weeds as she was for the finest arrangement of hothouse flowers. Whenever we were out in the spring and summer, I would hunt down every blossom I could find…"

Smiling, Evelyn listened as one story grew into two, bringing more moments with it. Smiles and tears accompanied them in turn, and she only wished she could've met Mrs. Josephine Payne in the flesh to thank her for protecting and nurturing the dear man at her side.

Chapter 41

A month was not a long time. As a lad, it had seemed an insurmountable stretch, but with each passing year, the weeks grew shorter. Thirty days was hardly worth noting. However, when December had dawned, Gideon hadn't anticipated the new year ushering in an entirely new life. Yet here he was. One month ago, he hadn't given courtship and marriage much thought.

He certainly wouldn't have dreamt of doing this.

Standing in his bedchamber, Gideon gave the room a final inspection, making certain the last of his things had been packed and taken downstairs. No empty spaces littered the shelves or mantle, signaling the missing mementos and trinkets he'd removed from their places of honor; someone had decorated the room, so it was not an empty shell, but it looked precisely the same as the day he'd first occupied it, testifying that he hadn't moved a single object during his tenure there.

Knowing a thing and witnessing it were two vastly different experiences, and Gideon was struck by the physical manifestation of that unease he'd always felt in Linden Place. This had been his bedchamber for many years, yet he'd never made it his own. However, standing here, staring at that cold, empty bed-chamber was merely avoiding what needed to be done.

Gideon was no coward. He'd faced many troubles in his life and done so alone, but at that moment, he felt Evelyn's absence keenly. Not that he was incapable of managing on his own, but he no longer needed to. In one short month, he'd grown accustomed to having her there to buoy his spirits and to hold him together when his heart threatened to shatter into a million pieces.

A cough echoed through the house.

Despite the prickling along his skin and how he longed to march to the front door without stopping, Gideon needed to face the old man. Taking a steadying breath, he followed that familiar path, going down the stairs to pause at Father's open doorway; Gideon refused to step past the threshold, for he wanted nothing more than to simply speak his piece and leave.

Despite the physician's dire predictions, the fellow looked better than he had in a fortnight. Lying amongst a mountain of blankets and pillows, his father was applying himself to the lunch tray, giving his son only a cursory look before turning his attention back to his meal.

Evelyn's words came back to him, wrapping around his heart and strengthening it as Gideon stared at the man. It had been only two days since that mighty conversation, but she had used those hours to reiterate those sentiments again and again.

"You do not deserve such treatment, Gideon. You do not..."

The sentiment felt so foreign that he struggled to accept it, but he trusted her with all his heart. Stuffing his hands in his pockets to keep them from shaking, Gideon held fast to Evelyn's belief, relying on her faith to carry him through.

"What are you doing with all those trunks?" asked Father, not bothering to look up from his luncheon, though there was a stiffness to his posture that made Gideon wonder if the avoidance had more to do with embarrassment rather than Father's usual apathy.

"I am leaving," said Gideon, forcing his voice to remain

even and strong. "Mr. Lewis Finch has helped secure temporary lodgings until I find a more permanent situation."

His fork clattered to the plate as Father turned and scowled at Gideon, finally deigning to meet his gaze. "You would leave me to die alone?"

Gideon dropped his head, shaking it slowly. With a few long breaths, he let that question linger in the air before replying.

"Had you said anything else, I might've felt guilty. But even now, you only care about yourself. I am finished. You may have thought to avoid the consequences of your actions by confessing them with your dying breath, but unfortunately, you spoke too soon. I shan't be your whipping boy any longer."

Father's chest heaved, and he shoved aside the lunch tray, the food scattering; Nurse Johnson jerked from her stupor, giving the mess a cursory glance before settling back in for her nap.

"Useless woman!" barked Father, pulling her to consciousness again. "Clean it up!"

"I am your nurse, not your maid," she replied, crossing her arms and drifting back into slumber.

The old man rounded on Gideon, his eyes blazing. "I am your father. How dare you treat me with such disloyalty. You owe me—"

"Nothing," cut in Gideon. "I owe you nothing."

"I gave you life!" A cough broke up his words, but Father's anger wouldn't slow for such a menial thing as breathing. "I put a roof over your head. Paid for your education. Found you a position in the army. I have given you everything, and you have done nothing but repay my generosity with scandal and disappointment."

Gideon's own lungs heaved, sucking in a deep breath, and he stiffened, staring down that wretch of a man. "When I thought you were the man who took me in, despite my mother's—"

"Hush, boy!" shouted Father, glancing at the nurse, who was studying the backs of her eyelids.

Letting out a sharp sigh, Gideon tried to ease away the

tightness in his muscles, but the feeling only grew, making him fairly tremble as his heart burned like fire. "Before, I thought your actions were generous, for there were plenty of men who would not do such a thing. But now, I know the truth, and you disgust me."

"Do not speak to me that way. You haven't earned the right—"

"Do not demand respect of me, old man," said Gideon, his voice rising as years of unspoken words poured out of him. "I owe you nothing, and you certainly haven't earned anything but contempt. Your giving me a roof over my head and clothes on my back is not some great debt I have to bear. It was your re- sponsibility—your obligation to your offspring! You had your fun and brought me into this world, and then wish me to thank you for making it a misery simply because you didn't allow me to die in the gutter?"

"You are my flesh and blood! You—"

"Do not speak to me of flesh and blood! I am your son, yet you've treated me like a burden, despising everything I said or did." Before the fellow could say another word, Gideon contin- ued, struggling to keep from shouting at the fool as he gaped at this affront. "Should you wish to treat me with respect and de- cency, I welcome the opportunity to know you properly. But un- til then, I will not darken your doorstep again."

Father threw off his bed covers, but when he tried to rise, he fell back onto the mattress. Spine bowed, his lungs heaved and his eyes burned as he glared at Gideon. "I will cut you off. Leave you without a farthing to your name!"

Gideon huffed and shook his head again, shifting in place, and replied in a monotone, "And what would the neighbors think? A falling out between father and son is odd enough at this juncture, but to cut him from a company he has successfully managed on his own would be scandalous."

Before his father could rave about his son's impending pen- ury (no matter how untrue it was), Gideon added, "But if you cut me off, so be it. I have the talent and knowledge to find another position. I do not wish to start over, but I will if you force me to."

Father scoffed. "No doubt you think to live off your woman's dowry."

Gideon met that with a scoff of his own.

"You think yourself such a grand gentleman now, don't you?" said Father with a scowl. "That woman has given you airs, boy. Making you believe yourself better than you are."

With an amused huff, Gideon gave him a genuine grin and nodded. "Yes, she has. And I thank the heavens for it."

Father's gaze darkened, that shadow spreading across his whole expression. "And what do you think she would say if she found out you're some lightskirt of a maid's bastard? Would she be so keen to welcome your attentions?"

"There is no need to speculate. I can tell you how she responded when I confessed the truth." Though he had no desire to torture his father, Gideon did get a slight thrill of pleasure at the gaping shock twisting Father's expression before a flicker of fear flashed in his gaze.

It was gone in a flash, and the old man scoffed once more. "So, the spinster is so desperate she will accept a bastard into her bed."

Heat flared bright and hot in his chest, burning in his gaze as Gideon stared the man down. Only when he was certain he could do so without shouting did he allow himself to speak.

"Do not speak about Miss Finch in such a fashion. Or my natural mother, for that matter." Gideon's tone was low but did not hide the threat rife in it. Only the memory of Evelyn's temper flaring on his behalf while she cursed his father in every conceivable fashion allowed him to remain calm. And it even brought a hint of a smile as he added, "I shan't waste your time relaying all the threats Miss Finch has made against your person—for they are vast, indeed—but know that neither she nor her family have kind feelings towards you."

Perched on the edge of the bed, Father fumed and glowered, his weak limbs trembling as they held each other's gaze.

"I never should've allowed Josephine to bring you home," he said, his voice matching the venom in his gaze. "You've been nothing but a disappointment from the very beginning. Never worth the bother."

Gideon hated how easily those words pierced his heart. His father had never loved him. That truth had crept in over the years by inches, but now, it settled in him with a sickening finality as the man railed against every aspect of his son, both real and imagined. Yet even while Gideon knew and accepted that fact, the words still pained him.

Despite the quiver in his heart born from habits that would take longer than two days to break, Gideon bowed, giving a curt, "Farewell, Father" when the man paused long enough for him to speak. Father's voice echoed in the hall behind him as Gideon turned on his heel and stalked away, not giving the old man a backward glance as he strode from Linden Place.

Chapter 42

Despite all the festivities and food surrounding Twelfth Night, Evelyn couldn't help but find the day a tad melancholy. True, it ended Christmas in a grand manner, but the holidays were now complete and not to be seen again until the next November when the whirl and swirl of the season would begin again. The walls looked bare without their greenery, and the room seemed all the darker without the Christmas tree. So much work for such a short amount of time. Evelyn wished they might keep the decorations up a bit longer, though she supposed that they'd lose their magic and sparkle when the clock struck twelve.

Puffing out her cheeks, she stood to the side of the gathering and clung to those thoughts, but they were hardly a suitable distraction. Family and guests mingled about the drawing room, exchanging pleasantries before the games began in earnest, and her thoughts wandered back to the subject that had stolen the whole of her attention today.

Mr. Gideon Payne. With everything he had to do, it was little wonder that he was late, just as it was little wonder that she could think of nothing else. Thoughts of his father and worries for Gideon's well-being buzzed through her like an angry hornets' nest, never leaving her be. Evelyn's head swam, and she forced herself to breathe.

If only he would arrive.

Her hands worried the edge of her gown as she shifted from foot to foot, her gaze darting back to the doorway every other second. Despite it being thoroughly improper, she wished she'd been there with him as he'd said farewell. Of course, Evelyn couldn't trust herself anywhere near Mr. Winslow Payne, but she couldn't help but long to be at Gideon's side, helping him to face down his dragons.

Odious man! Sucking in a breath, she held it for several long seconds, hoping it might ease the pressure in her chest that increased whenever she thought of that hateful creature.

From the corner of her eye, Evelyn noticed Mama watching her. The lady was hardly subtle in it or in how she nudged Papa toward their daughter.

"He will show," said Mama.

"I know," replied Evelyn. "I am simply worried for him."

"He's a good man, he'll sort it out," said Mama. For his part, Papa frowned, though his gaze was unfocused as though his thoughts were far from this conversation. Mama patted his arm, and he turned his attention to them with a gentle smile.

"I rather like your Mr. Payne," he said.

Evelyn's heart warmed at that, though her eyes flew from her father to the floor and then across the room to the doorway. "I rather like him myself."

Leaning forward, Mama pressed a buss to her cheek. "I am happy for you. Have you two decided anything?"

With a blush creeping across her cheek, Evelyn didn't know what to say to that.

"Leave her be," said Papa. "She doesn't need our meddling."

Mama scoffed, her laughing eyes narrowing with a good-natured scowl. "That is quite the fine philosophy to preach now, Lewis Finch. And courting couples need a little meddling, for we all tend to make a mess of it at times."

"We've certainly done that," said Evelyn with a huff. "I am afraid we've bungled it quite thoroughly, but all seems to be..."

A figure appeared in the doorway, and her words died on her lips. Gideon's gaze scoured the room, ignoring everyone else as he searched for her. When their eyes met, he smiled, and Evelyn hoped she would never tire of seeing that expression. He seemed taller somehow. Or lighter, perhaps. Evelyn's heart panged at the tinge of sadness in his eyes, but she couldn't deny that he seemed the better for whatever had transpired.

Moving through the crowd, he came straight to her, bowing low, though his gaze never left hers, and he took her hand in his, giving her knuckles a buss.

"Good evening, Miss Finch," he whispered.

Evelyn thought she managed an appropriate greeting, but it was difficult to pay attention whilst her mother and father snickered like children.

"You look a little flushed, Evelyn," said Mama, nudging her daughter forward, a laugh rife in her tone. "Perhaps Mr. Payne might escort you as you take the air. It's a bit chilly, but I am certain it will do you some good."

Evelyn shifted in place, her cheeks were now as flushed as her mother claimed them to be, but she couldn't hold onto her embarrassment when it provided her with such a reward. Gideon offered up his arm, and she took it while the questions she longed to ask him hovered on her lips.

"Five minutes, Mr. Payne. Not a moment longer, or I will come hunting for you," said Papa while Mama waved his warning away, shooing them towards the door.

In short order, Gideon had her bundled up and wandering out into the evening air. The moon was not full, though most of it was shining bright in the clear sky with the stars sparkling around it. The snow crunched beneath their feet as they wandcred along the front of the house, the light from the parlor windows guiding their footsteps.

With her by his side, Gideon felt as though he could breathe again. Between the shift to his temporary lodgings and that wretched business with his father, the day had left his head and heart so clogged that he could hardly make sense of the world around him. But there she was, clearing away the fog.

"How are you?" Evelyn asked.

Gideon sighed, uncertain how to answer. Instead, he launched into a description of what had transpired. At various intervals Evelyn huffed and scowled, growling dreadful epitaphs describing his father, and grew teary-eyed, seeming to feel everything he'd experienced.

Sighing, Gideon shook his head. "I fear your influence is filling me with boundless hope for better things to come. Despite knowing this was the likely outcome, I cannot help but be disappointed. Even now, my silly heart wishes things might be different."

"That is not silly," she replied, holding tight to his arm. "It only shows just how foolish that hateful man is for tossing you aside so callously."

Gideon didn't trust himself to speak for a long moment, his throat tightened as her confidence drifted through him, settling into all those lonely parts of his soul that had been neglected for far too long.

When he trusted himself to speak, he said, "But I am quite happy with my lodgings, and Charles even paid me a visit."

Evelyn stiffened, and Gideon struggled with what to say. Affecting a lighthearted tone, he added, "I told him I was not interested in continuing our friendship on his terms. You would've been proud of me, had you witnessed it. I am."

Pulling them to a stop, Evelyn faced him. Gideon kicked at the ground, scuffing the snow with his shoe, but he felt her attention on him. Slowly, he raised his gaze to meet hers, and he found understanding shining in those warm depths, which helped to pull the last of the story from him.

"He was..." Gideon paused, his throat constricting once more, but he forced himself past it. "He seemed rather unconcerned by the whole affair. Put out, I suppose, but mostly because I wouldn't be funding his entertainment until he returned to London."

Evelyn's jaw slackened, her brows furrowing, and Gideon shrugged.

"He didn't say that outright, but it was plain to see." Clearing his throat, Gideon shifted in place. "I don't know if he ever considered me a friend or a pocketbook."

"You do not deserve that, Gideon," she whispered, those words seeming like a prayer as she repeated it again and again, holding him close as he finally found some peace. Here was someone who cared about him. As much as the pain of the day ate away at him, that knowledge settled deep into his bones, strengthening them when they threatened to break beneath the strain.

Straightening, Gideon sloughed away the remnants of those regrets as he met her eyes.

"I do not know how to thank you. Though it doesn't look like it at present, I am happy. Or I will be, at any rate. And that is all your doing."

"Oh, Gideon," she whispered, her chin trembling as she studied him. The moonlight colored the landscape in grays, but still, Evelyn stood out like a shining beacon, coloring his world as no one ever had.

And then she was kissing him. Gideon knew he would never tire of such tender touches. Or he hoped he never did. Having spent so much of his life with so few displays of affection, he swore to never take her love for granted.

Could any woman hear such beautiful words and not swoon? Evelyn had never done so before, but she felt very close to it. The strength of Gideon's words and the depth of his conviction swept over her, consuming her heart with such fire that she was liable to burst.

To say nothing of how delightful his kisses were. In many ways, such embraces were nothing like she'd pictured them to be. There were moments of ardor and passion, but those fiery moments were not the pinnacle of affection she'd imagined them to be; no, that was found in these sweet, gentle kisses that conveyed more heart than heat.

Gideon kissed her as though she were precious and every touch were a gift. And Evelyn supposed they were; their lives had been headed in different directions until her father had meddled. Now, they were different people. Better, in fact. Evelyn's heart pulsed, as though Gideon's strength of character leached into her, and she only hoped she gave it back in equal measure.

Then their kiss ended, and he merely held her, which was nearly as wonderful.

"Now that the holidays have ended and life is settled once more, I look forward to courting you properly, Miss Finch," he murmured into her ear.

Evelyn stiffened, drawing away just enough to meet his eyes, her brows arching upward. "Pardon?"

Gideon's preferred smile was more of a quirk of a grin, and every time she saw it, she swore she heard that low chuckle of his. "Do not tell me that you are mistaken yet a third time, Evelyn Finch. I shall have to call myself the worst beau in history if you still do not recognize I am courting you."

"Of course not, but it is you who is mistaken now," she said with a huff. "I have declared myself madly in love with you multiple times, kissed you soundly even more often, and I do not do such things for a mere beau. A husband-to-be, on the other hand—"

Gideon silenced that with another kiss, and Evelyn lost herself in the feel of his lips. Oh, he was such a magnificent kisser. Granted, her experience with such things was limited, but she couldn't imagine anything finer than this. But she refused to lose her grasp on the subject at hand, recognizing a distraction when she saw one.

The moment he released her (which was a good while later), she continued, "I know my mind, Gideon. I know my heart. And I want you, forever and always."

He sighed and frowned. "I must not be doing this right."

And then he kissed her again, leaving Evelyn breathless in the process. He certainly was doing it right, but he underestimated her determination.

"I know you might think I am rushing things, but I know what my heart wants," she added when they parted once more.

Gideon chuckled. "That may be the case, my love, but I am determined you shall have a proper courtship. One where you know you are being courted."

A smile slowly stretched across her face as she considered all that might entail, and judging from the determination in Gideon's gaze, she knew it would include every one of her dreams. But courtship did not end the moment the marriage vows were spoken.

Taking his face in her hands, Evelyn bussed his lips. Then, holding his gaze, she whispered, "I know you, Gideon Payne, and I know I shall never find another man as wonderful as you or better suited to be my husband, so why should we wait?"

Pressed so close to him, she felt his breathing still as his eyes held hers, shining bright and warm as he reveled in those words.

"My heart is yours, Evelyn," he said with a burning gaze, "and it doesn't matter whether we call it courtship or engagement as long as I can be by your side."

Evelyn's chest tightened, her heart in her eyes as she whispered, "Then engagement it is."

Raising her hand to his lips, Gideon pressed a kiss to the place where her ring would one day sit. Then, reaching into his pocket, he pulled out a bedraggled bit of mistletoe.

A bright smile blossomed as she echoed the words she'd spoken that night of their first kiss. "You came prepared, did you?"

"I came with a lot of hope in my heart."

Evelyn huffed, her eyes sparking with laughter. "It's bad luck to have mistletoe out after Twelfth Night."

Gideon drew closer, his lips brushing hers as he gave her a lazy grin. "Then we shall have to make use of it while we can."

And they did.

Epilogue

3 Months Later

"It's beautiful, isn't it?" Evelyn's question concerned the landscape stretching before them, but Gideon's gaze was firmly fixed on her.

"Yes."

When her eyes turned to meet his and noticed where his attention was pointed, she laughed and took his arm, their steps meandering across the hill as they led their horses along.

Evelyn was correct. Though she was certainly the loveliest creature in the area, the view from that crest was a sight to behold. They'd passed along this way many times during their winter outings, and it only grew more entrancing with the passing months as winter gave way to spring, the signs of new life sprouting amidst the soil and along the tree branches.

They walked along in silence, and it still surprised Gideon how comfortable such a thing could be. Not needing words to fill the void. Simply being together. But Evelyn was too chatty a person to allow it to linger for too long, and he felt her question simmering beneath the surface a moment before she asked it.

"How are you faring?"

Gideon huffed, a wry smile twisting his lips. "With the fact that my father was so spiteful that he put off dying until the week of our wedding?"

Evelyn held fast to his arm and sighed. "I am certain even Winslow Payne cannot control the moment of his death. It is an unhappy coincidence. That is all."

There was wisdom in that, but Gideon couldn't help but feel the old man's determination had allowed his body to hold on longer than it ought. One last spiteful act.

"I should be asking you how you're faring," he said. "We shall have to postpone our marriage for some weeks."

Evelyn pulled him to a stop and faced him, taking his hand in hers. "You are worth the wait, Gideon Payne."

His gaze fell to the black ribbon fastened to the neck of her gown, that symbol of mourning matching the band on Gideon's hat and arm. The signs were as much a lie as any spoken from false lips, yet Evelyn willingly wore the mourning color without bidding, although brides-to-be were not required to do so by the rigid strictures of society. But then, she was not wearing it as a sign of respect for his father.

Taking her horse's reins in his hands, Gideon gathered both sets together. It took some maneuvering to lead both horses with one hand, but it was well worth it to fit her snugly into his other arm. His dearest Evelyn.

"I am sorry for the delay," he said.

"It is disappointing, but as we've raced through our court-ship, it is only right that our engagement moves slower," she replied with a grin. "Though I will say that no fewer than three ladies told me on Sunday that I ought not to allow mourning to set back our plans. They assured me your father would under-stand."

Gideon laughed, and she joined in, their voices ringing out in the afternoon air. "Spoken by people who did not truly know him. He is likely sitting by a calendar, counting out the exact number of weeks I must remain locked in this horrible mourning band, determined to ring a peal over my head in the next life if I withhold even one day."

Evelyn's hands came up to hook around his neck, and Gideon smiled at the feel of her fingers brushing along the nape of his neck. Though he didn't care for the tiny wrinkle between her brows.

"The posturing frustrates you," she said in a low voice.

"I hate the duplicity of it," he said with a sigh. "You are lucky that ladies don't attend the graveside service, for it was impossible to stand there, feigning sorrow when I felt none. He may not have disowned me in his will, but he took the secret of my natural mother's name to his grave."

Her hands tensed, that wrinkle deepening. "I have rather a lot of things I would have liked to say to the man on that score."

"And I despise myself for bowing to public opinion. How does it make me any better than him?"

Sliding her hands down, Evelyn tugged at his lapels, forcing his gaze to hers. "You are nothing like him."

She spoke with such vehemence that Gideon had no choice but to agree.

"You may not be mourning him, but you are mourning the loss of what may have been." Evelyn's gaze grew tender, seeing him more clearly than he saw himself. "You wanted so dearly to give him your affection, and he refused to accept it."

After spending so many years managing his life in a solitary manner, Gideon could not believe how much his situation had altered. During that Christmas season, he'd lost his father and closest friend, but Evelyn had given him so much more in return—not only her love but that of her family, who had become as any mother, father, and siblings could be, and the best friends a man could wish for.

With her kindness, she molded him into a man far better than he was, yet she looked at him as though he was Hercules of old sprung to life. But that hero's wife had not fared well in the tales. Achilles? No, his bride's story was hardly a happy one.

Odysseus? No. Gideon frowned and wondered if there were any myths in which the hero's love had met a happy fate. No glory or honor could overcome the agony of losing his Evelyn.

But why was he thinking of such things when he had his bride-to-be wrapped in his arms?

Analogies aside, Evelyn made his world better, bringing love and laughter like nothing Gideon had ever known before. He longed to be a poet so he could describe how much she meant to him, but he was not. So he did the next best thing. Closing the distance, Gideon pressed a kiss to her lips, showing with all his fervor how he counted the hours until they would be irrevocably bound as man and wife.

Forever one.

No matter how many times they kissed, Evelyn still felt giddy. She hoped it never altered, forever filling her with that lightness of spirit and surge of electricity that enhanced every touch. In all the times she'd imagined the sort of man she'd marry, she had never pictured someone quiet and unassuming like Gideon. But then, she had never understood just how important patience was in courtship, and she was blessed with a partner who had an abundance of that.

Evelyn had never felt more connected to another soul before. Lost in the feel of his touch, she swore his heart beat in time with hers, separating the distance between them until they were one. Her dearest Gideon.

Despite their kiss ending, Evelyn refused to move from her place, enjoying the feel of him so close. However, the horses had other ideas, nudging and nipping their master and mistress.

"I suppose we ought to return home before Papa sends out a search party," she said with a sigh.

"He threatened me with bodily harm if I kept you out too long," replied Gideon as his thumbs rubbed along the small of her back. He remained in place, not moving away, and the wicked glint in his eyes had Evelyn laughing.

"One more month, and you will be free to keep me by your side all the day long," she whispered.

Gideon frowned. "One month."

"A month is not so very long."

"It is an eternity," he whispered, his lips pressing to hers once more.

About the Author

Born and raised in Anchorage, M.A. Nichols is a lifelong Alaskan with a love of the outdoors. As a child she despised reading but through the love and persistence of her mother was taught the error of her ways and has had a deep, abiding relationship with it ever since.

She graduated with a bachelor's degree in landscape management from Brigham Young University and a master's in landscape architecture from Utah State University, neither of which has anything to do with why she became a writer, but is a fun little tidbit none-the-less. And no, she doesn't have any idea what type of plant you should put in that shady spot out by your deck. She's not that kind of landscape architect. Stop asking.

Website: www.ma-nichols.com
Facebook: @manicholsauthor
Instagram: @m.a.nichols
Goodreads: www.goodreads.com/manichols
BookBub: www.bookbub.com/profile/m-a-nichols

Join the M.A. Nichols VIP Reader Club at

www.ma-nichols.com

to receive up-to-date information, freebies, and VIP content!

Printed in Great Britain
by Amazon